•⁻ PRESS

ERE I SAW ELBA

ERE I SAW ELBA

A NOVEL

DREW BANKS

•‒ PRESS

.— PRESS

Dot Dash Press
270 Liberty Street
San Francisco, CA 94114

Printed in the United States of America.
10 9 8 7 6 5 4 3 2

With the exception of referenced historical personages and events, the characters and events in this book are fictitious. Any similarity to real persons, living or dead, is coincidental and not intended by the author. Non-fictional excerpts include:

- Antibes and the Antibes Road, from The Selected Poems of Max Jacob. Oberlin College Press. 1999.

- Picasso's Sentinel. Art in America | February 1, 1998| Tuchman, Phyllis | COPYRIGHT 1998 Brant Publications, Inc.

Book design by White Space, Inc.
Author photograph © Duane Cramer
Cover Art © Camilla Newhagen
Genealogy chart inserts by White Space, Inc.

www.dotdashpress.com

ISBN 978-1-60145-903-9

For my
father

Forgiveness is the fragrance the violet leaves on the heel that has crushed it.

- Mark Twain

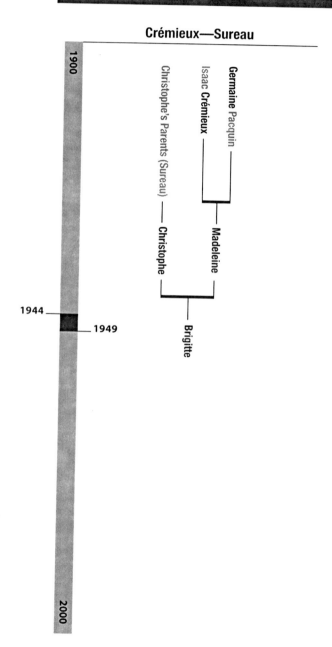

MADELEINE

Crémieux—Sureau

1900

Germaine Pacquin

Isaac **Crémieux**

Christophe's Parents (Sureau)

Christophe

Madeleine

1944

1949

Brigitte

2000

Padua Railway Station, January 31, 2000

"*Violette per la signora?*"

Brigitte smiled. "Violets, in winter?" The last time she had seen Parma violets was in this very train station, more than forty years before, and yet her response was one of simple pleasure, unscathed by memory. Time had healed her wounds.

The girl's eyes sparkled with the possibility of a sale, but her tight-lipped scowl persisted. "Oh yes, they're protected."

Unable to sleep, Brigitte had risen early and arrived at the train station a half-hour ahead of schedule. She was exhausted, but at least the morning's leisure had dispelled the anxiety that had plagued her since her rash decision to come to Padua. She strolled the small station's kiosks, bought a magazine for the journey, and was sitting on a bench flipping through its pages when the young girl approached. Though no more than nine or ten, the girl wore a stern expression that stole her youth. Her faded dress, once likely reserved for special occasions, had over time become common with wear. Still, for a *zingarella*, she was well kempt. Her hair, while unwashed, was neatly braided and her nails were clean.

When Brigitte bent over to smell the flowers, her two miniature reflections stared up from the girl's white patent leather shoes. The curvature of the shoes' leather widened her eyes and elongated her jaw, like tiny Munch portraits. The shoes' pristine condition was a paradox instantly overshadowed by another: the flowers had no scent. Nonetheless, Brigitte feigned intoxication. "They're lovely. How much?"

The girl's eyes darted toward the tracks and then back again. Her shoulders folded in, her body contracting in secrecy as she whispered, "Two thousand lira?"

Pulling her wallet from her purse, Brigitte replied, "I think that's fair."

Brigitte's train departure was announced and she stood in preparation to leave. "Do you have change for a five thousand?"

The girl pulled back in dismay. Now it was Brigitte who leaned forward. She handed the girl the bill and said, "Don't worry, you keep the change. Buy yourself something pretty." Finally, an impetuous grin spread across the child's face—a smile of such expanse it should have transformed her sad demeanor to one of innocent beauty, but alas, it was disfigured by two broken teeth.

On the train, Brigitte settled into her seat. She had booked an entire first class compartment to be alone and therefore had ample room to spread her things out on the seat beside her. Next to the posy of violets, a manila envelope sat on top of her magazine, *Maria Viglietti* scribbled across its front. Brigitte struggled to picture Maria as a fifty-year-old woman, Brigitte's own age when Maria had moved to New York. Brigitte unconsciously raised her hand to her face and traced the lines that confirmed the passage of time. It was hard to believe that, after fifteen years apart, she and Maria would again be face to face, all thanks to the duplicity of a professed stranger. Brigitte fingered the envelope's edges. She knew its contents would bear on both the past and the future. What remained unclear was the present.

The train's electrical system switched on with a flicker of lights and its accompanying subsystem drone. Brigitte rested her head against the seat cushion, picked up the small cluster of violets and held them to her nose. Their fragrance was barely detectable. A botanist friend had once told her that greenhouse flowers were odorless because in their shelter, they no longer needed their perfume to attract or repel. That must be the explanation, for Parmas were ordinarily exquisitely fragrant. Brigitte stared out the window recalling the girl's words: *they're protected*, and wondered how a gypsy had access to a greenhouse.

As if summoned by thought, the girl appeared, walking down the landing toward a vagrant standing on the edge of the tracks farther out from the station. Filthy and disheveled, he rubbed his hands together over wisps of flame that danced above a large steel drum. It was an image from an era long past, one of wartime depression and isolation. The girl held out her hand to the man and for a moment he stared into her open palm before he bent down to her level and regarded her eye to eye. He gently clasped her open hand and curled it back onto itself, over the bill that Brigitte had given her, and then pulled her to him and buried his face in her hair. A single raindrop struck the window with a surprising thud. The man, the girl, and Brigitte all looked to the sky. Suddenly the storm clouds that had been threatening since Brigitte's arrival to Padua broke, and it began to pour. The man swept the girl under the wing of his tattered overcoat and together they ran toward the shelter of the station.

At last, Brigitte succumbed to her weariness, redirecting her attention to her magazine whose cover decried the U.S. presidential election. Yet the cover photo was no longer the vainglorious George W. Bush but the face of her mother, from whom she had been separated for far longer than Maria. It was a face that spawned a lifetime of memories, many she had struggled throughout her life to forget. Retreat lulled Brigitte toward sleep where phantoms from her past swarmed until they dissolved into a million pieces raining from a gray summer sky. The posy fell from her hand and with its descent a remembrance of violet perfume filled the cabin. As the train lurched forward, Brigitte was drawn back.

2

Cinders covered the ground and lifted with the group's shuffle. Brigitte and her mother had been among the first released, and they huddled together apart from the others. Ashes swirled about them like a dismal water globe of some forlorn urban setting, where soot-blackened snow forever blanketed an eternal landscape of oppressive, bleak concrete. Whatever had been incinerated the previous night, there had been plenty of it. Few had slept, kept awake either by the fear that they were being burned alive or by their near suffocation from the smoke that filled the complex. Outside, waves of clamor rose and fell against Drancy's gates. Brigitte folded herself into the pleats of her mother's skirt. Despite it magnifying the already intense mid-August heat, she had grown accustomed to the coarse linen against her bare arms and legs. She looked down at her unblemished white patent shoes wedged between her mother's. Her mother's shoes were also white, but of a softer leather with no patent sheen. They were also badly scuffed. Madeleine had not been as careful as she.

Less a month prior, Brigitte's father, Christophe, had taken a Friday off from work and accompanied them on an expedition to the chic La Samaritaine, which had just reopened as part of the Vichy's commercial revitalization plan. Brigitte was awed by all of the fashionable things on display, though in reality most stores had few items to choose from and even fewer shoppers. All three of the Sureaus bought outfits—even her father. How funny he'd been, standing before the department store's full-length mirror with his puffy-armed siren suit.

Her mother had chosen a simple utility dress with two plunging pockets on the skirt. Made of stiff cream-colored linen, its fitted bodice flaunted her perfect figure. The dress's color (or lack thereof) was of no surprise since Madeleine Sureau was known for wearing white. As they walked to the girls' section, Christophe leaned down and whispered, "Today, you will select your own dress. I believe you are old enough to choose for yourself. Don't you agree?" Brigitte was stunned. Her mother had always picked out her clothes, usually something practical with sufficient balance of distinction and constraint to last multiple seasons.

They inspected every option at least twice before Brigitte made her selection: a white charmeuse silk dress. Madeleine, though flattered by the imitation, thought the sleeveless dress with its inset waist accented by a satin bow was too frivolous. But her father kept his word. After handing the dress to the clerk, he took hold of his wife's hand, kissed her cheek, and pulling out his ration card, said, "We could all use a bit of frivolity."

Afterward, they had enjoyed siphoned sodas and tea biscuits at Le Toupary, La Samaritaine's newly added rooftop café. From its vantage, the resplendent panorama of Paris could be imagined untouched by war's encroachment. They sustained this reverie down the dizzying staircase, carrying all of their purchases except for Brigitte's new shoes, which her father allowed her to wear only after her promise not to muss them. Their illusion shattered when, upon their exit, they confronted a street filled with two columns of soldiers, mirrored in matching lockstep. Christophe's hand squeezed around Brigitte's, and he backed into the crowd of solemn onlookers. Brigitte had resisted her father's pull, careful not to misstep. She had looked not out at the soldiers, but down, safeguarding her shiny white shoes as, with each cautious step, she avoided the grime of the hundreds of other careless feet that surrounded hers.

Now, three weeks later in Drancy's apocalyptic courtyard, Brigitte's world was again fixated upon her careful step. She imagined the past soldiers a parade, the present ash confetti, and her shoes the transport between reality and fantasy.

The crowd's frenzy surged and deepened. The stream of people spilling into the courtyard was no longer made up of only women and girls but also men and boys from the upper floors. There were euphoric reunions as mothers found sons and husbands found wives. Brigitte scanned the sea of bedraggled strangers for her father, but found him nowhere. For solace, she turned to her mother whose face was magnificent even in distress. It was a face so beautiful that it had twice graced the cover of *Vogue* and had prompted François Coty, one of France's most famous *parfumeurs*, to create a special scent for her thirtieth birthday party, a grand *fête* that had drawn the Paris elite. He named the cologne "Parma," after the particularly aromatic violet from which it had been derived, and from that day forward Madeleine had worn it without fail. It had become so intrinsic to her persona that Christophe sometimes referred to her as *ma violette blanche*. Even after their protracted internment, Brigitte could detect its faint smell. Its persistence was as inspiring as Madeleine's indomitable beauty. Her ivory skin did not sag from lack of sleep or appear sallow from disregard. Rather, it pulled taut across her angled bone structure such that it became almost translucent. It was as if she radiated an interior light made brighter by adversity. Brigitte buried her face into the rigid folds of her mother's dress.

The Sunday after their excursion to La Samaritaine, the Sureaus had dressed in their new clothes and attended Brigitte's first mass. Brigitte had been enchanted by the ornate grandeur of Notre Dame, past which she had walked so often with her parents. The cadence of the Latin liturgy was as exotic as the sconces of burning sage that flanked the cathedral's massive central doorway. The incense had billowed smoke so thick that upon leaving after the service, she'd ducked her head and run beneath its smudge.

Within a few feet of the cathedral, they'd seized her. She was still laughing when she opened her eyes and realized that her captors were not her parents but two German soldiers. As they were escorted away, Brigitte had been terrified until she saw that her mother was serene and defiant. In the three weeks since, every time she felt afraid, she would examine her mother's gray eyes, intractable from either certitude or denial, and would again be reassured.

Today, Brigitte was especially comforted by Madeleine's defiance. She peered out from her linen refuge at the other faces, faces far less stoic than her mother's. Those not joyous were shadowed with despair, and certainly there were none so beautiful. One was frantic. It was a woman she recognized from her cell. Like most of her fellow inmates, she wore a black canvas scarf tied beneath her neck. It flattened her hair and framed her face so that her equally black, desperate eyes, though small and narrowly set against the wide expanse of her round, cartoonish head, were magnified by contrast. As she tilted her head back, her eyes mirrored the drab gray of the clouds. With her hands raised to the sky, she began to wail. Brigitte tried to turn away but couldn't. And so she looked on, collecting memories to be locked away in the mental vault she would soon construct.

Since their imprisonment, Brigitte hadn't once left her mother's side. Having arrived at Drancy hours after a deportation train to Germany, the Sureaus had been among the first of a new batch of detainees. During Christophe's interrogation, Madeleine and Brigitte had quietly waited in a large reception area under the surveillance of a fat bespectacled guard seated behind a desk, who glanced up every so often with an almost apologetic expression on his face. Brigitte strove to emulate her mother by staring straight ahead without making direct eye contact with him. But after a while, she got bored and looked about the room. Absentmindedly, her eyes strayed to the desk, and when they did, the guard gave her a wink so jovial she had to catch herself to keep from smiling.

The second guard, who had taken Christophe away, returned and commanded they follow him. Madeleine did not respond but gracefully uncrossed her ankles, rose from her chair and took Brigitte's hand in hers. Brigitte felt panic swell within her chest—where was her father and why were they leaving him? She calmed herself by again mimicking her mother, shadowing her every step: one in front of the other, in front of the other, in front of the other. The guard escorted them out of the main administration offices, through the courtyard to the detainment quarters, to an empty room barren of decoration or furniture except for three rickety cots. They chose the cot farthest from the door. Although the other two remained empty for three days, they slept together in the one small bed.

In the early days of their isolation, Brigitte's every thought was of her father, but on the third day, when others began to arrive, self-preservation emerged as a competing concern. By the end of the first week, the room had become so crowded that to make space for everyone, those on the floor were forced to sleep on their sides and those in beds, like Madeleine and Brigitte, slept upright, leaning against the cell wall. Sometime in the second week, one of the younger girls developed a cough. By day, the sound was absorbed by the crush of bodies, but at night it found its way to the concrete rafters. It echoed from the tiny opening in the door that wasn't small enough to obscure the fury of the eyes that repeatedly peered in to silence her. Just the day before, she was taken away, her cough replaced by her mother's whimpering.

It was this woman who now stood before Brigitte, her wail so haunting that Brigitte was paralyzed by its eerie discord, unable to escape the misery that had summoned it. The woman's face drained of hope. Her ankle-length charcoal skirt deflated as her legs crumpled beneath her. The thud of her body landing a few feet away broke Brigitte's trance and she retreated to her mother's skirt. In her tented sanctuary, she stared down at her shoes, counted to three, and then closed her eyes and inhaled deeply.

Day and night since their detainment, Brigitte and her mother had remained seated upon their cot, Brigitte in Madeleine's lap even in slumber. When awake, Brigitte passed the time by staring into the reflection of her shoes and imagining the day of their release. She made up her mind to leave exactly as they had come, with her dress and shoes immaculate. Yet now that the day had arrived, neither Parma nor the shoes' hypnotic charm could disguise the creaking of bending knees or the approaching voices of those who came to the woman's aid. There was one voice more distinct than the others: "There are no more girls." Parma's sweet fragrance gave way to the pungent smell of unwashed flesh.

Suddenly Brigitte was standing alone. Cinders were eclipsed by falling stars as people tore the damning yellow badges from their chests and threw them into the air. Brigitte spun around too fast, one foot tripping over the other. This time the arms that caught her weren't banded in red. They were her father's. He picked her up and drew her to him. The scruff of her father's beard scraped against her scalp. Its roughness soothed her. She craned her head back from his chest so she could see his face, her eyes glistening with uncried tears. Like Madeleine, Christophe appeared unfazed by his three weeks at Drancy, though his distinguished features had not hardened in resolve. They'd instead retained their soft reserve. Even with his beard, Christophe was more pretty than handsome—a distinction that before Drancy was an accurate reflection of his gentle disposition, but afterward would become more and more at odds with the man he came to be.

As Christophe rocked her in his arms, Brigitte's disbelief turned to adoration. The meager sunlight reflecting off her jostled shoes sent playful glints dancing about them. Idolatry conquered fear, and Brigitte's brimming eyes welled with tears of joy and relief. Christophe cradled her cheek in the palm of his hand, wiped away her tears with his thumb, and with mild censure lowered his voice. "Never let them see you cry." Obedient, she stopped.

The Red Cross guards urged everyone to wait for transport, indicating that it was too dangerous to leave the grounds without an escort. Christophe decided otherwise, and he led his family through Drancy's gates to freedom. Before he did, he turned to one of the young guards and asked something that neither Madeleine nor Brigitte could hear. The red-haired, red-cheeked, Red Cross youth nodded toward the center of the courtyard, to the nucleus of large steel drums, above which flames still flickered. "I'm not sure we'll ever know, as they've burnt all of the records."

The garish green and yellow deportation buses were lined up outside the gates. When Christophe asked if any were headed into Paris, the guard said that someone had sabotaged their engines, rendering them inoperable. At first Brigitte was happy not to ride in the same vehicle that had brought them to this place, but after twenty minutes of walking, she longed for its cushioned seats. But though she was tired and had been experiencing repeated waves of nausea since her father's reproach, she did not complain. At last, they approached a corner with a car stopped at a traffic light. Christophe scooped Brigitte into his arms, ran to the open window and asked the driver, "*Excusez-moi*, could you direct us to the nearest train station?"

The suited driver, a dark-featured man with an Eastern European accent, chose to ignore the question, and Christophe reached in and turned off the ignition switch. After a heated exchange, an agreement was reached. Madeleine took the front passenger seat, and Christophe and Brigitte squeezed alongside a well-dressed couple that huddled in the back. Christophe sat hunched forward, Brigitte upon his lap, and stared over the chauffeur's shoulder as if through his intent, he could hasten their journey. He neither touched his backseat companions nor deigned them his regard. Following her father's lead, Brigitte dared not acknowledge the couple beside her, but she did glance over to appraise the woman's beautifully manicured hands. They were diminutive and intricately formed, like the hands of a porcelain doll. One was tightly enmeshed with its antithesis: her husband's monstrous, bloated hand. The other rested upon a small white box tied up with a pink ribbon. Brigitte watched as the hand's delicate, precise fingers deftly untied the ribbon, disappeared into the box and reemerged with a small puff pastry. The hand reached toward Brigitte, and instinctively, Brigitte toward the hand. When Brigitte bit into the pastry, sublime deliciousness oozed from its core.

"*Arrête!*" Christophe snatched the pastry from Brigitte's mouth and threw it out the open window.

Brigitte's stomach lurched from the shock of both the rich cream and her father's spite, and she buried her face into his sleeve to avoid further rebuke. Overwhelmed, she finally surrendered to her exhaustion and the world dissolved.

When Brigitte awoke, they were on a train and she was again sitting upon Madeleine's lap. Everyone stared at them. Brigitte averted her eyes to the train floor where there lay a handwritten leaflet entitled *Operation Anvil Wields Heavy Blow. Hitler's Hold on Paris Weakening.* She tried to read the small print of the article, but her attention was drawn to one of her shoes that was scarred with a black smudge. It must have happened in the commotion of the morning. She told herself that it was unimportant, that they were going home, but then she noticed the red blotch on her dress. Again, her eyes welled. Standing over them, Christophe angrily licked his thumb and blotted a similar red stain from the arm of his shirt, the arm on which she had collapsed. Brigitte covered her face and wept. This time he was not so tender. He pulled her hands from her face, pressing his thumbs so hard across the bottoms of her eye sockets that they would both be blackened the following day. "I told you, never let them see you cry." But this time she couldn't stop and Brigitte sobbed until she depleted her tears. She would not cry again for over fifty years.

3

Paris, August 18, 1944

Brigitte arose a second day to smoke. The smell seeped into the room through the window that her father had left cracked open. She lay in her bed, staring at the ceiling's ornate rosette high above her and took a few moments to reorient herself to her bedroom, finally crawling out from under the sheets to tiptoe to the window. In the courtyard, her father had built a fire out of—from what she could tell—the few remaining items from their home: the kitchen table, the tattered Persian rug from the salon, and the mangled vanity at which, before Drancy, her mother had sat every morning to paint her face. Upon the table was a haphazard pile of Madeleine's beautiful dresses. Christophe stood before the fire, feeding the dresses one by one into the flame.

When they had finally arrived home the evening before, the house was a disaster. Much of the furniture had been stolen or was broken, and Christophe's and Madeleine's clothes were strewn throughout the house. The house reeked of urine and there was what appeared to be human excrement smeared across the entrance threshold. For whatever reason, Brigitte's was the only room left untouched by the pillage.

Madeleine had been certain that the rug and most of the clothes could be salvaged, but apparently, Christophe thought otherwise. He tossed each article of clothing into the fire, staring at the flames until it was completely consumed, after which he tossed another. It wasn't until Brigitte saw the satin bow that she realized the dresses were not just her mother's. For some time she remained at the window and watched her father's savagery before crossing the room to her empty wardrobe: no dresses, no hats, no shoes. Brigitte walked barefoot from her bedroom and silently descended the stairs. She pulled the nightgown over her head, and went from room to room, wearing only her *culottes*. As she passed the kitchen, she recognized a storage trunk that Christophe must have retrieved from the attic. The makeshift table was set with three place settings of unfamiliar china. Upon each plate was a full *entrecote*— an unfathomable expense, given the city's food shortage. Brigitte hadn't eaten meat in over a month and was entranced by the sight of three steaks. In awe, she entered the kitchen, but as she neared the table, the smell of the rare meat made her stomach revolt, and she rushed to the kitchen sink and threw up. Crouching to the floor with her head between her knees, Brigitte tried to collect herself, unable to even glance at the table for fear that she would again vomit. At this level, she was in a direct line of sight of the courtyard, and her father stared at her through the kitchen window. Though she cowered in nakedness, Brigitte made no effort to put her nightgown back on. When at last Christophe turned from her to resume his pyromania, she rose, holding her breath to avoid the slightest scent of the breakfast that would go uneaten. Still, as she ran from the kitchen, she couldn't help look one last time. Spreading across each plate was a shallow film of blood that had leached from the cooling steaks.

Brigitte found Madeleine in the salon. Handing her mother the balled-up nightgown, she asked, "Does he want to burn this too?"

Madeleine had aged ten years overnight. Lines creased her forehead and the skin above her upper lip cracked like dry paint when she attempted a placating smile.

Dropping her cleaning rag in the bucket of water, Madeleine took Brigitte's nightgown and gently slid it back over her daughter's head. Like the rag, her hands were stained from the vandals' paint she'd scrubbed from the walls. "There is so much I hope you never understand." Brigitte looked over her mother's head into the dining room. A crude Magen

David had been scrawled on the wall where the original photograph of Madeleine's first *Vogue* cover had hung. The star was whimsically painted in pastels—yellow and pink—as if the intruders had intended to ridicule them with the modesty of their color choice. As if their act was a trifle of no consequence. "But there are some things you must know."

As her mother explained both fact and fallacy, Brigitte stared at the chandelier that hung in the center of the vacant room. It, like she, had been stripped of every teardrop. In seven days Paris would be liberated. For Brigitte, it would take far longer.

4

Paris, Autumn 1944

In the weeks and months that followed their return, the Sureaus struggled to rebuild their lives. As Christophe and Madeleine worked tirelessly, Brigitte kept her distance and spent most of the time alone in her room, coming out only for meals. These brief moments provided her the occasional observation of her parents' mania. Brigitte would creep out to the landing and peer over the balustrade to spy on them with a mixture of emotions that were similar but far less containable than the fear she'd denied at Drancy. It wasn't fear she now experienced, but dread. She was terrified that the future would displace the past. This feeling had begun with her bleeding—which Madeleine had explained away as premature, but normal—and now spilled over into her every thought. Would she and her mother resume their bedtime ritual where they brushed each other's hair and conspired on what to wear the following day? Would her father come in afterward and read to her as he used to? When Madeleine tapped the underground network for knowledgeable medical advice about Brigitte's premature menstruation, her diagnosis was confirmed. She was told that it was a simply a "physical misfire," probably a reaction to sensory overstimulation, and that back home, in their natural surroundings, everything should indeed return to normal. Guided by this premise, Brigitte lay in her bed day after day and waited for a familial rapprochement that was never to be.

Once, when her mother was out and her father was working in the study, Brigitte sneaked into their bedroom. She admired Madeleine's modern Lucite vanity, appraising her countless accessories, each in its exact placement as mandated by the vanity's transparency. She rummaged through every drawer, turning various items over in her hand, searching for some remnant of their past, until she found Madeleine's new Bakelite powder boxes and pearlized brush set displayed prominently in the vanity's topmost drawer. Brigitte opened one of the boxes and a small cloud of beige powder erupted from within. She giggled, softly. Closing her eyes, she recalled a distant image of herself as a young child, sitting at her mother's vanity. Poised over her, Madeleine applied her make-up, explaining to Brigitte the purpose for each tube and jar. Madeleine was dressed for the evening but repeatedly conceded to Brigitte's pleading to be shown every beauty secret, again and again. "*Otwa fwa, otwa fwa,*" Brigitte had cooed at each plume of powder emitted by the puff Madeleine patted against her face. When Brigitte opened her eyes, the memory vanished. These modern accessories were too sterile, too different from Madeleine's pre-Drancy tastes to prolong any sentiment.

After dusting the vanity top and returning each item to its proper place, Brigitte crossed the room to Christophe's dresser. In the first drawer she opened, sitting atop his monogrammed handkerchiefs, was his razor. This was also newly purchased, but it was the same style as before—a ten-centimeter blade encased in a simple stainless steel sheath. She remembered the first time she had ever seen her father shave. Cradled in her mother's arms, Brigitte had been mesmerized by his new white beard. She could almost feel the dollop of lather he had smeared on her nose. The memory of her parents' laughter was silenced by a sudden outburst of their arguing from downstairs in the foyer. Brigitte tucked the razor into the folds of her skirt and slipped quietly out of the room.

That night at dinner, when Christophe asked Madeleine if she had seen his razor, Brigitte kept her attention on her food and the moment passed without suspicion. Afterward, Brigitte took the blade from under her pillow and hid it in the bottom drawer of her new vanity, a miniature version of her mother's. There was one drawer with opaque sides where the contents couldn't be viewed from the outside. *For a woman's little secrets*—the vanity's designer had advertised.

At night when she was alone in her bed, after her mother had again forgotten to wish her good night, after her father had again shunned her throughout the day, Brigitte would retrieve the razor from its hiding place and stare at it. She would recall their life before Drancy. But after a few months, she could no longer distinguish memory from hope. With time, it would no longer matter because both would fade.

In public, Christophe Sureau established his manner of retribution—humiliation. In an attempt to restore their former lives, they returned to La Samaritaine and various other stores, replacing the goods that had been stolen or destroyed. Christophe would insist upon sales clerks of Aryan attitude or feature and then debase them by exaggerating the subservience of their position, openly ridiculing any hint of equality. Every new grocer, tailor, and doctor was—if they wanted the Sureaus' business—subjugated to Christophe's condescension. Madeleine countered the overt nature of Christophe's scorn with disinterest. She all but ignored the Germanic tradespeople with whom she was forced to interact, deferring every instruction or interaction to her daughter. As such, at the age of nine, Brigitte became the matron of the Sureau household, responsible for the logistics and oversight of the new staff. To counter her father's offense, her chosen weapon was civility. At times, she appreciated and commended; occasionally, she charmed and flirted; she sometimes even curtsied. She won over everyone except the most resolute, which included Christophe. The more considerate she became, the more exacting his command—as if leaving the administrative details to his daughter was part of his humiliation tactic and, by her decorum, she undermined his plan. If he witnessed her slightest accommodation or hint of gratitude, he interrupted the transaction to reinsert his disdain. If her breach were severe, his recrimination would result in the servant's dismissal and her reprimand. Once, she'd laughed at something the cook said, and Christophe stormed into the kitchen and demanded to be told what was so funny. When Brigitte defended the cook, Christophe had sent her to her room without dinner. At least it was attention, something she received less and less of from either parent as they established their new regime.

Like Brigitte, Madeleine enacted her role with dignity rather than derision. She reclaimed her beauty and her social status. Though a converted Catholic who before the war had eschewed any religious tradition or practice, she was now the victorious Jewess, the beauty who had escaped Hitler's clutch with her family intact. She was profiled and photographed for every major Paris magazine, balancing the tragic images and stories of many less fortunate than the Sureaus. One magazine even traced her Jewish lineage back to her great-great-grandfather, the statesman Adolphe Crémieux, noting that his famous appeal to Louis Napoleon to be a "standard for reconciliation and not of disillusionment" rang true with modern day currency. The journalist mistakenly used Madeleine's maiden name throughout the article and from that point forward, Madeleine's *nom publique* was that of her former self—Madeleine Crémieux.

Madeleine Crémieux was proof that beauty and perseverance could triumph over hatred and repression. She was the future to a world that so desperately needed to look forward. With her fame, her husband's stature grew as well, as did that of Brigitte, the innocent child who had a grace and style all her own. Soon the Crémieux-Sureaus had surpassed their prewar social standing. In the selection of her new wardrobe, Brigitte was again allowed to choose. This time she opted for color. Not just color, but opulence: vibrant reds, lavish blues, fertile greens. Even the yellows she chose were the richest in hue.

In December, the inaugural edition of a new Paris daily called *Le Monde* ran a story on Madeleine. For the interview, Christophe and Brigitte sat quietly at Madeleine's side, and though no photo would accompany the article, Madeleine had them dress for the occasion.

Christophe donned his light gray suit and Brigitte a bright orange wool dress with a fanciful black soutache trim. Madeleine wore a cream modern gabardine dress, cut mid-shin like a fitted overcoat. With wide lapels, cuffed sleeves and deep accentuated pockets, it was similar in style to the utility dress she had worn at Drancy, except that this dress stressed form over function and was thus far less modest. Madeleine called it her "reconstruction look." Christophe and Brigitte were silent throughout the interview except when, at the end, the journalist took note of Brigitte's contrasting attire and addressed the final question to her:

> *Journalist:*   *"You have obviously inherited your mother's looks and sense of style. Anything else?"*
>
> *Brigitte:*   *"The love of my father."*

The article was entitled "Reconciliation."

5

Paris, October 2, 1948 - Morning

It was the morning of Brigitte's thirteenth birthday. She was in the bathroom, engrossed in her morning ritual. For her last birthday, her mother had given her a bathroom key of her own so she could lock the door as she saw fit. It had been after dinner, after the table had been cleared and Christophe had retired to the study. Kissing Brigitte goodnight, Madeleine handed her a small red envelope and said, "You are a young woman now. You will need your privacy."

Behind the locked door, Brigitte's hand guided the razor precisely, almost mechanically. As always, she entered a trance and once finished, would remember very little. The voices from the heating vent in the bathroom that, unbeknownst to her parents, transported the slightest sound from their bedroom, were channeled from conscious to subconscious like memories from a fading dream.

Madeleine appealed, "Darling, I don't see why we must put her through this today of all days."

Christophe contradicted, "You know far better than I that this is not normal. We can't bury our heads in the sand."

Brigitte finished and wiped herself clean. After putting everything back in order, she turned on the faucet and, due to a new invention that Christophe had recently installed, hot water was magically dispensed.

Madeleine called out, her voice no longer a tinny echo from the vent but her distinct articulation from just beyond the bathroom door.

"Brigitte dear, are you just now running your bath? You know we have to be there within the hour."

"Yes Mother, I know. I will be only a few minutes longer."

It was her second bath of the morning. When it was drawn, she gritted her teeth and stepped into its heat. She bore its scald and in return, she was once again clean.

The new doctor's prestigious Champs-Elysées address was directly across from the Arc de Triomphe. The building was one of the pie-slice wedges whose tip directly abutted the world's most famous roundabout. The Sureau family walked in silence up the six flights of steps and down the elegant hallway that seemed more like a luxury hotel than an office building. The hallway, however, paled in comparison to the doctor's waiting room with its fourteen-foot ceilings hemmed by at least a meter of ornate nested carved moldings that capped the rich sanguine-colored walls. Brigitte stared up at the room's grand chandelier that made their own recrystalled dining room chandelier look diminutive in comparison.

"I don't see why I can't accompany her. I always have in the past," Madeleine told the reception nurse who sat behind a prodigious Louis XIV desk that cut the room in half.

"Dr. Godard will call you back if you are to be consulted." The nurse was a young woman, in her early twenties perhaps, who had powder-white skin and thick blond hair waved like frosting. Her navy blue blouse was clasped with a gold floral pendant at the throat. She didn't look at all like a nurse, but like a stylish clerk in one of the tony Saint-Honoré boutiques. While she appeared solicitous, her voice was callous and stern.

The nurse led Brigitte down the hallway to a large triangular corner room whose window looked out over the Place de l'Etoile. She held open the door and talked into the room as if Brigitte were in front of and not behind her. "Sit on the table. Dr. Godard will be in shortly."

As Brigitte walked past, she noticed the nurse's pendant was not floral, but figurative—a mob of people huddled, the one in front holding a thin flag that trailed back and over the entire group. The gold buckled as though the flag were fluttering in the wind. Shutting the door, the woman added, now speaking into the hall, again in the opposite direction of Brigitte's presence, "At *his* convenience."

For thirty minutes Brigitte sat as she was told, waiting for the doctor's convenience. She looked around the room, which, like the building and the reception salon, revealed little of its medical facility. On two of the three walls were oil paintings of Paris, both of the Arc de Triomphe: one in winter, the other in spring. Even the white enamel table, from which her bare legs dangled, was more akin a kitchen pastry table than the austere stainless steel tables of the other doctors' offices she had visited in the past. Brigitte flicked the enamel with her finger and its ping resounded throughout the office. She finally lifted herself off the table and walked over to the window that looked directly out to Napoleon's Arc. It was more ominous from this vista, like a giant, headless beast marching across Paris. She could even make out the detail of the Arc's intricate frieze: carved armies marching as to war.

"It's quite a view, isn't it?"

Startled, Brigitte turned to confront a beautiful Aryan man—undoubtedly her father's choice. His face was formed by wide planes, and his thick curls of hair, so blond they were almost white, floated like clouds above eyes the color of a clear winter sky. He stood with superior posture, certain of his command. His physical perfection was that of a triumphal statue, as if he had been molded for Arc or pendant. He didn't wear a doctor's coat but a double-breasted charcoal suit that was tailored for eveningwear. He had no accent, per se, though his distinct pronunciation made his French sound like a foreign language: "An astonishing monument to a false victory soon overturned."

They stood side by side for a moment looking out the window, until he finally asked, "Brigitte, is it?"

Brigitte nodded in compliance.

"Please disrobe and sit on the table."

6

Paris, October 2, 1948 - Midmorning

Christophe clutched the steering wheel but made no attempt to start the ignition. He stared straight ahead through the windshield, his evenly modulated voice underscoring the extent of his anger. "He said her pubic hair follicle maturation indicates that she's probably been doing this since—"

"Darling, calm down. Can't we talk about this when we get home?" Madeleine adjusted the rearview mirror to see herself and took a handkerchief from her purse to blot her eyes.

Christophe turned to his wife. "It's nothing she hasn't already heard, Madeleine. If you recall she was in the room too, sitting naked with her legs spread wide open while I was shown her shaved stubble through a magnifying glass. *Quelle horreur!*"

"Horrible for whom?" Madeleine looked past her image to that of her daughter.

Christophe ignored her implication. "I can't believe you didn't know."

"Darling, it's not as if I perform daily inspections of her *hygiène personnelle.*"

Christophe readjusted the mirror, replacing its reflection of Madeleine's concerned wince with that of his harsher scrutiny. The mass of keys on his bulky keychain clattered together as he jerked them from his pocket. "We're not talking about a day, Madeleine. We're talking about three years."

"Christophe, please!"

Brigitte sat alone in the backseat, transposing her parents' raised voices onto the scene outside the window: a couple who stood immobile on the sidewalk, ogling the Arc de Triomphe. From behind, the woman's petite frame made her appear younger than she probably was. She wore a slim-waisted dress with a flared skirt, but on her short legs, the skirt didn't show well nor did its flare create the illusion of any womanly curves underneath. In contrast, the uniform of her lover transformed the boy into a man, though since Brigitte couldn't see his face, she could only imagine his as one of the many war-wizened faces of the uniformed youth that filled Paris. In Brigitte's storyline, the American soldier had brought his new bride to France to see the country in which he'd fought. Their dialogue was shrouded in mystery, an allusion to some recently shared intimacy.

Clapping his hands in front of him, the soldier joked, "I can't believe you didn't know."

His newlywed nuzzled closer to him. "Darling, it's not as if I perform daily inspections of your *cuisine personnelle.*"

He rubbed his face into her hair. His voice was garbled. "We're not talking about a day; we're talking three years."

The girl raised her slender arm to point at the monument. A tiny *Tour Eiffel* jingled from her wrist against untold other charms.

"Christophe, please."

The soldier put his arm around his wife's shoulder and led her farther down the sidewalk. As Brigitte watched them stride away, she felt her father's scowl from the mirror, but it was an anger to which she had grown accustomed. She did not acknowledge his contempt but remained looking out the window as the couple turned the corner and disappeared from view.

The Sureaus arrived home with less than an hour before the party was to begin. Christophe drove Madeleine and Brigitte to the front entrance, but instead of waiting for him to park as they usually did, Madeleine ushered

Brigitte into the house. "Darling, *depeche-toi*! Go change into your party dress. We'll talk about all this later." Brigitte ignored her mother's urgency and was unhurried in her ascent, showing neither excitement for the day's celebration nor anxiety from the morning's exposure of her deceit.

Upstairs in her room, Brigitte undressed. She walked over to her armoire and took from one of its hangers the dress her mother had bought the day before from the new couture shop that had recently opened in La Samaritaine. It was signature Madeleine style, a simple cut with a white chiffon overlay and a low neckline. Brigitte threw it across the room and stood naked in front of the mirror opposite her bed. The reflected body was not that of a twelve-year-old girl but the emaciated image of a stunted child. When the doctor had questioned her eating habits, she told him the truth, "*Je n'ai pas faim.*" She had never regained the appetite that had withered in Drancy.

Brigitte ran her hand up her side, caressing the contours of each rib as she passed, and then across her aching nipples. The pain had started again. She could feel the insistent swell beneath her skin. She would need to contrive some way to skip breakfast this week. Given the doctor's strong words to her parents, she knew that it was going to be harder than ever. But she would find a way.

Certain that she had locked her door, Brigitte gasped when it swung open. She lunged for her robe but Christophe stepped in front of her before she could reach the bed. She immediately sank to the floor to shield herself from her father's gaze.

"*Lève-toi.*" He took hold of both of her wrists and attempted to pull her back up to her feet.

Though she had balled herself into deadweight, he easily lifted her into the air. "Twenty kilograms—" the doctor had said, "—dangerously underweight." She dangled before him like felled prey.

"Father please, you're hurting me!" she screamed. Her shoulders felt as if they were about to dislocate, but Christophe continued to hold her in suspension, forcing her body to his as it uncoiled from fatigue.

"*Qu'est-ce que tu fais?*" Madeleine's shriek was desperate, emanating from somewhere behind her father's body, which eclipsed Brigitte's view.

When Christophe finally released her, she collapsed to the floor, followed immediately by her mother. In her descent, Madeleine took the bottom hem of her coat and like a mother hen's protective wing, fanned its full drape across Brigitte's crumpled body.

"Madeleine, we can't go on pretending anymore." Christophe stormed over to Brigitte's vanity and yanked each drawer from its frame.

Brigitte felt oddly safe in the asylum of her mother's coat, even as she watched her father's enormous black-shod feet stomp and kick in rampage. But though the coat's wool muffled Christophe's swearing and destruction, it magnified the clang of the drawers' contents upon the floor, especially metal objects. When the razor fell from its hiding place, Brigitte retracted into her own refuge just as she did when she guided the blade's edge. She receded to the edge of consciousness.

From her daze, Brigitte felt the increased swaddle of her mother's weight as Madeleine splayed her body over her daughter's. Christophe picked up the razor and waved it in front of his wife's face. "How could you not know she had this? How could you make us go through the humiliation of that man's inquisition?" He swung the razor again, this time closer to Madeleine's unscarred beauty. She didn't flinch. The only reaction to his threat was to remove her coat completely and gently spread it over Brigitte's exposed legs.

The blare of Christophe's disembodied voice was now a soft hum as Brigitte retreated into a cloud of white wool.

So withdrawn was she that she didn't register the shatter of the vanity's glass, nor her father's final threat: "Tomorrow the rest of her mirrors go as well."

Madeleine didn't speak to Brigitte as she dressed her. She was methodical, first sweeping up the mirror shards, and then Brigitte's toiletries, returning them to the vanity's broken drawers. Her preparation of Brigitte's appearance was as meticulous as her own. Madeleine was far more adept than Brigitte at embellishing the most modest of features, as well as dissembling the least conspicuous of flaws. Even after three years of subterfuge, Brigitte had not discovered her mother's tricks of camouflage. At last, Brigitte stood before the floor-length mirror that her father would, as promised, remove from her room the following day. Madeleine stood behind, inspecting her work: the reflection of her beautiful coming-of-age daughter ready to attend her thirteenth birthday. She smiled as she leaned down and whispered into Brigitte's ear, *"Demain est un jour nouveau."* They walked downstairs hand in hand, past Christophe's study, and went directly to the kitchen to address the servants.

7

Madeleine had spent September planning the party. She had spared little expense in developing the party's *Alice in Wonderland* theme, and had even convinced Christophe to replace the house's exterior gutter pipes with a whimsical art nouveau dolphin design that would be a permanent complement to the party's temporary fantasia. She also managed to obtain a private reel of the American movie version, which was no small feat, given the studio's tight rein on all private distribution. In an additional coup, *Le Monde* had planned to run an article the day before the party describing the Sureaus' courtyard, staged as the Mad Hatter's tea party. Worried about the perceived excess of the affair, Christophe demanded the interview be kept short and the article was relegated to a trifle in the culture section about the resurgence of the Jewish community in the Marais district. The journalist ended the piece with a tongue-in-cheek comparison of the party's *Alice in Wonderland* motif to the Sureaus' internment. Madeleine smiled widely when she picked up the copy of the morning paper that Christophe had left on the pantry's *confiturier* and discovered that yesterday's mention had ballooned into today's front-page controversy, with Jewish leaders calling for the journalist's dismissal over suggesting an analogy between Drancy—France's most notable symbol of Nazi compliance—and a children's fairytale.

As the hour for the party approached, Madeleine's increasing anxiety manifested in a scrupulous re-inspection of every detail. Brigitte sat alone in one of the courtyard's miniature chairs, looking very much like a forlorn Alice, though her wonder was of a subject less fanciful: whether or not her father would attend the party. This deliberation was interrupted by the early arrival of Geneviève. Brigitte's immediate inclination upon seeing her former best friend was to escape to her room. But there was only one door from the courtyard, and in it, Madeleine and Geneviève's mother stood conversing. Geneviève pardoned herself and made her way toward Brigitte.

For three years, the Perroys had not spoken to the Sureaus, a difficult evasion since they were next-door neighbors who shared an abutting courtyard. Most neighbors had reconnected over the course of the days and weeks following the Sureaus' return from Drancy, as liberation took root throughout the city. Many had come immediately to express their horror and offer what help they could. Others found sheepish or obsequious ways to make their condolences known, or they managed to reenter the Sureaus' lives with the mannered equanimity of their shared class. But the Perroys, the Sureaus' dearest pre-war friends, had made no expression of regret or attempt at reunion. On the contrary, they had made every effort, short of moving away, to avoid any interaction with the Sureaus.

Long ago, before the war, Geneviève and Brigitte had professed their undying friendship, going so far as to steal keys to their respective homes and bury them in a secret ceremony to signify their lifelong commitment to one another. "Friends forever," they had promised. Brigitte hadn't then known just how ephemeral *forever* was.

Not certain she could withstand Geneviève's first words face to face, Brigitte remained seated, resulting in an awkward greeting suitable to the occasion.

"You're so small." Geneviève giggled with nervous tension as she sat down next to Brigitte. "I guess that's the whole point of the theme, no?"

Geneviève was Brigitte's opposite: tall, long-featured, with perfect hair—or Brigitte's idea of perfect hair: straight and bodiless, so that it fell evenly on all sides. She wore a sleeveless icicle-blue dress with an empire waist meant for a younger girl who hadn't Geneviève's emerging curves for the satin's sheen to accentuate. In response to its suggestive cling, Brigitte unconsciously plucked from her skin the blouse of her own dress.

In the courtyard doorway, another mother had joined Madeleine and Mme Perroy, and two of Brigitte's classmates stood beside them, staring up at a large Queen of Hearts marionette that dangled from one of the upstairs windows. With the wind as the queen's master, she danced in midair. The party was about to spark.

Sensing their intimacy would soon be lost, Geneviève leaned into Brigitte with a whisper: "I've missed you so much."

And so the party began.

Fortunately, the other children knew one another, because for the next half-hour, Brigitte gave Geneviève a tour of the redecorated house, regaling her with details of this artist and that piece of furniture.

In the salon, Brigitte plopped down onto a chaise longue rocker of chrome and leather. "Mother adores everything modern these days. She was keen on this designer Jean Prouvé but she discovered his style was somehow related to Bauhaus and, well, as you can imagine . . . " Brigitte paused, conscious of her words. If Geneviève noticed, she didn't show it. " . . . that was the end of that."

"Anyway, as of late, she prefers women designers. This entire room is by Charlotte Perriand, who's becoming quite the luminary, admired by the likes of Le Corbusier and Léger. Except for that puffy chair in the corner. That was designed by some Irish woman named Eileen Gray who Mother says was modern far before modern was chic."

Brigitte again became aware of her chatter. She was so happy to have regained her friend that her tongue overcompensated. This time it was Geneviève's reaction—a blank stare—that made Brigitte realize she had been bragging. "Oh whatever, just come sit on it. It's like a teeter-totter."

The girls' laughter resounded throughout the house, enhancing the general gaiety of the party. Finally, upon one last teeter to Geneviève's totter, Brigitte's manners resurfaced. "We should get back to the party."

Geneviève stood, crossed the room to the salon door, and peered around it to survey the crowd. She looked back at Brigitte, and with a Cheshire grin, said, "Come next door. I want to show you something."

Standing in the Perroys' vestibule was more disorienting than Geneviève's renewed friendship. Everything looked as it had before, and suddenly Brigitte felt as if she'd fallen down the rabbit hole to her past.

Geneviève ran up the stairs, calling out behind her, "Wait here. I've got to hurry. If *Maman* finds out I brought you here, she'll be livid." In her excitement, Geneviève did not comprehend the implication of her words. Nor, for that matter, did Brigitte, who had already tiptoed down memory lane to M. Perroy's study to see if the infamous Bellangé *bergères* were still there. Brigitte smiled in remembrance of how her mother once envied these chairs, whose ornate detail was so different from her simple linear tastes of today. Her smile vanished when she saw the sketch that hung above M. Perroy's desk.

8

When Geneviève reappeared, Brigitte had returned to the staircase landing. Geneviève didn't notice Brigitte's malaise for she was too excited by a revelation of her own. Brigitte somehow mustered appropriate awe over Geneviève's miniature Hermes mannequin, an exact replica from Le Théâtre de la Mode (the identification of which reminded Brigitte who the braggart was in this friendship). Geneviève was so overcome that she invited Brigitte upstairs to see her newly painted room, but Brigitte convinced her that they needed to go back to the party so she could mingle with her other guests.

Adrift in the crowd, bewilderment gave way to conjecture as Brigitte realized that the stolen sketch that she'd just discovered hanging in Geneviève's house was a link not only to the past but possibly to the future as well. She mindlessly chatted with various neighbors and classmates while secretly polishing the looking glass of her mind's eye. When her mother shepherded the party into the dining-room-turned-home-theater, Brigitte trailed behind the crowd, eager for more time to reflect. For the full hour and a half of the movie, Brigitte wondered not at Alice's adventures, but at one of her own that had transpired six or seven years prior.

She remembered waking to a commotion of raised voices that were silenced by the bleating of a lamb. It had been a cold day but the sun was out, and there was that indescribable tingle in the air that signals the beginning of spring. By the time Brigitte dressed and made it downstairs, the lamb had been tied to a stake in the courtyard, and her parents were in the salon arguing with Grandmother Germaine in hushed tones. From what Brigitte could deduce, her grandmother had somehow acquired the lamb with the idea that it would bring the family good luck, but both Madeleine and Christophe were opposed to the idea. Brigitte stole past them into the kitchen to get a closer look. As soon as she spied the lamb, it spied her back, and in her memory (though it contradicted her mother's unequivocal assurance that such behavior was impossible from a lamb), the lamb wagged its tail. By the time the three adults discovered her in the courtyard, Brigitte had wrapped her arms around the lamb's neck.

Christophe threw his hands in the air. "*Sacrebleu*, now our daughter has been sullied by the beast." Brigitte wasn't sure how long they argued or when Tío Piquot arrived, because at some point she had been sent to her room. All she could remember was looking out to the courtyard as her father stormed out of the kitchen, untied the lamb and scooped it up in his arms. He carried it, kicking and bleating wildly, to the corner of the courtyard, where he cut its throat.

Brigitte had cried for days during which her mother tried to comfort her by explaining the meaning of Seder and the salvation of innocent families through the blood of the lamb. Grandmother Germaine had been raised with such beliefs, her mother explained, and had only done what she thought was best. Two weeks later, when the sketch arrived, Brigitte was horrified and there was no amount of convincing her that hanging it in their salon would honor the poor creature's sacrifice. Every time she passed it, she shuddered. She never understood, nor did her mother ever explain, why Tío Piquot had drawn it in the first place.

After their return from Drancy, Brigitte had reasoned that the theft of the gruesome drawing was the one benefit from the destruction of their home. To think that now she found it right next door, and that this drawing and this memory that she detested could indeed be the salvation of her family! When the movie was over and the lights turned back on, Brigitte was upset to find an empty plate in her lap. In her distraction, she had eaten an entire piece of cake. It was a careless mistake, one that before two hours ago would have made her rush to the bathroom to remedy. But though her stomach ached, it was now of no consequence. Her focus was elsewhere. Brigitte rose and returned her plate to the kitchen. She went to find her father but was intercepted by Geneviève and her mother, whose oblique regard conveyed, at most, mere tolerance. Had this encounter gone unwitnessed by other guests, Brigitte was certain Mme Perroy would have heeled her daughter to prevent Geneviève's hug and parting birthday wish that she whispered in Brigitte's ear: "Friends forever?"

Brigitte returned Geneviève's embrace. Her steady voice concealed competing emotions. "Yes, forever."

As the party thinned out, Brigitte repeated perfunctory farewells while mentally scripting her imagined conversation with her father. He would sneak up to her room to apologize, and just as he was about to speak, she would interrupt and let him know that she understood how difficult it had been for him. She would tell him how much she loved and admired him for working so hard to rebuild their life. He would smile his radiant smile that she hadn't seen for three years and would come over and lie down beside her, and it would be he who would cry, and she who would dry his tears. She would then tell him that she had found a cherished thing from their former life and that everything would be as it once was.

Brigitte rehearsed the scene over and over while she prepared for bed. Her heightened anticipation became unbridled delirium, so much so that she was unable to contain herself and unwittingly foiled her plan.

It happened when her grandmother came in to kiss her goodnight. Though Brigitte was raised Catholic, Germaine Crémieux still made subversive attempts to teach her granddaughter a bit of Jewish culture. Tucking Brigitte into bed, she said, "If you were a Jewish boy, today's party would have been called a Bar Mitzvah." In Brigitte's response, unpracticed words sputtered from her mouth. "*Mamour*, do you remember that drawing of Father with the lamb?"

Her grandmother's face darkened as she replied with a slow wistful timbre of regret, "Of course I do, dear. I am so sorry you had to witness such a thing. Such a superstitious fool I was."

Brigitte flushed, and though having been rendered almost breathless by her dither, she managed to prolong a pensive demeanor and sufficient delay in her response to honor her grandmother's remorse. Finally, she asked, "Do you believe Father would be happy if I found it?"

Germaine's face went blank. She raised a hand to her large cloistered bosom.

"The drawing, I mean. What if I found the drawing?" Brigitte looked over to the wall where her vanity had been; her father must have taken it sometime during the party. Her head began to throb. She imagined the drawing hanging on the empty wall: Christophe's blank visage staring out from the canvas gave no hint of his fury while the lamb struggled against his clutch.

Germaine's upper lip quivered and revealed her snaggletooth. When Brigitte was a baby, the exposed tooth had frightened her, and to this day it still triggered a visceral response. A shiver jolted through her body. "Brigitte, the past is past. We need to live in the present and look toward the future. My dear, we are the lucky ones. We survived. If you found that drawing, it would only remind us of all the innocent people who didn't."

The lamb kicked in her father's arms and, craning his head to the side, it shrieked.

"My dear, we must try to forget memories that cause us pain. It is this that will make your parents happy. It will make us all happy." The room echoed with the lamb's bleating. When Germaine kissed Brigitte on the forehead, she recoiled from her granddaughter's feverish brow. "Brigitte, *tu as de la fièvre*—are you feeling well?"

9

"Mother, Daddy promised." Brigitte squinted from the midmorning sun that reflected up from the sand, giving the beach a shimmery glow.

"Darling, I'm sure he'll be well by noon. Allow him a little more time. He was awake until very late." Madeleine was fully shaded by the tremendous umbrella that Tío Piquot had lent her. Not that it mattered, for she had barely any exposed skin, given the billowy sheer scarf tied around her waist and the tightly knit faille turban that bound her head. With her painted nails and rhinestone cat-eyed sunglasses, she looked like an American movie star. She didn't look up from her *Vogue* and punctuated her response by flipping the page. She was always reading *Vogue*.

Brigitte knew better than to interrupt her a second time, so she turned back to the sea. She still couldn't get over how big it was. Two days ago she had seen it for the first time. Nothing they had told her prepared her for its scale. She asked her father question upon question. "How far away is the other side? How deep is it? How can that man so far out in the surf be standing? Is he able to walk on water?" But they were all tired, and he promised he would answer her questions in the morning. When he broke that promise after she waited inside all day for him to get out of bed, he made another. Now, on day two, Brigitte waited again. At least today she waited on the beach, but its proximity made her anticipation worse. To allay her worries, she closed her eyes and listened to the waves.

In the darkness, they enthralled her even more, their gentle surf a lullaby teasing her with a recurring verse. *What caused them?* she wondered. She knew why rivers had motion; her father had told her. It was during one of their Sundays together at Square Barye where they sat together on a park bench while he read his paper. Brigitte never tired of watching the Seine sweep by, especially from the tip of Square Barye, where it rushed and split, dividing itself around the Ile St. Louis where they lived. She wasn't allowed to go alone, but on occasion, usually on Sundays, he took her with him. Most of their neighbors would be in church, so often it was just the two of them. She rarely disturbed him, but one morning she asked what made the water rush so. He stopped reading and spent what seemed like hours explaining how rivers were made of rainwater or melted snow streaming from higher to lower elevations. He told her how, since there was no way to predict rain or snow, people built dams and levees to try to control rivers so they wouldn't flood or run dry, but that sometimes the river still had its way, as with the great flood of 1910, which forced the city to reconstruct the levees. He had walked her over to the park's fence and given her a *centime* to throw into the water. Her toss was more of a drop and they both watched in silence as it bounced from and then rolled down and across the reconstructed levee, coming to a rest on the concrete just short of the river's edge. If only he were here now to tell her about the sea, about its waves that washed against the shore. If only he would walk her to its edge so she could drop a *centime* into the water. This time she wouldn't miss.

In the darkness of her mind, the waves began to swell. They crashed against the shore, louder and louder, until she could no longer distinguish thought from sound. She knew that if she didn't open her eyes, she would be swept out to sea.

Brigitte awoke from the dream in her father's shadow. She lay alone in his bed. He stood beside her, his face darkened by the contrast of the afternoon sun cast from the window behind him.

"*Ca va?*"

His calm voice erased the pain, but when she tried to speak, her throat rebelled. All she could manage was a squeaky lie. "*Bien.*"

Christophe's hand swept from the darkness into light as he reached toward her and stroked her forehead. "Everything's going to be all right." He left before she saw his face. For years she would think back to this morning, recasting his expression as anger, betrayal, or even disgust, anything but a face that mirrored the smooth evenness of his voice—a face filled with tenderness and love. And forgiveness. But as he walked away it was this inviolable purity that she imagined, and thus Brigitte would forever wonder: if on that morning she had seen his face for what it was, would everything have turned out differently?

10

Paris, Winter 1948-49

Brigitte's recovery was slow. Doctor Godard said it wasn't just the Scarlet Fever, but that her body was weak from malnutrition. His insinuation of neglect was clear. As before, his diagnosis infuriated Christophe. Christophe insisted that Brigitte be monitored. Madeleine finally agreed. The following week, Madeleine's mother moved into the guest bedroom.

Under Germaine's watchful eye, Brigitte started eating. By Christmas, she had gained ten pounds and her teenage body began to take shape. She also menstruated for the first time since Drancy. Brigitte was distraught by these changes, but her grandmother, who made no attempt to discover the cause of Brigitte's concern, was frank and stern.

"Brigitte, try as you may to retard nature, you are maturing into a young woman. While there are some unfortunate realities in this process, there are fortunate ones as well." With this she began a discourse on sexual pleasure, something she insisted one should never be ashamed of.

During this time, Brigitte had very little interaction with either her mother or father. Madeleine's career had taken off again. A new clothing designer named Christian Dior had selected her as one of his "New Look" models and when America's *Time* magazine featured an article on postwar style, her tuxedo dress photo from his debut collection ran as its cover. Even the article's title, "A New Look for a New Day," paid homage to Madeleine. When asked how Dior had convinced her to wear a black dress when there had never been a published photo of her in any color but white, Madeleine replied, *"Aujourd'hui est un jour nouveau."* (The magazine printed her response in its original French.) Upon reading the quote, Brigitte felt cheated. Her mother had parroted to the public words of solace that Brigitte had thought were meant for her alone.

When the "New Look" toured in America, Madeleine was the one model Dior insisted accompany him. The six-month trip was sponsored by Chambre Syndicale in an effort to boost France's flagging fashion industry, with a particular focus on a revitalization of *haute couture.* Everything about the tour was to be new and one-of-a-kind, including the transportation itself: the inaugural transatlantic flight of an enormous plane dubbed *Deux Ponts* because it was big enough to have two full passenger decks. Madeleine was terrified of airplanes, especially flying an untested prototype across the ocean, but Mr. Dior convinced her to go and went so far as to hire a car to chauffeur the entire Sureau family to the newly reopened Villeneuve-Orly airport to see her off.

On the ride to the airport, Christophe sat in front and Brigitte in the backseat between designer and model. Although it was a large car, they were crowded, and Brigitte's dress caught under Mr. Dior's leg. In pulling it free, she attracted his downward gaze. It was the first time she'd seen his face up close and her immediate thought was that he had too much skin: it sagged from the top of his bald head, down his face, to the thick folds that comprised his neck.

"You must be very proud of your mother," he said.

Madeleine took Brigitte's hand, her touch warmed by vanity. Brigitte too blushed with pride. When she looked back up to address Mr. Dior's remark, he had already redirected his attention out the window, to the narrow winding streets of the Marais.

Photographers lined the red carpet that stretched from airport to plane. The following day the paper would be filled with photos of *Christian et Madeleine.* There was also one of Christophe and Brigitte together on the tarmac. It was a casual snapshot in which the blur of Brigitte's waving hand matched that of the plane's double propellers. It appeared as though her other hand was enclosed in her father's. It wasn't.

11

Paris, Spring-Summer 1949

The moment Madeleine had decided to go, Christophe isolated himself even further. After she left, he stayed later and later at work, leaving Brigitte and her grandmother to dine alone. No matter how early Brigitte awoke, he would be gone. Whenever she did manage to place herself in the same room with him, she employed every contrivance imaginable to attract his attention. But the harder Brigitte tried, the more distant he became. She began to lose weight again as her grandmother's vigilant eye was redirected to the oversight of household duties that, in her parents' absence, Brigitte had begun to neglect. Christophe wasn't around enough to take notice.

After the third week, he started spending weekends in Antibes. Germaine said that Christophe was trying to buy the seaside house they used to rent before the war. Brigitte doubted her grandmother's defense, but every mention of Antibes would nourish her dream. It was always the same—she and her mother together on the beach, waiting for him—except that each recurrence brought with it added detail: the deep red of her mother's nail polish, the light breeze of the wind off the sea, and the increasing anxiety that her father might break his promise again. Every time, she would awake before he came. Until one night in the midsummer's heat, when the dream changed.

It started the same, except that her mother wore the black Dior tuxedo dress with long black gloves. She still had on rhinestone sunglasses although they were no longer white, but black like the rest of her outfit. On the cover of the *Vogue* Madeleine was reading was a photo of herself in the same dress and glasses that she was currently wearing. Brigitte sensed that soon they would leave and she would never be allowed to discover the sea. She prayed for her father to come. It was an odd feeling to pray. Brigitte knew nothing of praying except what she had intuited from the other women at Drancy—how when they closed their eyes, their faces would soften, causing their jowls to droop and quiver with the minute movements of their lips. For their stark contrast to her mother's beautiful tightlipped countenance, Brigitte had pitied the ugly praying ones. But now Brigitte too closed her eyes, relaxed her face and prayed that Christophe would come. This time he did.

She was in his arms and they were in the surf before her mother had time to notice she was gone. He kept running until he was knee-deep, the water he kicked splashing over them like the Place de la Concorde fountain she and her grandmother had visited just the week before. When he stopped, the water's spray continued to rain around them, shielding them from view, containing their voices to them alone. He whispered, "Promise me you won't tell your mother. You must promise me." After Brigitte nodded, he directed her, "Now, wrap your legs around me and hold on."

She straddled his waist, readying herself the best she could, tensing and clenching her every muscle as he dove backwards into the surf. She closed her eyes in preparation for the water's splash that never came, and held her breath for the plunge that didn't follow. Instead, they skimmed across the water's surface with Brigitte riding atop her father's stomach as if he were a giant upside-down fish. The sea spread out before them as they sped farther and farther from the shore. Terrified, she focused on her father's gaze. His smile was like none she had ever seen. It was intense and full of adoration. She relaxed and enjoyed the wind as it warmed her. It was surprisingly without odor, unlike the briny smell of the shoreline. When she was finally able to look into the sea, she noticed through the clear water bright coins glittering up from the seafloor like stars.

The next thing Brigitte knew, they were on dry sand, sitting on a park bench. Her father was reading the paper, and the curtain of water that enshrouded them was now clear and silent. "Daddy, where are we?"

Christophe glanced up from his paper. He looked funny in his siren suit. This was the first time she had seen him wear it since the day he bought it. "We're on a sand bar. Remember I told you, it's a little hill on the seafloor. Look, it's just big enough for you and me." As he went back to reading his paper, Brigitte contemplated her feet, dangling from the bench's edge. She admired her new white patent leather shoes. Aglow with the sun's reflection, they were perfect. But as she stretched her legs out to get a better look, her feet penetrated the fountain's curtain. The water pelted down with such force upon her legs that it knocked them back down and splashed a spray of seawater into her lap. She giggled, thinking it was funny at first, until out of the corner of her eye, she saw the black scar across the toe of her right foot. Suddenly, it was colder and she wanted to go back. "Father," she tried to say, but the word wouldn't come. He continued to read his paper. The water's veil was no longer clear, but murky; she couldn't see through it. It was then she noticed that the seawater had stained her dress. A red spot had appeared in the center of her lap, and the dress's wet cloth weighed heavy upon her skin. Her gasp at the stain caught her father's attention, and when he looked up, his face had changed. It was flush with disappointment. "Oh Brigitte," he said. He stood from the bench and walked through the wall of black water, leaving her alone. Brigitte's eyes burned, but she did not cry. She knew that he would come back if only she did not cry. The fountain's curtain faded into a sky of ash falling upon the water that stretched out around her for as far as she could see.

12

Brigitte's relapse happened so fast that by the time Christophe was notified and caught the first train back to Paris, he arrived to a large yellow *quarantaine* flag draped upon their front door. Christophe ripped down the flag and marched into his home. The day nurse did her best to convince him of the risk, but Christophe stormed upstairs to find Brigitte delirious with fever. After escorting the recalcitrant nurse out the door, Christophe returned to his daughter. He cradled Brigitte's limp, wasted body in his arms and carried her to his bedroom, where he gently tucked her into bed.

The next morning Christophe telephoned a friend of his at the Office International d'Hygiène Publique to discover that there was no precedent for publicly quarantining someone with rheumatic fever and, furthermore, there had been recent discoveries that the new miracle drug, penicillin, might be effective in eradicating the bacteria. After Christophe hung up the phone, he stood motionless for some time until he finally again lifted the phone's receiver. He first called an ambulance, then his mother-in-law, whom Dr. Godard had sent home for her own safety, and finally Madeleine. It took several hours for the international operator to get through and when she did, Mr. Dior's secretary answered the line.

"I'm sorry, Mr. Crémieux, Madeleine has accompanied Christian to dinner."

Christophe's silence was magnified by the telephone's delay. At last, he said, "Could you tell her that her daughter is seriously ill and that she should come home as soon as possible?"

Though she was released from the hospital the day after Madeleine's return, Brigitte's recovery was again hindered by her frailty, although this time her debility was far more profound. Her physical health did improve gradually and, again, she began to put on weight. Still, her disposition remained that of a sickly child. She responded when spoken to and complied with the routine required of her, but she was vapid and morose.

Three months later, when Madeleine took Brigitte to the doctor for a follow-up appointment, the question of Brigitte's sudden weight gain led to the discovery that she was pregnant. Madeleine was stunned. "I'm afraid your daughter has traded one perversion for another," Dr. Godard had informed her, his monotone disaffection laced with judgment. Back in the car, Madeleine wept.

For the first time since her illness, Brigitte's curiosity was spurred. *Am I dying?* she wondered. It was comforting that through her impending death, she'd managed to affect her parents. Just maybe, for however long she had to live, they could be a family again.

On the drive back, Madeleine's interaction with Brigitte was tender. She asked about school, particularly the boys and teachers to whom Brigitte was drawn. Brigitte's responses were less rote than usual and included modest embellishment of feigned crushes and wayward glances. She assumed that such behavior would provoke Madeleine's intrigue and would disguise the truth: that Brigitte was even more reclusive at school than at home.

Once home, Madeleine's attention abruptly ceased and she asked Brigitte to wait in her room until her father returned home from work.

For two hours, Brigitte sat with her ear pressed to her bedroom door, listening to her mother's repeated phone calls and muffled conversations. She imagined that Madeleine was breaking the news to family and friends. Brigitte's mood continued to lift and she became restless, a welcome reprieve from her months of stupor.

When she heard her father come in the front door, Brigitte's heartbeat slowed to the attenuated tick of the glass-domed clock that sat on a stand in the hallway just outside her door. She knew that everything hinged on his first words, but they were words she never heard. Madeleine and Christophe's whispers were too guarded to carry upstairs. Thirty minutes later, Madeleine came to Brigitte's room, alone. She sat down on the foot of the bed and told Brigitte of their decision to move to Antibes. The words rushed over Brigitte, bringing with them a torrent of emotions she couldn't decipher, neither those of her mother's nor her own. That night, Brigitte dreamt again of Antibes, a dream not of the past but of the future. The shoreline was the same, as was her mother's presence and attire. Yet everything was somehow different. The most obvious change was that her father was there as well. Like in her previous dreams, Brigitte was distraught with anticipation, not anticipation for him or her discovery of the sea, but rather for her imminent death. She asked him question upon question and with Christophe's unwavering attention, her anguish slowly dissipated. Yet in its absence, there was nothing. With each question he answered, she felt lighter and lighter, until she finally floated up from the beach, above her parents who waved goodbye, above the sea that stretched across the horizon. After she woke, the dream quickly faded, as did the residual optimism when over the course of the two-week preparation for the move, her father never spoke to her once.

The morning before their departure, Madeleine explained the situation to Brigitte. She was not dying but was pregnant and would have a baby sometime in the new year. Brigitte did not understand, nor did she ask questions. She simply listened to her mother's plan. Madeleine had made arrangements for her to go away to the island of Elba until the baby was born. Afterward, Brigitte would come back to Antibes and Madeleine and Christophe would raise the child as their own, as Brigitte's sibling. At some point, when enough time had elapsed to avoid suspicion, the family would return to Paris.

Later that night, long after her parents had retired for the evening, Brigitte crept into their bedroom. Her conviction gave her the fortitude and the grace to slip in unawares. She paused to gaze upon her parents in slumber. They slept back to back, Madeleine deepening night's resolve with a sleep mask and Christophe by burying his face into his pillow. They were perfectly still, no snore or twitch invaded their escape. Christophe's dresser was in the far corner of the room. It didn't take her long to find the razor. Afterward, she tiptoed back to the door, stealing one last glance at her parents.

She didn't bother to change from her nightgown; her trip was a short, desolate one. The cold air should have invigorated her, and yet her torpor was too deep for her to notice autumn's early arrival, feel its dampness cling to her gown and bathe her skin. The year before, summer had held on through September as she and her mother ran the final errands in preparation for her birthday party that was less than a week away. This year, there had been no mention of such celebration.

Square Barye was empty, its midnight darkness brutal in the postwar rationing of electricity. A single light trickled through one of the *chambre de bonne* windows atop L'hôtel Lambert, its flickering that of a lone candle. As Brigitte approached the park's edge, a light breeze off the Seine greeted her. With the razor in her hand, the trance came easily, its familiar otherness seducing her as before. She disrobed and deftly shaved her pubic hair, but this last time she intended to go further, much further. In the final moment, the blade glinted and broke the spell. Brigitte looked out over the river. There was no moon from which the light could have emanated, and the stars were too distant to intrude. For now, her decision had been thwarted. She retracted the blade back into its sheathing, slipped back into her nightgown, and walked the few short blocks home.

In Brigitte's distraction, she found herself at the Perroy's front door instead of her own. Since Brigitte's birthday party a year prior, the Perroys had again distanced themselves from the Sureaus, creating excuse upon excuse for Geneviève's absence whenever Brigitte inquired. Brigitte's illness had further sealed the girls' separation. As Brigitte looked up the house's façade toward Geneviève's window, a cold wind raised goose flesh on her exposed arms as it whispered the twice broken promise: *Friends forever.*

Brigitte turned around and crossed the street to the steps that led down to the river. Here the Seine's rush was ever present, but Brigitte did not heed its beckon. Her compulsion had found another target. She had been the one who had chosen the tree, and she hadn't forgotten. She passed two lovers sequestered in the dark, but neither they nor Brigitte acknowledged the illicit intent of the other. When Brigitte unearthed the small metal box, she opened it and found the keys still there, untouched. The key to her house would no longer work because Christophe had replaced the lock. She withdrew it from the box and tossed it into the river. The lovers paused to watch the key plummet through the air, but upon its imperceptible splash, they retreated into the shadows. Brigitte tucked the other key into her pocket.

Back in front of the Perroys' house, Brigitte slipped back in time as she turned Geneviève's key and the door opened. She crossed the formal vestibule, walked to the stairwell, and stood for a moment with a faint desire for her friend's descent. It was a short-lived sensation and soon Brigitte turned to go. Before she did, she followed yet another impulse. She found her way to M. Perroy's study, guided by memory to the *bergère* chairs. She ran her hands down their ornate carved frames to the thick embroidered upholstery silk. From the chairs, she felt her way to the desk and followed its edge to the wall behind, sliding her hand over the plaster until she found the frame's lower edge. She quietly pulled the desk chair over and climbed up onto it. This impulse she followed to fruition. The room's darkness was complete with no ambient light to glint from the razor's retracted blade as Brigitte cut the drawing from its frame.

Upon the Perroys' doorstep, Brigitte folded the sketch into a manageable size while Geneviève looked on from two stories above. Geneviève had awakened suddenly from a nightmare. She sat in her dark windowsill, unable to shake the vague sadness that lingered from the dream, and watched her friend turn and walk away.

13

Antibes, October 1-3, 1949

The train ride was long and silent. Christophe read a book, Madeleine her magazines, and Brigitte stared out the window. City after city, station after station bore the pockmarks of the war's destruction, scars that had not yet been effaced through the country's widespread renewal efforts. It was dusk when they reached Antibes but still light enough for Brigitte to recognize the charm of the small Mediterranean port. Here there was neither destruction nor renovation as the town was sufficiently insignificant and remote to escape the Germans' reach.

The day before Brigitte sailed from Antibes was her fourteenth birthday. Her mother had awakened her with a kiss upon her forehead. *"Bonne anniversaire, ma chérie."* The three of them spent the day touring the town. They were a family on holiday—a family that spoke little and enjoyed less. They stopped for dinner at a magnificent seaside resort called Eden Roc. The maître d' recognized Madeleine, which secured them a reserved table on the terrace. It was a place where few words were needed and overt enjoyment was scorned. The Sureaus fit in nicely and ordered their meal one exemplary course at a time. As their dinner dishes were being cleared, Brigitte excused herself and walked to the edge of the terrace. She leaned into the rail and stared out into the unobstructed blackness of the Mediterranean. There was a light wind that carried the smell of the sea.

Their waiter came over and leaned down to ask if she would be having tea. He was tall and slender, with olive skin that she would soon discover was generally classified as Mediterranean, and an instant appeal that she would years later realize as sexual. He was far closer to her parents' age than hers, but unlike most of the patrons, he had a casual ease about him that dissembled any distinction of generation or class.

She kept her gaze to the sea. "Are you familiar with the island of Elba?"

"Certainly—" He answered without affect, as if her question were a natural response to his. It was that kind of place. "—the island that Napoleon was exiled to."

"How far away is it?" Brigitte gently placed her hand on her barely swollen abdomen.

He joined her stare. "I'm not certain. It must be pretty far or they wouldn't have exiled him there. At least far enough so that he couldn't easily come back. Why?"

Brigitte almost said, "He did come back," but held her tongue.

"Darjeeling please."

Cake was brought to the table—thin slices, no candles. Each of them had their own individual tea set. That night, back at their new home, Brigitte heard a muffled argument between her parents, whose bedroom abutted hers. The centuries-old stone walls were thick so she couldn't make out what they said, except her father's final words: *"Le pardon est impossible."*

The next morning the Sureaus stood upon the beach of which Brigitte had so often dreamt. They were finally all three together and though the occasion was anticipated, it was not with joy. Madeleine and Christophe each kissed her goodbye. He said nothing, and Madeleine whispered only, *"Adieu, ma chérie. Je t'aime."* Yet her touch lingered, as did her perfume. It took two weeks to wash the tenacious scent from Brigitte's dress and years before the smell of violets, real or imagined, was more pleasure than pain.

The two couples on the sailboat greeted Brigitte with a warm welcome. The women, both pregnant as well, showed Brigitte her accommodations while the men helped Christophe load her luggage onto the boat. As they sailed away, Brigitte saw her father take her mother's hand. It was the first act of physical intimacy she had seen between them since Drancy. Everyone waved, a final sentiment. The looming stone bell tower of Antibes cathedral chimed the hour. It was 7 A.M. October 3, 1949. It would be far longer than a few months before she would see her parents again. In fact, it would be a new century. She would spend her lifetime trying to both forgive and forget. She would accomplish neither.

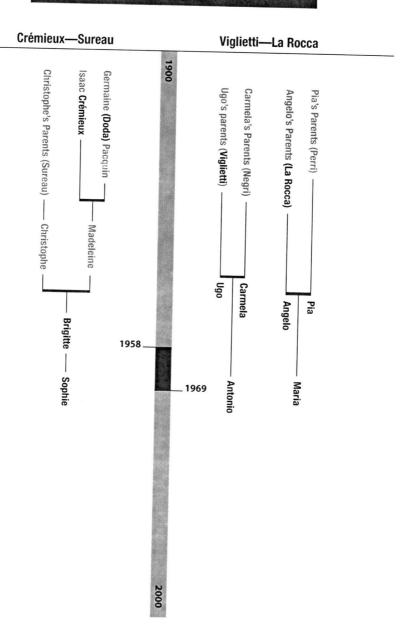

14

Train from Padua to Rome, January 31, 2000

The short train ride from Padua to Ferrara had been a quiet one, enabling Brigitte's subconscious to reenact long-suppressed memories without intrusion. Although it had been fifty years since her initial journey to Elba, the Mediterranean was recast with the same iridescent shimmer of that long-ago morning: an eerie meld of sea and sky that both reflected and absorbed the light. The sixty-four-year-old Brigitte twitched in her sleep as her adolescent dream-self shivered on the bow of the strangers' sailboat, waving to her estranged parents upon the shore. Both Brigittes held back their tears—the younger from five years of constant practice, the elder as a matter of course. As the memory of Christophe and Madeleine faded into the distance, the sounds of children playing in the neighboring compartment jolted Brigitte's dreamscape forward, not to the present, but past her awkward welcome to Portoferraio, past her transformation under the tutelage of her new friends, and past the birth of her daughter, Sophie, and the ugly legal battle that ensued. It came to a rest on May 17, 1958, the morning of Sophie's eighth birthday.

Sophie was begging Brigitte to try one of the new ice cream bars the café had started importing from England when Brigitte's grandmother, Germaine Crémieux—the surprise trump card of the family dispute who had moved to Elba to help Brigitte raise Sophie—walked through Caffè Roma's door in a state of confusion. This was particularly disconcerting because Germaine had recently had an alarming fainting spell and Brigitte thought she had convinced her to stay out of the heat. It was a memory that would record not only Germaine's initial signs of dementia, but also Brigitte's attempt to crack open an emotional window, one that she couldn't before bear to consider and would soon after seal shut forever, only to peer through it from afar.

15

Portoferraio, May 17, 1958

"So I've finally managed to attract your attention." Donovan was from San Piero, a small hillside village on the other side of the island. He was a medical student attending university in Padua, but at the insistence of his parents, had returned to Elba for the summer break. Having grown accustomed to an urban life, Donovan couldn't bear to spend the entire summer in his tiny hometown and persuaded his parents to let him live in Portoferraio with the promise of at least two weekly visits. With his red hair and pale skin mottled with freckles, his name suited him, though it was hard to believe with such fair complexion that both of his parents were Italian.

Brigitte watched Sophie run to welcome her great-grandmother. When Brigitte turned back around to face Donovan, her features had hardened. She presented the facts as if she were a lawyer arguing her case. "If something as enticing as ice cream in an edible container is advertised in front of a child a mere forty-eight hours before her birthday, the child's mother is not going to hear the end of it until it has been tasted."

When the fourteen-year-old Brigitte had first arrived on Elba, public suspicion due to her inability to speak Italian turned to distrust of her French manners and eventually to scorn as her pregnancy began to reveal itself. Her hosts, the Vigliettis and the La Roccas, were her fearless protectors, and they soon became much more—a surrogate family who displayed an unconditional love that she had only read of in books.

Ugo Viglietti and Angelo La Rocca were social idealists who met at university and had been conspiring ever since. They argued constantly and agreed on everything. They met their future wives, Carmela and Pia, at a communist rally protesting the *Casa Savoia*'s support of Axis aggression. Ugo had just given a speech condemning the King's loyalty to Mussolini when Carmela came up to him and challenged the statistics he quoted. It was love at first bicker and Ugo insisted she join him for dinner to finish the debate. To boast (and ensure) his conquest, Ugo asked Angelo to chaperone. Carmela brought her best friend, Pia. From that night forward, the two couples were inseparable.

Unfortunately, their four families each found the others socially, geographically and ecclesiastically undesirable. To avoid continued confrontation, Ugo and Angelo dropped out of school and eloped with Carmela and Pia, and the newlyweds eschewed all family ties and struck out on their own. They moved to Elba and started a small boating company, and Ugo and Angelo combined their surnames to call it Le Voci. Years later, Brigitte would see an episode of the American show *The Honeymooners* and be wistfully reminded of the Viglietti-La Rocca dynamic. If the actors had had mustaches and the actresses black hair, and each of them had been a shade darker, shorter and thicker (except for Jackie Gleason who, with the exception of the shaven face, was a pretty accurate representation of Ugo), then the two fictional couples would have been indistinguishable from her friends. Any Portoferraiese who saw it would agree.

Within days of being on Elba, Brigitte had begun eating normally again, and it was Carmela and Pia who coached her to hold her head up high and look the puritan *fascisti* in the eye (for the Vigliettis and La Roccas, anyone they disapproved of was labeled a *fascista*). After regaining her post-pregnancy figure, it was tempting to pretend to new people that she was Sophie's nanny, but Carmela and Pia convinced her that such chicanery would be demoralizing and give the *fascisti* the upper hand. Now, almost eight years later, every time someone confused Sophie for a younger sister, Brigitte would take a deep breath, prepare an unapologetic glare, and correct them, bracing herself as their winsome regard became shock, derision or at best, embarrassment. She had also developed an unconscious habit of divulging their mother-daughter relationship in an initial comment or response so that she could control the disclosure.

Donovan didn't flinch. "Ah, so that means your daughter's birthday is today—how fortunate for me." He winked at Brigitte before asking, "*Due novantanove?*"

"Excuse me?" Though after eight years on Elba, Brigitte had finally become comfortable speaking Italian, she would still second-guess her ears.

"*99 Flake*—it's the name of the ice cream. It's British."

Behind her, Brigitte heard the boisterous entrance of little Antonio and Maria. Antonio (Ugo and Carmela's son) and Maria (Angelo and Pia's daughter) were born within six months of one another. The three children were so close that at times, it almost seemed as though they, like some twins or in this case triplets, had yet to recognize themselves as independent beings. Brigitte felt their swarm around Doda (the pet name Sophie had given Germaine). To the children, Doda reigned supreme, due in part to her unmitigated excess. Her latest indulgence was a Grammont console from Paris, one of the few privately owned televisions on the island. Every Thursday, rain or shine, the children crowded into Doda's salon to watch *Lascia o Raddoppia*, one of the only shows the television's poor reception could pick up.

"*Otwa fwa, otwa fwa*," Maria implored, commanding Doda's repeat performance of something she had done to delight the children. Brigitte shivered. Maria had picked up a few French words from Sophie, though the crude way that she pronounced them always made Brigitte cringe, which she thought odd given her own difficulty with languages.

Ignoring the commotion, Brigitte asked, "Why 99?"

Donovan was tongue-tied and neither he nor Brigitte responded with the requisite gestures to dismiss his hesitation as inconsequential. The two confronted each other, dumbstruck. Windowed on both sides, Caffè

Roma was situated between the harbor and Piazza Cavour so at any time of day, sunlight streamed in one side or the other. At the perfect midday hour, it shone evenly through both. It was this perfect hour, and Brigitte and Donovan's faces reflected the opposing light.

Donovan broke the tension. "I'm not sure why, but I have a guess." He took a pen from behind the counter, reached across the counter and took Brigitte's wrist. Brigitte clenched her hand into a fist, attempting to pull away, but with his gentle coaxing, she relaxed her fingers to an exposed palm. In its center he wrote *IC*.

Donovan's skin was smooth and cool against hers. They were the hands of a student, not a *barista*. "What's that?"

"The Roman number *99*." Donovan's grip loosened but Brigitte no longer tried to retrieve her hand.

"So?"

Donovan's face beamed with self-gratification. "The English name for *gelato* is *ice cream*. Get it—I. C."

"You figured this out by yourself?" Brigitte slid her hand from his and bent down to address shy little Maria who tugged at her skirt.

Donovan's smile broadened. "*Sì.*"

"Sig.ra Cremiù." Maria hadn't learned to pronounce the French *eux* and so she substituted the Italian *ù*. "Doda's upset."

Brigitte followed Maria to the table where the children surrounded their Doda.

The next few minutes were a tangle of confusion. Brigitte tried to hide her concern as her grandmother revealed that she had suddenly found herself outside in the square without any recollection of having left the flat. And when Donovan brought them all *99s*, presenting them with a deep bow to Sophie as a birthday present, the children's squeal caused their Doda to scream and duck, a reaction she couldn't explain.

Donovan wouldn't accept payment for the ice cream and even left the café to escort the family across the square to Brigitte's apartment building, a modest sienna three-story *palazzina*, one of the few on the square whose bottom floor had not been converted to retail space in the postwar reconstruction of Portoferraio. With her grandmother and the children safely ensconced upstairs in front of the television, Brigitte remained downstairs with Donovan at her doorstep.

"Is there anything else I can do to help?" he asked.

The door was wide open and they stood mere inches from one another, and yet the threshold that stretched between them maintained decorum. Brigitte asked, "Shouldn't you be getting back?"

Donovan rocked back and forth on his feet, his hands behind his back. "It's just a summer job. In September, I return to school anyway."

"Oh."

"Padua's a beautiful city. Have you ever seen it?"

"No, I've never been to the mainland."

Excitement freed Donovan's bound hands. He thrust them into the restricted zone and stepped over the threshold into Brigitte's flat. His response began as an exclamation. "You must be kidding!" Adjusting to her alarm, he lowered his voice. "Everyone should see Padua once. It's so vibrant."

"As you can see, I've got my hands full." Brigitte went to close the door but Donovan stood his ground.

"Yes, but I also see you've got a resident babysitter who's a Pied Piper of Hamelin."

"A what?"

"Nothing, it's just that your mother appears to be adored by the children."

"Doda's not my mother; she's my grandmother. My parents are dead." Brigitte pressed the door into Donovan's leg, a clear signal of her intent to end the conversation.

"I'm sorry. I assumed . . . " Donovan blushed as he retraced his step back over the threshold. "I guess I should be getting back. I hope to see you tomorrow. Now, there's a reason for you to drop by the café more than once a week." Donovan turned to leave but after a few steps, he turned back to clarify his comment. "The 99s I mean, the kids seem to—"

He didn't complete the sentence because Brigitte had already closed the door.

16

Portoferraio, December 1949 – May 1951

It had been early December, barely two months after her arrival, when Brigitte decided to stay. The night before, Carmela had begun having contractions and was doing everything short of hanging herself upside down to keep Antonio in until he was due. He was supposed to be a New Year's baby, a good omen, especially on a jubilee year like 1950. Pia stacked two piles of books on the bed and Carmela lay there like a swollen cockroach with her short legs propped up in the air while Pia opened a bottle of dessert wine because alcohol was supposed to stop premature labor. No one knew where Carmela had heard such a thing, but when Carmela was determined to do something, there was no challenging her. As Pia and Brigitte watched Carmela try to drink the glass of wine without raising her head from the bed, Pia got the giggles, which soon spread to Brigitte. Carmela tried her best to hush them, but it was hard to take her seriously, lying there with her feet on two wobbly stacks of books, holding a glass of dessert wine that she couldn't put down because the nightstand was out of her reach. She finally joined in with a belt of laughter that caused the books to fall and scatter across the room. The contractions, instead of being worsened by the commotion, stopped. To be safe, Carmela asked Pia for another glass of wine, which started the hilarity all over again. Brigitte was so moved by the experience and the women's evident love for one another that the next day there was no question in her mind: she would not return to France.

She asked Ugo to help her. "I can't go back." Ugo balked at first, until she confessed her reasons.

In her short time on Elba, Brigitte had traveled a long and painful journey from total ignorance of the sexual fundamentals of pregnancy to the realization of her rape. Whether she had blocked out the incident or it had happened during the delirium of her fever, she didn't care. She was glad that she remembered nothing and hoped she never would. While she had no desire for a confidant, nor would she ever tell anyone the exact truth, she did need an ally. So she told a half-truth: "The man who did this is . . . an acquaintance of my parents." Ugo looked at Brigitte with skepticism until she started to tremble and her voice wavered. "They're protecting him, Ugo. I can't go back while he's still alive." She made Ugo promise confidentiality, though she suspected he told Carmela, and of course Carmela would have told Pia, who then certainly told Angelo. The four of them shared everything. It didn't matter for she was certain that they would never tell anyone else, not even their children and especially not her own.

Ugo was enraged by Brigitte's revelation and had he not had three pregnant women to care for, Brigitte was certain he would have jumped on his boat and set off that very night for Antibes to discover the truth. So when she told him her plan, Ugo agreed to help. Lawyers were contacted and phone calls made, and by Christmas Brigitte had a bank account with enough cash to buy an apartment building, which is exactly what she did. Convincing Ugo of this decision was yet another provocation, even though Brigitte wasn't planning to move out anytime soon. This time she turned to Carmela for support. Carmela was clearly the business-savvy one of the four. It was she who recognized Le Voci's growing tourism opportunity and managed the boating company's books. Brigitte knew that Carmela would understand the need for an income stream independent of a contract that had yet to be legally endorsed. Carmela agreed and felt that they must move quickly before minds were changed and monies revoked. They found the apartment building in two days. It was one of the few buildings in the piazza that remained fairly unscathed from the city center's heavy bombing. Despite his desperation to offload it, the owner didn't want to sell the building to a fourteen-year-old pregnant French girl so Carmela had to issue some strong threats and even convinced Pia to come along to stage a bit of pregnancy activism for effect. The following day, they were proven right in their haste: the Sureaus' lawyers contacted Ugo, demanding to know what had been done with the money.

On New Year's Eve, the five of them toasted the second half of the century as Carmela paced the floors trying to induce her labor. To her chagrin, Antonio was born on January fifth, with five days of Carmela's kvetching in between. In early February, Pia gave birth to Maria and, three and half months later, Brigitte to Sophie. All mothers, fathers, and children fared quite well. Sophie's birth caused a flurry of letters from the Sureaus' lawyers, and at the point that Brigitte thought she would be forced to publicly indict her father, Doda stepped in.

Germaine Crémieux was the unexpected witness to the unsummoned prosecution. Her announcement of her intention to relocate to Elba ceased all legal inquiries. On June 23rd, Germaine arrived in Portoferraio, followed by a stream of Crémieux deliveries that would pellet the island throughout that summer and continue on and off for the remainder of her life. Her predilection for French design was a discrimination she had passed on to her daughter and granddaughter and would to her great-granddaughter as well. She established herself in Brigitte's apartment building, unapologetically choosing the preferred top flat, and decked it top to bottom in *Louis Quinze.* Though she didn't particularly ingratiate herself to the townspeople or even to the adult Vigliettis and La Roccas, she was the only grandparent that any of the three children had, or for that matter, required. She spoiled all three of them and, to her credit, showed no favorites.

Two weeks before Sophie's first birthday, Brigitte and Sophie moved out of the La Roccas' house. It was a day of mixed emotions, full of tears and promises that would surely be kept, especially from a half kilometer away. It was also the day of Sophie's first word, and the whole Crémieux-

Viglietti-La Rocca clan was there to witness it. Brigitte was introducing Sophie to the elaborate Victorian bassinet, a gift from Germaine that had just arrived from Bordeaux. "Your *nonna* bought this for you so you have someplace to sleep when you come upstairs to visit her."

Sophie cooed, "Doda." From that point forward, the name *Germaine* would never be used again.

17

"Allegria!" The television's blare echoed throughout Brigitte's bedroom, situated one floor beneath her grandmother's salon. Brigitte sat on her bed, her suitcase beside her. She hadn't opened it in over a year, but for whatever reason, meeting Donovan had rekindled her old desire.

"Awwwwwwwww."

The collective groan from upstairs meant some poor soul on the show had just *raddoppiato* and lost everything when they should have *lasciato* with the money they had. Brigitte didn't understand everyone's interest in the game show. Maybe it was because she had personally doubled too many bets in real life and ended up forced to leave almost everything behind.

Though Brigitte had cut open the suitcase's lining several times over the past six years, she took such great care in mending it that it was next to impossible to see its defect. As always, there was the anticipation of heartache, but the last few times, another emotion had transcended the pain: curiosity.

The paper on which the sketch was drawn had aged and its corners were curled. She had considered reframing it but her grandmother's move to Elba had squashed that idea, probably for the best since Brigitte wasn't sure she could lie about its origin. She laid the sketch on the bed and scrutinized it line by line to see if maybe there was something she had missed before. She was certain the image was that of her father. Of that, there was no question—she had seen him slaughter the lamb. Brigitte smoothed out the drawing upon the bedspread, her hand lingering for a moment on the lamb. Like the rest of the portrait, it was just an outline, unformed. Tío Piquot had not taken the time to shade in the detail. Yet the few lines he had drawn were sufficient to convey the lamb's inescapable terror.

On the boat ride to Elba, Brigitte had locked herself in her cabin and for the first time examined the drawing up close. It had been less than an hour since they had set sail and she'd already begun to forget her father's face. Rather than remind her of him, the figure's simple contour replaced her memory. From that point on, whenever she would try to picture Christophe, he was not of true human form, but the faceless silhouette of the sketch. There was one exception: the image of his face above her sickbed. But in that recollection, he had no features whatsoever. His entire face was hidden in shadow.

Brigitte's memory of her mother remained intact. There were rational explanations for this disparity. One was that Madeleine would still occasionally be featured in the French fashion magazines to which Brigitte subscribed. A less escapable reminder was the Crémieux nose that had been passed down from Germaine to Madeleine to Brigitte and now, to Sophie. It was odd how it was a distinction for each of their faces, but one of varying esteem. On Germaine, it was Jewish; on Madeleine, regal; on Brigitte, the Elbans called it Roman (a compliment, Brigitte thought, for a man, not a woman); and on Sophie, it was downright Aryan. Regardless, with three Crémieux noses in the household, it was hard to forget the fourth. Madeleine also remained vivid in Brigitte's dreams. Even in the Antibes beach dream, which, like Christophe's image, had become distorted in its rendering, Madeleine was indelible.

Fortunately, most of Brigitte's nightmares faded over time, although the Antibes one would haunt her throughout her life. As would one other. But whereas the Antibes dream became more and more abstract, this one became increasingly real. It was of a party where there were candles and music, and everyone was dressed up. Brigitte's tiny hand was held tightly by her father, and she felt the cool metal of his wedding ring against her palm. When she looked up, he and Madeleine were smiling at one another. He held her hand too. Tío Piquot was also there with a friend, and they were all laughing. Brigitte looked around, spying on the other guests who were separated into groups of different sizes. Everyone was talking in German, and Brigitte was intimidated by the room full of strangers whom she could not understand. Christophe knelt beside her and asked, "*Ca va?*" Brigitte timidly nodded, to which Christophe replied with a whisper: "You need to look after your papa tonight because I'm not wearing my glasses. You can be my eyes and watch everything that goes on and then later tonight you can tell me what happened. Will you do that for me?" He then kissed her on the cheek and as his warm lips grazed Brigitte's skin, her nervousness vanished. When Christophe stood back up, Tío Piquot's friend leaned into the group and said something that made everyone laugh except for Madeleine, who immediately swept Brigitte into her arms and walked away, thus forcing Christophe to release his daughter's hand. Brigitte's eyes blurred with tears as her mother waded through the crowd, bidding her farewells as she went. Brigitte sensed her mother's anguish but didn't understand why they were leaving the party—why they were leaving her father behind, why he had let her go. She always awoke from the dream as soon as the door closed behind them.

Brigitte's first thought was that the dream was purely a subconscious fabrication, but the recurrent detail of the party was too exact. At some point, she began writing down whatever specifics she could remember—who wore what, who talked with whom, the music that was playing. Over time, this codification transformed the dream into a memory, and the memory into an iconic representation of her past that overshadowed other childhood memories. Years later, after Brigitte finally framed and hung the drawing of her father above the hearth, it lost its significance and became simply a sketch of a man holding a lamb. She could walk past it time and time again without reflection. But whenever she had this dream, she would spend days afterward trying to unravel its mystery.

There was a knock on Brigitte's bedroom door followed by Sophie's voice. "Mother, can Antonio and Maria stay over? Their parents already said yes."

"*Bien sur.* You know where the bedding is. Pull it out and I'll help you in a minute."

Brigitte folded the drawing, slid it back into her suitcase lining and went to her vanity to fetch her sewing kit.

18

Portoferraio, Summer 1958

For Brigitte and Donovan, the summer of love came nine years early and with no psychedelics to hasten its pace. It was a deliberate courtship spurred by, to the children's fortune as well as Brigitte's, a different overindulgence. The day after Doda's *début tragique* (which was how Brigitte would come to refer to the onset of Doda's illness), Donovan showed up at Brigitte's apartment asking about Doda's health and bearing ice cream for all. Brigitte's polite refusal was easily countered by the delighted cries of the children. Donovan later confessed that he had spent the morning stationed behind the café's bar where he could observe Brigitte's apartment building in wait for the daily visit of Antonio and Maria, unwitting accomplices to a scheme that he had planned. It was a ploy that hinged on the insatiable sweet tooth of children and their disbelief in the insurmountable. He enacted the second half of the plan in short order and with perfect timing. Donovan waited until after the children had taken their first 99 licks and interjected his proposition before the party moved upstairs where either Doda or the television could divert the children's attention. They were on their way out the door when Donovan wagered that the children would not be able to eat a 99 for ninety-nine days in a row. The challenge provoked Antonio's contrarian bravado that, when mixed with the general commotion of the children in transit, negated any possibility of a refusal. The most resistance Brigitte could muster was a weak "I'm not sure we can afford it," which everyone knew was not true, and to which Donovan upped the ante by offering to pay, a stratagem that could have lost him ground had it not been drowned out by Antonio's caterwaul. When they reached Doda's, Brigitte silenced the children and said, "Maria and Antonio will have to ask their parents." Donovan's tentative smile belied his certain victory. He replied graciously, "I'll check back again tomorrow."

As spring approached summer, Brigitte's days lengthened with impatience for the appointed hour. At three o'clock, Brigitte and her boisterous pride would cross Piazza Cavour to Caffè Roma. The warm sea air would greet them, having wafted over the buildings and through the square's harbor gate, which had been recently widened for the increased automobile traffic that was forcing Elba to upgrade its roadways for twentieth-century thoroughfare. On the short journey, they would detour at least once to retrieve a dropped ball, run a quick errand, or sometimes engage in a casual conversation. To afford conversation with their overly attentive *barista*, they sat at the table closest to the bar that was remarkably always empty upon their arrival. The public setting and children's presence ensured genteel conversation, though Donovan always found ways to incorporate a subtext of innuendo. By June, the children's anticipation had wilted from the unfailing routine while Brigitte's had blossomed in its ritual. She looked forward to Donovan's wry smile when they entered the café, his immediate attention over other (often resentful) customers, and his daily intimations of his attraction to her. As Sophie, Antonio, and Maria became increasingly exasperated by the café's chatter and manners, Brigitte compensated with heightened deference to Donovan's every chattered word and mannered gesture. Sometime in mid-June, Antonio convinced Brigitte to let the children eat their 99s in the square. Brigitte toyed with disapproving the change of rules. "How will Donovan know that you really ate it? You don't want to lose the bet, do you?"

Before Antonio had the opportunity to recant, Donovan appeared, dish rag in hand, to secure his advantage. Wiping down the already spotless table, he said, "I'm sure we can trust them. Besides I can see the entire square from the bar." As quickly as he swept in, he swept back out again.

With the children playing in the piazza, Brigitte sat alone, diffident in her solitude. Donovan was haggling with two regulars over their bill, and though she wanted to look on, Brigitte couldn't bring herself to even glance in his direction. Instead, she surveyed the café. Despite Elba's increased tourism and harbor location, Caffè Roma remained a local establishment. A giant bar divided the café in two, and over the years, the patrons as well. On one side, young couples wooed over shared sodas; on the other, fishermen and families dined on the day's catch; and in the middle, huddled around a shared carafe of house wine, were mostly older men from town gossiping about their gossipy wives. The tenderness of the scene struck a chord for which Brigitte was wholly unprepared. It was Donovan's good luck that he chose this moment to sit down beside her.

"*Buona sera, principessa.*"

Brigitte nodded and the intensity of her hazel stare made Donovan blush and stand up again, though he remained at her table. "I wasn't sure you'd be okay here all alone."

"I didn't realize I was alone."

Donovan managed a few lines of small talk before two new customers sidled up to the bar. He looked to them and then back to Brigitte's rapidly diminishing ice cream. Realizing that she would likely finish and leave before he could return, he blurted, "Will you go out with me on a date?"

Their relationship took root on hot afternoons spent at the café watching the children play in the square while sharing casual (and for Brigitte, cautious) selections of their pasts and spirited hopes for their futures (with which, again, Brigitte was cautious). While selective in her disclosure, Brigitte did reveal that she had lied about her parents' death and gave only a cursory and severely abridged sketch of her life before Elba. During this discourse, Donovan abandoned his usual high-spirited inquisitiveness. He listened with intent but said nothing.

She concluded as if denying his unasked question. "That was a long time ago. I've learned not to dwell on the past." It was clear that she never wanted to discuss this topic again. By July, a deeper affection began to bloom, and the couple took twilight walks, hand in hand, through Portoferraio's narrow, winding streets and small piazzas. If home is the place whose contours are most indelibly etched in memory, then that July, Elba became Brigitte's home.

By August, a first kiss had been repeatedly pursued but, alas, uncaught. Then on the evening of their ninety-second *99*, two weeks before Donovan was to return to Padua, the kiss was granted and rewarded with an invitation for a family dinner in San Piero to meet the parents.

On the night in question, Ugo and Carmela drove Brigitte to Donovan's. It was their *cena fuori* (the Vigliettis and the La Roccas shared Friday as date night, switching off every other week) and so they took the opportunity to try a new restaurant in the neighboring town of Marina di Campo. There was a brief debate as to whether they should take the bus or the company car that they had just bought. Carmela, as always, won.

Italy's *miracolo economico* had brought a host of new sailing enthusiasts to Elba and with their influx and disposable income, the little La Voci boating company was suddenly no longer so little. Its success brought with it a Marxist quandary that was an infinite source of entertainment for everyone who knew the Vigliettis and La Roccas. Carmela and Pia, being women and mothers who had married into *comunismo*, found it easier to compromise here and there. Ugo and Angelo, being Italian and men who were as stubborn as mules, endeavored to stick by their ideals. But they were also the husbands of Carmela and Pia. When Pia wanted to move to a nicer house, she argued that proximity to Le Voci's offices was proximity to the workers. When Carmela wanted a car, she found a used car that could be a company car for all, yet parked it in their driveway. Every personal use would be justified and processed. Tonight's drive across the island was a rare excursion that they would permit any Le Voci worker. That was true, Ugo finally agreed, and the threesome climbed in for the ride.

It was Brigitte's first time in the car and somehow during the month-long argument for its purchase, she had missed the fact that it was the same car that her parents had owned when she was a child. When she stepped into the backseat, she stepped back ten years in time, into the new car Christophe had brought home one night after work. Madeleine had been surprised but cautious. "Darling, can we afford this?" Christophe replied, "It's German, of course we can afford it."

"Brigitte, what's wrong? Are you nervous?" Carmela was in the front passenger seat, and Ugo was still in the office looking for the ignition key that Angelo had supposedly left on his desk when he had returned the car earlier in the day.

Brigitte wore a cerulean blue dress that hid the healthy bosom that had never receded after breastfeeding Sophie. The dress brought out the blue of her eyes, as did the complementing silk turquoise scarf that she had pinned over her shoulder. Pia had given her the scarf along with a card, inscribed with one of her infamous double entendres—*a bit of the sea to subdue the mountains.* "I'm not sure, I guess so. To be honest, I don't feel anything."

Carmela turned around abruptly. "What do you mean?" Carmela and Pia had become overly protective of Brigitte ever since they found out about the 99 bet and more so after Brigitte and Donovan had begun their twilight walks. "Brigitte, if you are in any way uncomfortable with this, you don't have to go."

"Carmela, please don't worry. Donovan couldn't be more of a gentleman."

They were quiet together as Brigitte smoothed her scarf over her collarbone and Carmela searched Brigitte's face for any sign of misgiving. Ugo's exclamations could be heard from within the house even though the car's doors and windows were closed, as were the house's. Brigitte looked up. "Carmela, what was your first kiss with Ugo like?"

The concern in Carmela's face deepened the few lines around her mouth, and her oval face rounded in restraint. "Have you two kissed?"

Brigitte was slow to respond. "I think so, but I don't remember it."

"I think you'd remember." Carmela stifled her laugh when she realized Brigitte was serious.

"We had climbed up to Fort Falcone for a picnic. I made up my mind I would let him kiss me. When he leaned in, I closed my eyes and waited. For a second, the world disappeared. When I opened my eyes again, Donovan was grinning wider than I've ever seen him. I felt the moisture from his lips on mine and tasted the salt from his skin but that's all I remember."

"Are you sure it was only a second?"

"I think so but that's not the point, is it?" They both looked out the windshield at Ugo who had just slammed the door and was barreling his way to the car.

Ugo got in and slammed the car door as well. "Angelo needs to learn the difference between a desk and a shelf."

"*Caro,*" Carmela said as she laid a placating hand on the nape of Ugo's neck.

Ugo put the key in the ignition, swearing, "*Che stronzo,* everyone else seems to be able to hang the key back on its hook—why not Angelo?"

Carmela took the wheel. "Don't you go flying out of here *come un pazzo.* Get your wits about you." The engine slowed and Carmela released the wheel. "Now, couldn't we get Angelo his own key made?"

"*Ma no,* how many times do I have to tell you that this car is a company car. There's either one key for all, or we have a key made for everyone." Looking into the rearview mirror as he shifted the gear into reverse, he also reversed the subject to the inevitable. "So Bri, are you nervous?"

19

San Piero, August 16, 1958

"So, you're from Paris?"

Arianna was short and thin, almost elfish. She was one of those women who tried to fend off aging through weight loss but instead ended up accelerating the process. She wore a white pantsuit and had a stylish short haircut, curled like a tumultuous sea and bleached the foamy color of its capping waves. The powder on her cheeks, the false lashes, the bluish tint that varnished what there were of her lips, did not mask her middle age.

"Yes, that's right."

Brigitte had been in the Gazzettas' house for over three hours but felt that if asked, she still couldn't sufficiently describe the family dynamic. And Carmela and Pia would certainly ask as soon as Brigitte walked through the door. They had already speculated from information they'd gathered from the island's extensive rumor mill. *Who names an Italian "Donovan?" You mean the son of Arturo Gazzetta, the owner of the tourmaline quarry—farmer's son done well and married some snotty Milanese woman. I've heard she rules the roost and makes him work day and night to support her mainland tastes.*

"And how did you come to Elba?"

Arianna Gazzetta smoked. Her long thin cigarette was made longer by the mother-of-pearl cigarette holder she used, light enough in color that even at a short distance it was indistinguishable from the stark white of the cigarette's paper. She held it between her middle two fingers and when she pulled the cigarette to and from her mouth, she kept her neatly manicured hand perfectly straight so that it turned like a vacillating rudder, her white-tipped nails sweeping through the smoke. Her overstated femininity was only one of the idiosyncrasies that reminded Brigitte of Madeleine, and that was just one of the many things that put Brigitte on the defense.

"By boat."

"Oh, you didn't swim?" Arianna's rudder swept out. Her nearly lipless mouth formed a small *o* and she exhaled a plume of smoke as thin as her cigarette.

Throughout dinner, Arianna had been gracious, or rather, civil. She had inquired mostly about the growing success of Le Voci. She had heard of its recent acquisition of the only other small boating company on the island. Arianna also knew that Ugo and Angelo had attended (but not finished) university in Padua, the same university as Donovan. There was no pride in her underscoring of Donovan's medical studies, simply fact.

After the *digestivo*, Donovan accompanied his meek father—who had said at most five words the entire evening—to the den and left Brigitte in the salon with Arianna. Brigitte was not totally surprised, though she'd never personally experienced such a domestic gender divide in the Viglietti and La Rocca households. And yet something told her that this division was unnatural in this household as well, and that it had been purposefully orchestrated for the evening's close.

"Donovan tells me you have a daughter."

"Yes, that's correct." Brigitte looked around at the salon's modern design, another reminder of her mother. Although it, like Arianna, had none of Madeleine's refinement. From the den, Brigitte heard the familiar musical jingles of *Carosello* and pictured Sophie, Antonio, and Maria crowded around Doda's TV.

"I assume your husband died in the war."

"Yes." Brigitte rearranged her scarf's drape. The result emphasized her ample endowment. It was clear that this was a test—that Arianna knew that Brigitte was far too young to have had a husband in the war. It was for this reason that Brigitte lied.

"*Poverina, che disgrazia.*" Arianna stubbed out her cigarette in an ashtray on the side table whose circular top had been adjusted so that it slid over the arm of her chair. The table was identical to the bedside table Brigitte had as a child. "You must have been so young when you married."

"Youth has its advantages."

Arianna ignored Brigitte's innuendo. "And your grandmother moved here as well. She's Jewish, no?"

Brigitte's nod was slight.

Arianna rotated the side table's top from her lap and stood. The interview was over. Donovan was called and reemerged from the den. Mother and son escorted Brigitte to the door.

"Brigitte, it was a pleasure to meet you. Oh, I can't believe I didn't ask about your mother—Madeleine Crémieux, am I correct?"

Arianna's tactical shift proved a success. There was no mistaking the accusation in Brigitte's terse response. "*Sì.*"

Arianna held one hand quizzically in front of her mouth as if she were still smoking and lowered eyes down the full length of Brigitte's dress. "What a beautiful woman. I can certainly see she influenced your sense of style, though it must have been difficult growing up under such a considerable shadow."

Brigitte glared at Donovan. She could forgive him telling his mother about Sophie and Doda., but not Madeleine. "Yes, it must have been."

Arianna looked out into the night's darkness, thickened by the surrounding mountains. "Well, let's not get you back too late. I'm sure your daughter is expecting you home soon." She turned to go inside. "You don't have to wait for your ride. I'll get Arturo to take you."

After she'd walked away, Donovan asserted himself. "Brigitte, I am so sorry." He hesitated, looking over his shoulder to inspect the empty foyer, and then asked, "Will you take a walk with me, now?"

Brigitte's anger at Donovan's betrayal was blinded by the need to wound this woman. "Yes, let's."

Donovan shouted into the empty foyer, "*Mamma,* Brigitte and I are going to take a walk around town."

Arianna's voice screeched from her hidden perch, "Donovan, it is far too late!"

Donovan didn't respond to it or the clatter of Arianna's heels as she scurried back across the Carrara marble floor. They were already to the end of the newly paved driveway by the time she reached the door. "Don't worry, we'll be back within the hour."

"You know I can't sleep when—"

Donovan began humming loudly, drowning out his mother's voice. He tried to take Brigitte's hand but she refused. He did not press her, but instead allowed Brigitte to set the pace and the distance between them as they walked to a small church on the outskirts of town. The crisp mountain air was cooler than in the city, and the dry, musky smell of the autumn pine soothed Brigitte, as did the repeated chorus of Donovan's hum. As they neared the church, his notes became more distinct and she realized that it was not a song Donovan hummed but the melodic cadence of the *Salutatio Angelica.* When they stopped in front of the church, Brigitte followed Donovan's gaze up the simple white façade.

"When I was a boy, I often came here at night." Donovan pushed open the weathered door; its creak heralded their entrance. He lowered his voice to a whisper. "Even though the church is always open, rarely do I find anyone else here, unless there are special services being held." They walked slowly down the nave's short aisle. Donovan stared across the apse at a statue of the Virgin Mary in a small alcove.

"And yet there is always at least one candle lit, as if she is expecting me." Indeed, two candles burned at the altar, casting a dim light on walls covered in what first looked like tapestries but what Brigitte later realized were frescoes.

"Alone, I would talk to her—not pray, mind you—but talk. I'd tell her about my day and ask her advice about this or that. I even shared with her secrets that I wouldn't tell anyone else. Hopes, fears, dreams—you know, all that kid stuff."

They stopped in front of the altar.

"I imagined that she listened to what I had to say, to what I wanted." Donovan was standing in profile and Brigitte couldn't make out the expression on his face.

"Brigitte, my mother is—"

Brigitte lifted their clasped hands to his lips, knowing what the denouncement of one's mother was to an Italian son. "Donovan, my mother is a strong woman too."

He caressed his hand against her cheek and choked on his words. "You're the first person to listen to me like she does." Brigitte was unsure whether Donovan meant the Virgin or his mother. With the candles' flicker, shadows danced among the frescoed figures.

Donovan leaned in and kissed Brigitte just below the ear, wooing her in *sotto voce*. "This church is one of the oldest," he kissed her temple, "buildings on the island," her cheek, "supposedly built upon Roman ruins," the corner of her mouth, "of a temple to the god Glauco."

Brigitte stopped the next kiss with a question. "And he was?"

His lips were so close to hers that she felt the punctuation of his breath with each word. "Poseidon's son who fell in love with the sea nymph Scylla and asked the witch Circe to make a love potion that would make Scylla fall in love with him."

"And?" Brigitte stumbled backward against his weight and in doing so knocked the two candles from their stand. In their fall the flames were extinguished and the church was engulfed by darkness. Brigitte stifled a scream, resisting Donovan's groping hand as it searched for hers. He fought her resistance, gripped her wrist and led them back to the door.

Outside, Donovan wrapped his arms around Brigitte's shoulders and pulled her trembling body into his. Across the horizon, the distant moon was replaced by the glaring headlights of the Gazzettas' car. Brigitte did not squint but kept her eyes open, welcoming the pain of their constriction against the light.

The next day, Donovan was not at Caffè Roma. Bartolo, the once standoffish owner who had softened toward Brigitte over the summer, told her that Donovan had quit a week early to prepare for his return to university. Brigitte thanked him and brought three 99s to the children out in the square. She didn't buy herself one. Three days later, the ninety-seventh day of the bet, Bartolo informed her that they had discontinued the ice cream bar because the expense of refrigerated shipping had risen. But not to worry, he added, the success of Donovan's experiment had convinced him to find an Italian equivalent and he planned to receive the first shipment of *Cremino* by the end of the week. The children were disconsolate, though Brigitte assured them that they had won the bet out of forfeit.

Carmela and Pia drilled Brigitte on every detail. They scoffed that Donovan was a typical Italian mama's boy and discouraged any continued affection. When Brigitte told them about the church and its legend, Carmela laughed, "*Dio mio!* If I'm not mistaken, that story ends with a jealous Circe turning Scylla into a six-headed monster."

Pia chimed in, "I think Circe Gazzetta has a nice ring to it. Stupid cow will probably think it's a compliment." The jokes and laughter helped in the moment, but at night, in her bed, Brigitte lay curled into herself and convulsed with the tearless sobs of one who cannot cry. Finally, she rose in the darkness and tiptoed to the salon so as not to wake Sophie. She sat in silence and watched through bare windows as the waning moon was overtaken by dawn. Portoferraio's awoke with the sounds of sweeping brooms and whispered salutations. When at last Brigitte made her way to the kitchen to make coffee, she noticed a card stuck halfway under the door.

> *Dearest Brigitte,*
>
> *This time you'll not be able to stop my apology for my mother. She's beside herself and doing everything possible to keep me from you. I have let her because my education depends on it. But I yearn to see you. In Padua, my mother has no influence on my life. Will you come visit me? Padua's a beautiful city but one I've yet to truly explore because I've*

had no partner to explore it with. We could learn its streets and sites together. Just like we have Portoferraio, like I hope we will Rome and London, and dare I say Paris. There is so much more I want to say but not in a letter that I can't even deliver to you myself. Please come and please let me pay for your trip.

Tuo per sempre,
Donovan

20

Brigitte's decision to go to Padua was met with intense scrutiny by all, except for one surprise supporter. When Brigitte shared her plans to visit Donovan, Sophie responded with conspiratorial glee, as if she were a childhood friend with whom Brigitte had a shared secret crush. "Oh Mother, he's such a nice man. I think you are perfect together."

Brigitte looked across the kitchen table at Sophie who was tall for her age, and at eight, already showed signs of maturation. Brigitte's heart began to race, anxiety triggered any time she pondered her daughter at length. Before Sophie was five, Brigitte had run every medical test imaginable to check for potential physical or emotional abnormalities stemming from her incestuous conception. Brigitte's concern for Sophie's early puberty was similar, but it was tinged by a visceral and compulsive panic. Though Brigitte now intellectually understood the cause for her anxiety, she remained terrified that any provocation could again produce its overwrought effect. Just recently, during a routine doctor's visit, Brigitte had become belligerent when the nurse told her she couldn't accompany Sophie to the examination room. Brigitte's hysteria was of such extent that the nurse had no option but to acquiesce, and Brigitte sat in the corner while the doctor performed Sophie's check-up. On the way home from the doctor's office, when an embarrassed Sophie asked about the incident, Brigitte trivialized her reaction: "You know me—I'm just overprotective." Thankfully, Sophie hadn't pried further because Brigitte wasn't prepared to dissemble motives she herself couldn't fully comprehend. Brigitte closed her eyes and took a deep breath.

"Mother, are you okay?"

When Brigitte opened her eyes again, Sophie stood beside her. "Yes dear, I'm just happy you like Donovan."

"Like him? Who wouldn't like him?"

As Sophie extolled Donovan's boyish handsomeness, comparing him to the American Hollywood star Mickey Rooney, Brigitte lamented her daughter's vanishing boyishness. Sophie's tall lanky figure was widening into its bone structure through her hips, shoulders and even her face. The planks of her cherubic round cheeks had flattened, bringing a severity to her face that the blunt cut of her thick bangs accentuated. Her blond hair had never darkened but conversely, it became lighter every day, especially in the summer. The three months of continual outdoor exposure had turned it almost white. The Sureau lineage was never as obvious as it was in Sophie. When Brigitte was a small child, Christophe had regaled her with stories of his ancestors who fled Norway in The Northern Wars, forced into the North Sea where they braved its torrential waters through the Strait of Dover and finally to France. They had taken a new family name from that journey *sur eau*—a name Brigitte had forsaken after she had been forced to cross a sea of her own. This Nordic bloodline was not as apparent in either Christophe or his parents, who were dark and more diminutive in stature, but Sophie was the embodiment of the stout blond, blue-eyed Norwegian.

"Mother, what is it? What's wrong?"

Brigitte reached out and took Sophie into her arms. "Nothing dear, it's just that you're growing up so fast."

Once Brigitte made up her mind to go, Ugo arranged everything. He first proposed that he escort Brigitte, indicating that it was inappropriate for a young woman her age to travel alone. Brigitte was moved by the magnitude of this request given that he, Carmela, Angelo, and Pia had all vowed never to return to Padua after Carmela's and Pia's parents had joined forces against the girls' unbefitting suitors, going so far as to convince the priests of their respective dioceses to refuse marriage rites. Still, Brigitte politely refused, laughing that her life was far from *appropriate* and that she was confident that she could fend off any untoward advances. Ugo protested until Brigitte finally said, "Ugo, I've learned a hard lesson, one that will never be repeated." At last, Ugo complied and focused on other precautions. He contacted some old friends to see if the hotel Donovan had chosen was respectable for a single woman. When one of his old *compagni* who was now a professor at the university agreed to put Brigitte up for the weekend, Ugo finally calmed down but still drew Brigitte an intricate map of the route from the Piombino ferry station to the Padua train station detailing all the stops in between. He included explicit instructions on how to purchase tickets, what announcements to listen for, and where restrooms were located in each station. Carmela and Pia took care of the more domestic matters, looking after Sophie and preparing Brigitte a basket of food that could have easily lasted her the entire weekend. At the dock, Brigitte's sendoff was worthy of a soldier's farewell. While no tears were shed, hugs lingered and hands remained airborne until the boat was well out to sea. On the water, Brigitte had a faint flashback of her original trip to Elba, but her excitement was too piqued for melancholy. She stayed on deck for the entire hour and enjoyed the sea air against her skin as Piombino spread into view.

Upon debarkation, Brigitte followed Ugo's careful compendium of the railway transfer logistics and, after purchasing her tickets, she sat on the bench to wait for her train. When she opened Carmela and Pia's basket, there was a note on the top.

> *Dear Brigitte,*
> *We know you can take care of yourself, but we are your*
> *family and we love you. Please be careful and please don't—*

"Is anyone sitting here?" Giovanni had already sat before Brigitte could respond. "Please allow me to introduce myself—my name is Giovanni Ferrari Bravo." He was remarkably thin, so animated that he resembled a spindly tree blowing in the wind. He stuck out his neatly manicured hand: small but with long, slender fingers. Although Brigitte had seen men shake hands, she had never experienced the gesture in person. Her hand was closed with her thumb pressed into her palm, forcing Giovanni's shake into more of a squeeze. "May I ask you where you are from?"

Charmed by his candor, Brigitte responded in kind. "Elba, Portoferraio."

"I would have sworn you were French. If I'm not mistaken, your accent is Parisian."

"Excuse me?"

"*J'ai dit que vous avez un accent Parisien,*" Giovanni said in perfect Parisian French.

The shock of the abrupt language change was disorienting, but Giovanni's gaiety mitigated the effect. Brigitte replied, "*Oui, je suis né à Paris mais c'était il y a longtemps.*"

"It couldn't have been that long ago; certainly you're younger than I. Do you like opera?" It appeared Giovanni was prone to non sequiturs.

Brigitte replied, "I must admit I'm not too familiar with opera." It was an admission that launched Giovanni on the first of many raves.

Giovanni was returning to Padua from a long weekend in Torre del Lago where he had met a friend at the *Festival Puccini.* He was thrilled to discover Brigitte was on her way to Padua as well and suggested that, if she didn't mind, he would accompany her. Before Brigitte could think of a suitable objection, he picked up her bag and started for the train that had just pulled into the station. From that point forward, Giovanni didn't stop talking and through his idle verbosity, he again put Brigitte at ease. He told her of his dual loves: opera and language. He was getting a degree in linguistics and his teachers had told him that he had an infallible linguistic ear, which was why he was able to place her accent just by overhearing her brief exchange with the ticket agent.

Giovanni had been standing two people behind her but had caught a *whiff* of her accent (as he described his auditory exploits, he used descriptors of every sense but sound). He said that he was certain that she was from Paris and concluded that, being a young French woman on her own, she must be a student. "But Padua," he exclaimed, "of all the luck." Brigitte squirmed with the attention and was contemplating how she would interrupt him when Giovanni, with finger to lip, shushed her (even though she wasn't speaking) while he identified the accents of all those within earshot. She could not bear to look as he introduced himself to the surrounding passengers to verify his surmise, but she was then awed by his easy engagement with every stranger and indeed by his accuracy—he only missed one of seven, and that one, who Giovanni had guessed was from Genoa, admitted he had spent his summers there as a child.

They had just passed Pisa when Giovanni excused himself to go to the bathroom. When he returned, Brigitte started talking before he had settled into his seat. She was allowed one sentence before he interrupted, but in those few words she managed to reference Donovan. Giovanni first said that he was devastated that she was visiting a beau but then confessed that he preferred women as friends. He said that he could really talk to women, something he'd always found difficult with men. It was an admission that led to a new subject: his friend Claudio Moretti who also lived on Elba, in Marciana, a fishing village that had recently become something of a tourist destination. At the mention of Claudio's name, Giovanni's monologue finally slowed. When he asked if Brigitte knew him, his pause for her answer was so unexpected that she had to ask him to repeat the question.

When she said no, he made her promise that if she met Claudio in the future, she would mention the name Giovanni Ferrari Bravo. Albeit perplexed by the inconsequence of the request, she agreed. Her affirmative response elicited Giovanni's effusive gratitude and thus stoked his mania back into a fevered pitch. He told her that he and Claudio had been pen pals introduced via letter by another friend and that they'd written to each other for six months before they decided to meet up at *Festival Puccini*. Giovanni described their first dinner together where both of them were so nervous they spoke only two or three words throughout the entire meal. She found it hard to imagine Giovanni speechless, but was touched by the sweetness of such girlish disquietude between men. Giovanni filled the next two hours recounting, note by note, each Puccini opera he and Claudio had seen at the festival. By the time the train reached Padua, he had convinced Brigitte to give him her address so he could contact her when he came to Portoferraio over Christmas break to visit Claudio. She saw no harm in it, taking the pen and paper that he'd pulled from his satchel, until she looked up and saw Donovan standing before them in the station. He wore an elegant burgundy suit that was misshapen on his short stocky frame, and in his arms he cradled a basket of crimson roses that his crestfallen countenance matched in both color and wilt.

Giovanni maneuvered a quick *pas de bourrée*, placing Donovan and Brigitte *vis-à-vis*. "So you are the handsome devil that I have been hearing about our entire trip." With Giovanni's exaggerated obeisance, Donovan's mood lifted and the three walked from the train station like old pals. Giovanni started in immediately. "You're from Milan, correct?"

"No, but my mother is."

"Well, she passed on to you a bit of Milanese dialect."

Brigitte was thankful for Giovanni's chatter as they walked from the station along the canal that encircled the city. He facilitated what could have been an uncomfortable reunion by asking Donovan about his planned itinerary for the weekend. His buffer also enabled expressions of romance between her and Donovan that might have been impossible had they been alone. By the time they turned to enter the fortified city through a massive stone gate that Giovanni told them was designed by a notable architect and depicted in some famous painting, Brigitte's fortifications had given way. Instead of Giovanni's voice, she focused on the moon's reflection upon the water and Donovan's hand warm within her own. She was so lost in the moment that she barely registered

Giovanni's commentary as they crossed the bridge, missing his final point about the unusual tier of steps alongside the river that "no longer was suited for mooring the bountiful Venetian merchant ships that once sailed its channel but rather the impassioned Paduan lovers who sauntered upon its banks."

Giovanni continued to chaperone the couple the few blocks to the address that Ugo had given Brigitte. When they arrived, Giovanni turned to them and said, "There's something I must confess." Before either his confession or Donovan's lift of the knocker, the door opened and a man appeared who was an older, shorter, balder version of Giovanni who, like his son, began talking immediately as he ushered the threesome inside. Giovanni whispered under his breath to Brigitte, "Dad's a friend of Ugo Viglietti's. I guess Ugo didn't want you traveling alone."

Inside, Giovanni's father apologized for having a widower's lack of both grace and tidiness. His immediate disclosure of his marital status reminded Brigitte of how she managed the revelation of her own circumstances. Assuming a similar subtext, she responded with a smile and a deferent nod and then excused herself to freshen up. After acquainting Brigitte with her accommodations in Giovanni's room (Giovanni was staying with a friend for the weekend), Professor Ferrari Bravo ushered the three men into the salon, where he recounted his and Ugo's conspiracy. "It was just like old times. We devised a foolproof scheme and recruited Giò as our envoy." Brigitte rejoined them mid-story, just catching the professor's admission. He slapped his knee when she confirmed that she hadn't realized that Ugo had convinced her to delay her trip a week.

"I thought it was our idea," she said, glancing over in Donovan's direction. Donovan had said very little, but his broad, unrelenting grin implied that he was enjoying how much ado was being made of their not-so-secret rendezvous.

"He was always the best. That one could convince a cow to volunteer for slaughter." The elder Ferrari Bravo's eyes had the same boyish twinkle as the younger's.

Getting out the door was much harder than getting in. The father's skill for continuous monologue surpassed that of his son's and Brigitte and Donovan had to back down the hallway through a flood of words. Also, the professor insisted that Brigitte's daylong journey must have left her too tired for an evening out. Permission was granted only with Brigitte's assurance that she was famished, and Donovan's repeated promise to have her back by ten.

Giovanni accompanied them out and then profusely apologized for his role in the affair. "I'm supposed to follow you throughout the weekend. In their defense, I think that is more from two old zealots' desire to relive their youth than to keep you from living yours." The three quickly contrived a story for Giovanni to share with his father, and Brigitte with Ugo, to ensure full corroboration that would satisfy the men's espionage. After Giovanni left, Donovan looked at Brigitte and exhaled a long sigh, which caused the two to erupt in stifled laughter as Giovanni disappeared from view.

When their laughter subsided, the couple began to stroll. Donovan spoke first. "You are certainly cared for."

Brigitte welcomed the acknowledgment of the devotion of those she had come to regard as her family. "Yes, I am lucky."

"What was all that about Ugo and the professor's collusion?"

"I'm not certain, except that Ugo and Angelo were *comunisti* when they were students here and from what their wives tell me, they attempted to orchestrate protests against Mussolini."

"That would certainly provide someone with the skills to protect a loved one from the encroachment of a dangerous suitor," Donovan joked. They walked a bit farther down the street on which the Ferrari Bravos lived, and then Donovan turned to Brigitte and asked in earnest, "Do you think I'm dangerous?"

"I think my feelings for you may be dangerous. That is probably what they sense." Before he could respond, she asked, "Are we going to the restaurant?"

"I lied about going straight to the restaurant. I thought I would give you a tour first."

"That would be lovely."

"*Principessa*," Donovan said as he pantomimed an aristocratic bow and then presented the crook of his arm to her. It was indeed one of the loveliest of moments she could have ever imagined.

They meandered through the mostly barren streets of Padua as Donovan elaborated details of his favorite establishments. "I was hoping to take you to the botanical gardens and the Libreria Draghi, but I didn't plan on our little diversion back there. I think they're now both closed, but I've got a couple of other ideas." They walked around the grand Prato della Valle, Donovan providing only cursory explanation of its graceful oval canal and the statues that lined it, filling in the gaps with facts about historical relevance of the Orto Botanico and the Draghi bookstore that paid literary connoisseurs to enlighten its customers. Donovan kept pulling a crumpled sheet of paper from his pocket, obviously reference notes for his tour.

As they made their way toward the immense basilica, Donovan went off script and the two began treading uncharted ground.

"You never talk about France."

The stars disappeared and the night's darkness deepened as the shadow of Il Santo loomed over them. The air was colder in the church's courtyard, as if the paving stones absorbed the fading warmth of autumn.

"It was a long time ago and there is much I have forgotten."

"I've always wanted to visit Paris. Is it as beautiful as they say?"

"To some, yes."

Standing before Il Santo's grand door, Donovan pulled out his notes and told Brigitte about Padua's patron saint, for whom the basilica was erected. "The building is over six hundred years old—its construction having begun just after the death of St. Anthony who, by the way, was originally from Portugal, but upon returning from a missionary trip to Africa— "

Seeping through the door's crevices was a faint scent of burning sage, and from deep within the church's sanctuary echoed the howl of a dog.

"—his ship was forced by a storm to Sicily, where he was given shelter by the Franciscans."

Brigitte interrupted. "Donovan, I'm suddenly exhausted. Perhaps I am in more need of rest than food. Can we skip dinner?" If Donovan sensed her unease, he didn't show it. On the way back, he continued the history of St. Anthony and how over the years, he had become the patron saint of sailors and fisherman. He told Brigitte of a poor Portuguese tourist he'd met who had spent her life savings on a pilgrimage to the basilica, claiming that St. Anthony had saved her husband when his boat disappeared in a storm. The woman told Donovan that her husband was found the next day unconscious on the rocky shore miles from where he was fishing, a solid gold St. Anthony medallion hanging from his neck. When he came to, he remembered nothing, including the origin of the medallion. He had since died and now his widow wore the medallion, (which Donovan admitted did indeed have a certain ethereal quality about it), but she'd always wanted to come to Padua to give thanks to the saint who had delivered her husband from the sea's claim and given her five additional years with him.

Brigitte was lost in memory and wouldn't remember the story until over ten years later, when, upon noticing a silver St. Anthony's medallion in a jewelry shop window, she recalled the absolute conviction of the Portuguese widow she had never met.

21

Insecurity and exhaustion summoned a labyrinth of dreams. Fragments of Brigitte's childhood were rendered and soldered to fantasy with no adherence to chronology or context. As if it weren't already sufficiently disjointed, the recurrent Antibes dream was coupled with images from her ninth birthday party—except the sandbar was recast not as her lush *cour intérieur* of quai d'Anjou, but as the barren courtyard of Drancy. Brigitte remained seated on the park bench, looking out to the horizon of cracked and stained concrete that stretched between Drancy's detainment cells and its imprisoning walls. Ash rained from an open sky onto birthday guests elaborately costumed as Alice in Wonderland characters. While they hobnobbed, freed detainees frantically pushed through their huddle, snatching the guests' masks as they passed in search of lost loved ones. Laughter comingled with cries in the heightened merriment and misery.

At the edge of the courtyard, sitting crossed-legged high atop Drancy's east wall, was Geneviève, dressed as Humpty Dumpty, her gaze fixed outward beyond the camp's containment. "*Bonjour, mon amie,*" Brigitte shouted above the crowd. Geneviève didn't hear or ignored Brigitte's greeting, but from her cradled arms slipped her cherished Théâtre de la Mode mannequin. Rather than free fall, it floated overhead, swirling with the ash in a lazy descent. Brigitte followed its arbitrary path. When it got close enough for her to see the doll's diminutive, intricately formed hands, Brigitte was filled with a jarring, unplaceable sense of *déjà vu* that was overtaken by instant recognition when she looked up from the doll's hands to its face and realized that it was modeled after her mother. Brigitte screamed and shielded herself as the miniature porcelain Madeleine dipped in its final plunge to the ground and shattered upon the concrete. When she opened her eyes, everyone had vanished except the real Madeleine, who stood before her holding the disembodied head of a lamb. Madeleine placed the lamb's head on the bench, offered her hand to Brigitte and said, "Come, it is time you knew."

Christophe waited for them outside Drancy's gates. The three walked together hand in hand across the street and through a set of double doors to greet the party of Brigitte's other recurring dream. In this occurrence, Brigitte had a wider perspective than before. There were people and books scattered across the room, clusters of each tucked away in corners and amongst shelves. Everything was magnified and Brigitte sensed that she had shrunk in relation to her surroundings. Her much taller parents were still beside her, Madeleine clad in her usual white elegance and Christophe in his dark gray suit. They were looking for something or someone. As they moved through the room, they greeted people in passing, stopping on occasion for idle prattle that often focused on Brigitte. People leaned over and stroked her hair or pinched her cheeks, some speaking to her, oblivious to, or disinterested by, her inability to understand them. Tío Piquot and his friend approached. Tío Piquot engaged Madeleine, while his friend chatted with Christophe. Both couples were so rapt in their respective conversations that they appeared to have forgotten her. Brigitte conformed to her role as the neglected observer and watched as Tío Piquot's friend leaned in to tell Christophe something. In doing so, he noticed Brigitte for the first time. He was bald like Tío Piquot and similarly large featured. Dominating his face was a bulbous nose and bushy black eyebrows set askew over slit eyes in a caricature of malice.

With his wink, the party paused; all movement and sound ceased. Even the candle's flame reflecting from his open eye was still, its flicker frozen within fixed halos against the blackness of his iris. His mouth twisted into a sneer as his words fell from his mouth like spittle: *Spickindekunz gertesklaun herrpusigian.*

22

Padua, September 10, 1958 - Predawn

Brigitte leapt from the bed repeating the cryptic German phrase to herself. *"Spickindekunz gertesklaun herrpusigian."* She stumbled over her shoes, just catching herself before twisting an ankle. The darkness was complete, giving no trace of the room's layout, but she knew that if she didn't hurry, the dream would fade. The rain's pelt against the window guided her to her open suitcase on the stand just below the sill. As she felt her way down the unfamiliar wall, Brigitte struggled to recall the dream's final transition.

She searched her suitcase for her notebook but then remembered that she had taken it out and left it on the bedside table. She didn't have time to make it back; the words were already muddled. She found her small makeup bag and quickly located the eyebrow pencil. Brigitte attempted to write the phrase upon her forearm but couldn't tell if the pencil's wax was just smearing against her skin. Though she was now whispering the phrase out loud, it was a jumble of incomprehensible words that she was no longer certain was from memory or rote.

She felt the outline of the sketch beneath the suitcase's lining. She had meant to remove it before the trip but had forgotten. Her decision was instant and the scarred silk tore easily. Brigitte unfolded the paper and quickly ran her hand across both sides. The artist's strokes had been confident, leaving a distinct indentation from the charcoal's tip. She turned the sketch over and found an empty patch of wall to serve as a writing surface.

After scratching out the message, Brigitte relaxed and sat upon the foot of the bed, listening to the rain and trying to remember the details of her dream. The newer scenes were now a fog and for the most part, the old ones were so deeply rooted in her subconscious that small differences from past dreams were as indistinguishable as subtle anomalies on a well-worn path. There was one exception: as she replayed the exact moment that she bolted awake, there was a vivid image of a blotch of blood on the bench beside her and out at sea, beyond the veil of raining ash, the distant bleat of a lamb. Now, as if to echo the lamb, a dog barked in the night somewhere on the streets of Padua.

23

Padua, September 10, 1958 - Morning

By the time the first rays of sun gave form to the room, Brigitte had completely forgotten the words of her dream and why she thought they were so important. When she inspected the back of the sketch, her writing was erratic but still readable: *Spickindekunz gertesklaun herrpusigian*. She wasn't sure of their pronunciation. Now, in the light of day, she questioned her urgency to write them down. After all, it was a dream and nothing more. She rose from the bed, restless. Although Professor Ferrari Bravo hadn't yet stirred, daybreak gave her an excuse to ready herself before their morning's interchange, which would require protracted courtesy. She left him a note and outlined her day's plan as best she knew it, indicating that she would likely be back after lunch.

Brigitte opened the door into a dense fog that absorbed the morning light and the dampness from the previous night's downpour. By providence, her overcoat had a hood and she haphazardly tucked her unruly hair into it. She knew the hood's billow must have appeared ridiculous, yet she didn't want to go back inside for fear of being sidetracked by her attentive host. And so, with a couple of hours before breakfast, she set out on the route Ugo had mapped out for her.

The previous weekend, Brigitte mentioned to Carmela and Pia that she wanted to see where they had grown up, as well as visit any other sites that held meaning for them. With Brigitte's promise that there would be no anonymous visits to either Carmela's or Pia's parents, they agreed, and then somehow the list took a life of its own with no fewer than thirty points of interest, including a dozen or so friends who could be dropped in upon and inquired about if, of course, time permitted.

Like Portoferraio, Padua had suffered from severe bombing during the war. Fortunately, most of the damaged buildings in the city center had been reconstructed with their original portico extensions, resulting in a dense network of arcaded sidewalks that enabled Brigitte to traverse the city without exposure to the elements. Brigitte's adventure wound within and along the city's twin river borders, and though it was far too early for a stranger's welcome, Brigitte stopped at each location where her friends had trodden. Across the street from Carmela's and Pia's side-by-side family homes, Brigitte was careful not to tarry and arouse suspicion. Pia had asked her to check and see if a flowerpot she had made as a child still hung outside her bedroom window. Pia told Brigitte that when she was eight years old she had begged her parents to buy window planters, but her mother said that all she needed was another chore like watering plants. So Pia made a planter in art class and got her father to help her hang it. Over the years, her mother must have changed her mind because planters hung outside all the windows. It wasn't until Brigitte passed directly in front of the house that she saw that one planter on the second story was different from the rest—instead of sculpted terracotta, it was a simple mold of dark brown clay with no distinguishing marks.

When Brigitte reached Piazza delle Erbe, the vendors were already setting up their stands. She looked up to the repeated arches of Palazzo Ragione, where, according to Carmela, Ugo had won her at first glance. Carmela had been waiting for her mother to finish haggling with the tomato vendor, as a dashing college student passionately orated for some cause Carmela couldn't hear and to which no one else appeared to be listening.

The Palazzo was far more imposing than Brigitte had imagined, with graceful arches hemming the roofline. Their elegant repetition reminded her of the flying buttresses of Notre Dame. The fog, which had been at most an inconvenience, now became a stagnant shroud.

"Signorina, si sente male?"

That the older gentleman held two tomatoes in one hand and was dressed in a double-breasted tweed suit two decades out of style that should have again piqued Brigitte's nostalgia for Carmela's undoing. It didn't, for she was blinded by her own.

Brigitte managed a feeble response. "Yes, I'm fine, *grazie.*" But she was unable to shake her sudden gloom.

An hour later, she stood entranced before a storefront's plate glass window. She didn't see the young clerk on the other side point to his watch and shake his head, nor, if asked, could she have identified what type of store it was. She just stared until jolted from her reverie by an unmistakable fragrance that she hadn't smelled for years.

"So I see you found the Libreria Draghi?" Donovan stood behind her and tipped his fedora. In the glass the hat's shadow momentarily covered his face.

Brigitte lied. "Yes, I thought I might get a book to read on my way home."

"Good, we'll come back when it's open and I'll buy you one. But this morning, I've something else for you."

In Donovan's outstretched hand he held a small cluster of violets. He mistook her shock for awe. "They are *violette di Parma.* They are extremely delicate and have to be cultivated in order to survive. In fact, no one knows their origin because they've never been found in the wild."

As Donovan pinned the violets onto her jacket, Brigitte reeled from the flowers' perfume.

"An intoxicating flower for an intoxicating woman."

During breakfast, Donovan resumed his role as the informative guide, laying out the plan for the day. She did not tell him of the sites that overlapped with her morning's walk and responded with enthusiasm that appeared genuine, though he noticed that she left the brioche untouched on her plate. As she watched him pore over his notes, she was reminded of Christophe's unwavering focus whenever he read the newspaper. She fought to ignore the sickeningly sweet redolence emanating from her corsage but no matter how hard she tried, her stomach lurched with nausea.

"You don't like it, do you?"

"No, it's not that."

"Actually, I never come here. It rests on its laurels. Even the famous zabaglione is mediocre. But tourists love it and I thought, with you, I can be a tourist."

Brigitte smiled. "No really, it's wonderful. I'm just not hungry. "

When Donovan put his arm around her as they left the café, Brigitte's body tensed. She pulled his arm from her waist and instead took his hand in hers. He accommodated what he assumed was her preference for one intimate expression over another.

"Our first stop is a surprise. It's a sight that few tourists get to see and not even many students."

As they walked, Donovan gave Brigitte hints: built in the sixteenth century, the first of its kind, allows for spectator viewing of up to three hundred people. His playfulness helped lift her mood, but the atmosphere of the university with all the students milling about made her self-conscious. It was almost two months before the academic year formally started, and yet the campus radiated erudition. Brigitte had educated herself the best she could with Sophie's text books and the clandestine assistance of Ugo, yet still, when she was around truly educated people, she was ashamed of her ignorance. For some reason, Donovan had not intimidated her. Now that she saw him as one of them, she began to doubt herself. They crossed a flagstone terrace to a grand three-story villa that was older than most of the other university buildings. The imposing cast metal entryway had stoic life-size figures on each of its double doors.

"An opera house?" she guessed.

"Wrong, but close. But there is a classroom in this building that looks far more like an opera house than a classroom. Supposedly, Galileo taught there. I'll show you afterward."

The stillness of the building's interior was churchlike and, in unconscious reverence, Brigitte was more cautious with her step. Even so, she couldn't silence the clacking of her heels against the marble floor. They passed from a hall into an outdoor courtyard flanked by an enormous clock tower. The few students that mingled here were more serious than those outside, and Brigitte felt both awed and alien. She surveyed the encircling balconies, trying to suppress her discomfort by continuing the game. "I know, it's an oratory or debate theater."

Donovan laughed. "Not quite."

They crossed the courtyard, to a wooden staircase that was blocked by a chain. Donovan pulled a large key ring from his pocket. "I'm only allowed access because I'm assisting Professor Rossi this year. Now, shut your eyes and let me lead you. I want your first view to be from the top."

Brigitte nodded but did not close her eyes completely. Through her squint, she saw a spiral of wooden slats.

At the top of the stairs, Donovan guided her to the rail. "Okay, now open them."

24

Padua, September 10, 1958 - Midmorning

The first impression Brigitte had was that she was looking down into the bedroom of a large dollhouse. Either her squinting or the distorted perspective caused a slight bout of vertigo and she had to close her eyes. When she again opened them, the distortion remained, as well as a hallucination of Genevieve's Théâtre de la Mode mannequin lying on what appeared to be a miniature table centered on the elliptical floor below. The doll's legs were spread apart and its voluptuous Hermes skirt hiked up to her open thighs. Brigitte abruptly backed away from the rail. Her eyes darted around the room that encased the wooden structure. "Can I sit for a moment?"

"Unfortunately, there're no chairs." Donovan walked her over to the window. "Just look outside for a minute. It can be disorienting the first time."

Across the street stood the imposing façade of Padua's city hall. Donovan's arm stretched around her waist as he told her the history of the anatomy theater that dated back to the sixteenth century. Again, Brigitte tensed as his arm slid around her, although this time she did not remove it.

Donovan gloated in his explanation. "It's called *teatro anatomico* and was built to study the anatomy of corpses. Come on, let me show you the dissecting table."

"Give me another few seconds. Can I open the window?" The fog had completely dissipated and the gust of air was warm and dry, intensifying the bouquet of her corsage.

Brigitte tugged at her lapel, pulling the flowers from her face. She asked, "Why on earth would someone build a theater to study the dead?"

Donovan instinctively jerked his arm from around Brigitte to help him orchestrate his answer but then returned it, subsequently waving his free hand about in even more grandiose gestures as if it had to pick up the slack for its otherwise engaged accomplice. "Geronimo Fabrizio, the professor who had the theater built, argued that the *teatro anatomico* would normalize the formerly inhuman science of *autopsia*."

Though she had never heard the word *autopsia*, Brigitte shuddered at its certain implication.

"He argued that there are certain fields of study or practice where achievement has historically been marked through unethical means. Take architecture, for example. The most notable monuments in the world—Egyptian pyramids, the Taj Mahal, the many grand cathedrals of Europe—have been built on the backs and lives of slaves. With Industrial Age construction technologies, we no longer require human sacrifice to build our cities."

"I'm sorry, but I don't see the connection." Brigitte turned from the window and again peered down into the theater. While the illusion of Genevieve's doll had vanished, the thought of a crowd of students watching a human dissection sent a shiver up her spine.

"Well, Professor Fabrizio argued that the science of anatomy requires dissection of human bodies and that it should be taught as a science instead of relying on plagues and war."

"Plagues and war?"

"Yes, before broad acceptance of human anatomy as a reputable science, most research consisted of simple observation done when dead, and often mutilated, bodies were readily available, like during times of war and plague. This condemnation of human dissect Brigitte turned from the window and again peered down into the theater. While the illusion of Genevieve's doll had vanished, the thought of a crowd of students watching a human dissection sent a shiver up her spine. ion meant that some of the greatest advances in anatomical understanding were the result of dubious practice. In fact, when the *teatro anatomico* was built, the church still condemned human autopsy so there was supposedly a canal under the Palazzo Bo that allowed gravediggers to deposit anonymous corpses without being seen."

Donovan closed the window and said, "Don't worry, there hasn't been an autopsy for years. Come on, it will only take a second. Be carful on the way down. Here, let me guide you."

Brigitte relented to his lead. Pressing into her back, Donovan's fingers ran across the ridges of her *gaine*, making her hyperaware of how the girdle's constriction exacerbated her shortening breath.

As they descended each of the six tiers' narrow elliptical aisles, the years peeled away. The small floor of the bottom level was just big enough for the dissecting table and dissector. Brigitte looked up to escape its narrow confine.

"Your window and the others up there were all bricked up to avoid any possibility of detection, even though they're too high up for anyone to see in." Donovan slapped the table, its metallic ping echoed through the theater's stalls. "They even say that in case of an emergency, the dissecting table had been designed to rotate, allowing it to be flipped over so that the human body would disappear and be replaced by that of an animal whose corpse was pinned to the opposite side. Although it's hard to tell the truth from folklore since so little was documented."

Brigitte lifted her hands to her ears. The ringing reverberated in the chamber, its pitch getting higher and shriller.

Donovan moved closer, "Brigitte, what is it?"

Brigitte reached out to the dissection table to steady herself. It was made of wood, not metal. And yet the ping from Donovan's slap kept growing louder and louder. The violets' suffocating fragrance was supplanted by the imagined putridity of rotting flesh. "I need to go." Brigitte's words caught in her throat, making them barely audible. If

Donovan heard her, he didn't acknowledge it but instead wrapped his free arm around her as well.

"You know last night when I asked you about Paris, I only wanted to say that whatever happened I don't care."

Brigitte couldn't respond though every cell of her mind and body screamed in protest.

"Actually, that's not true. I care about everything in your past because I care about you."

Above them, faces spun in the elliptical stands. There was laughter and the clinking of glasses and a disembodied German voice that boomed above the din. Donovan leaned in to kiss her and she lost the present entirely. When he backed her into the railing, she felt his erection press against her thigh.

Her vision dimmed as an inner voice chanted, "*Spickindekunz gertesklaun herrpusigian.*"

"Please, no." She wasn't sure whether she whispered it or screamed it and when questioned the next day by Carmela, she couldn't remember anything else until they were out of the building and Donovan was standing before her, apologizing profusely. It wasn't until during the train ride back to Piombino that Brigitte noticed that the blood from a deep scratch across Donovan's face had stained the front of her dress. Brigitte disembarked at the first stop, changed into her other outfit, and discarded the dress in the station's trash receptacle.

25

Brigitte sat by the window, her book in her lap. It was there because she didn't have time to put it in her suitcase. It also served as a guard against any conversation attempted by the passenger seated across from her, though such conversation was unlikely, given the woman's concentration on her knitting. The clicking of her needles seemed to mimic the clacking of the train's wheels so that the scenery shooting by Brigitte's window was set to a rhythmic orchestration. Brigitte welcomed its hypnotic effect in the hopes that it would purge the lingering sensation of her final hour in Padua.

Outside the Palazzo Bo, Brigitte's hysteria had subsided, but her anxiety remained. "Donovan, I have no explanation, nor can I imagine one sufficient to justify my actions. I will not impose on you for your forgiveness, and I'm sure you'll understand why I must return to Elba immediately."

Donovan insisted that it was he who was at fault, but his pleading only worsened her distress and led to repeated apologies that finally withered into an awkward lull—a silence that was barely pierced even for the curt explanation of Brigitte's early departure to the inquisitive Ferrari Bravos. On the way to the train station, Donovan had again attempted to make amends, but this time he did so by pretending that nothing was wrong. As they passed the Libreria Draghi, he said, "It's open. Let me buy you that book you were thinking about reading on the way back."

Of course, Brigitte couldn't refuse, but she faltered when the seemingly timid clerk asked what book she had in mind. "Do you speak, or rather, do you read English?" he asked.

Brigitte replied, *"Non molto."* The clerk's timidity vanished. He wore black thick-rimmed glasses and was tall and thin like Giovanni, without the meticulous self-grooming, and dressed with nonchalance as if to convey that the physical world was of no importance. He either didn't hear or ignored Brigitte's response, because he proffered a euphoric recommendation of a recently published novel called *Lolita*, which he called *"il romanzo più brillante del secolo."* He told them that many bookstores were banning it because of its subject matter, which he then went on to describe in graphic detail.

Both Brigitte and Donovan grew increasingly pale until finally Brigitte blurted out, "A dictionary, I want a German dictionary." But even he walked them to the language section, the clerk continued advocating for *Lolita*, reciting its verse as though he were an actor rehearsing the part. *"Lolita, light of my life, fire of my loins. My sin, my soul."*

Donovan finally inserted himself, asking Brigitte to wait outside. On their walk to the station, the silence between them resumed and was broken only by the logistics of the ticket exchange and their final agonizing goodbye.

"Brigitte, please call me and let me know you made it home safely."

"I will."

"Reverse the charges."

"Yes."

"Give Sophie, Antonio, and Maria my love."

"I will."

"And Doda."

"Of course."

As the train pulled out of the station, Brigitte was relieved to see him finally turn and walk away. When he was out of sight, she unpinned her corsage and threw it from the train's window, and though she shared a compartment with two others, collapsed into a deep dreamless sleep.

The train was halfway to Florence before Brigitte awoke, alone. In her lap lay the unopened German dictionary, bundled and tied. The clerk had insisted Donovan wait while he wrapped it with the loving care of one who cherishes books. Brigitte had watched this final transaction through the same plate glass window into which she had unwittingly stared hours before.

Brigitte took the package and slid the string from around it.

26

Piombino, September 10, 1958 - Mid-afternoon

Spickindekunz gertesklaun herrpusigian.

In the final hours of her train ride, Brigitte had searched the German dictionary for the words that rang in her head. She had come up with nothing until she showed the phrase to a German student whom she had met in the dining car. The woman said that the nearest translation would be: *Sprechen sie keines. Gerte es klein, Herr Pozigian* or "They do not speak. Switch it small, Herr Pozigian."

"What does it mean?" Brigitte had asked.

The woman laughed. "I don't know, it was your dream. Maybe you should ask an Armenian."

"An Armenian?"

The student responded, "The name Pozigian is most likely an Armenian name. I can't be sure, but when a surname ends in *ian*—and especially *gian*—it is almost always Armenian."

When Brigitte returned to her compartment, she took out the sketch and wrote the parsed German phrase and its translation in pen beneath her previous night's scribble. On her final leg home, she'd stood on the bow of the ferry, straining her memory to recall the name Pozigian or any of her parents' friends who could have possibly been Armenian. No one came to mind. She spoke the phrase aloud one last time into the wind as if to purge it from her tongue. Back in Portoferraio she would absolve herself of all that had happened in Padua, just as she had dispelled these words. There would be her grandmother and Sophie and the Vigliettis and La Roccas—they were her family. The past didn't matter. She even decided to frame and hang the sketch so that it would no longer haunt her.

When Brigitte found both her and Doda's flats vacant, she assumed everyone was at the Vigliettis or the La Roccas. When no one answered either phone, she began to worry. She called Le Voci. The secretary told Brigitte that both Angelo and Ugo were at the hospital in Piombino, and when Brigitte pressed her for more information, the woman confessed her ignorance but asked her to wait while she asked her other colleagues. Brigitte was halfway back to the ferry when the secretary returned to an off-hook signal blaring from her handset.

Everyone but Doda was surprised to see Brigitte. They had had a huge debate over whether or not they should call her and let her know about the accident, but Carmela had finally convinced the others that this was Brigitte's first time off Elba in eight years and, as everything was now under control, they shouldn't ruin her trip. When Brigitte walked into the room, Doda looked up from the bed, and through a drug-induced haze, she said, "I knew you would come back."

No one else said a word as Brigitte walked over to the bed and took Doda's hand. "What happened?"

After everyone had seen Brigitte off at the ferry, Doda had asked Pia if Sophie could stay at their place for an hour or so while she went to the market and ran a few errands. By nightfall, when Doda hadn't returned or called, Pia began to worry. She asked Angelo to stop by Doda's flat on his way home from work. He did, but Doda was nowhere to be found. The next twenty-four hours were harrowing as the La Roccas and Vigliettis engaged the police and friends and everyone they knew to find out if anybody had seen her. They kept Doda's absence from the children for as long as they could until the three of them stormed the kitchen and, with Antonio as their spokesman, demanded to know what was going on. Instead of crying, the children, Sophie in particular, joined the adults in brainstorming where Doda could be. In fact, it was Sophie who stumbled upon the essential clue. "Have you tried the synagogue?"

Everyone knew Doda was Jewish but it was never discussed and no one but Sophie, not even Brigitte, knew that Doda went to the—

"What synagogue?"

Sophie explained that since the armistice, some of the Jews who had ended up on Elba after the war had decided to use the bombed out lighthouse at Port Stella as a makeshift synagogue. Doda's Saturday morning *scopa* game was really a weekly trip to the lighthouse. She took Sophie once but made her promise not to tell anyone else—a promise Sophie had kept until now.

Afterward, Ugo and Angelo had driven to Fort Stella and found Doda walking in circles around the lighthouse's unrailed parapet muttering to herself in French. When Angelo and Ugo approached her, she was confused as to why her husband (dead for over ten years) had not come with them. The only way that they were able to convince her to leave of her own free will was for Ugo to lie and, in French, tell her that M. Crémieux had been injured and was in the hospital.

The doctor had said Doda was suffering from a case of unresolved grief that sometimes played tricks on the minds of loved ones left behind, especially the elderly. He also said that she was dehydrated, which had aggravated her delirium.

Brigitte held her grandmother's limp hand. She thought not of the spoiling Doda but the stoic *Mamour* of her childhood and her surreptitious lessons on Judaism. There was one particular outing that Brigitte hadn't thought about in years. It was one of Brigitte's earliest memories. Though the memory was vague, Brigitte recalled that it was just after a birthday and that she had tingled with excitement for the secrecy and splendor of her first visit to a synagogue. They had taken the long way so Brigitte could ogle the *patisseries* on rue de Rossier, an indulgence that detained them five minutes or so. As they approached the synagogue, Doda was explaining something about the *Belle Epoque* when there was an explosion just ahead of them. Doda wrapped Brigitte in her coat to shield her from the debris. "Don't look. Just keep walking and whatever happens, don't leave my side." Brigitte never did visit Agudath Hakehilot, or any other synagogue for that matter. After Germaine had moved to Elba, Brigitte would occasionally inquire about their Jewish ancestry, but Germaine refused to discuss anything related to Judaism. She'd appeared to have lost her faith.

Brigitte leaned down and whispered in her grandmother's ear, "Just hold my hand, and I'll never leave your side again." She never did.

27

Portoferraio, December, 6, 1958

Brigitte's apartment was uncommonly quiet. Sophie had gone with the La Roccas and Vigliettis and the rest of Portoferraio to the *Presepe di Greccio* mass that launched the Christmas season. While Brigitte still hadn't personally adopted the Italian zeal for Catholic ritual, she had acquiesced to Sophie's need to belong. Also, Sundays and holiday masses gave her time alone, a luxury that had become more precious since Doda had fallen ill and Brigitte spent much of her day tending to her grandmother's ever-increasing needs. But today's solitude was unusual because Sophie's absence and the lack of hubbub from the square were amplified by an emptiness that Brigitte at first couldn't place until she realized there was no familiar drone of Doda's television. Brigitte checked her watch; it was early yet. She basked in the morning's unfolding and considered her apartment anew. The soft light of dawn and dusk always enriched her dark mahoganies, richly colored fabrics, and satiny gilds. The *bergère* chairs flanking the door were resplendent. Brigitte smiled in her content.

When Doda's condition didn't improve, Brigitte had consulted the only medical resource that she knew. Donovan took up the cause with the zest of a lover who had been given a second chance. His research was exhaustive and the series of letters where he conveyed his diagnoses carried a confidence and compassion that gradually overshadowed the messy finale of the Padua trip. His conclusion was that Doda had a variant of senile dementia that had become known as Alzheimer's disease, after the German doctor who had documented a severe case at the turn of the century. Very little was known about it except that it often struck earlier than ordinary senility and it was progressive, which meant Doda's condition would probably worsen. In each letter, Donovan included recent data he'd discovered about the disease while availing himself of the closing paragraph to renew his courtship. It wasn't long before Brigitte was counting the days until his Christmas break, when they would see each other again. Unfortunately, that count was greater than either of them expected because, at the last minute, Donovan's mother decided on a Milanese Christmas spent with her family.

Though Brigitte was disappointed, her endearment to Donovan grew when his repeated testimonials of love were inflamed by his anger at what he termed *Accordo di Arianna*. Apparently, as far back as he could remember, Arianna had been scheming to marry him off to a Milanese girl. She had a list and for years had been working through it prospect by prospect. Introductions had been brokered by letter, by "coincidental" acquaintance, and the worst, as was certain to be the case with Christmas, by forced occasion. Donovan said that, since he had told his mother of his feelings for Brigitte, her matchmaking efforts had become obsessive, to the point of convincing one Milanese family to transfer their daughter from the Sorbonne, where she studied French philology, to Università di Padova, which had no approximate curriculum. Donovan wrote that the poor girl was so distraught that he had agreed to go home with her one weekend to convince her parents that he wasn't interested.

Brigitte wondered about the nature of Donovan's affection. He told her that he cared for her and certainly the time, effort, and money that he put into his pursuit of her had attested to this desire. She crossed the room to her newly refurbished lavatory. Since she'd put in a bidet and a hot water heater, it had been transformed from a necessity to a refuge, like the bathroom of her childhood. The new porcelain shone against the floor's aged terracotta. Brigitte closed the door, stood before the vanity mirror and studied her face. It was a distinct face but one, she thought, devoid of beauty or softness, and with no sense of relativity. Features were either too big or too small or set too far apart. She had her mother's bone structure but with sharper angles that were more rectilinear, with the Crémieux nose dividing two halves of an inverted pyramid. Her pointed chin terminated a pouty French mouth that was far too small and appeared to be rounded into a perpetual whistle, a caricature accentuated by narrow sunken cheeks. Overlooking her enormous eyes was a preposterous expanse of forehead, made more expansive by the lack of bangs, an absence that was not from lack of trying.

Brigitte's hair was a dense nest of auburn with a frizz that was untamable on the driest day of winter. For Brigitte, long hair meant unwieldy hair, and so she maintained a standing weekly appointment at the salon. But no matter how short she kept it, it would not lie flat, and during her youth and into her twenties, Brigitte would often look as if she had just awakened from a nap. Doda said that even as a baby, Brigitte had a ring of wispy fuzz that stood out from her head like a cherub's halo. In the mid-sixties, Brigitte would adopt the curling iron to attempt to exert control, but after an intense two-month battle, would give it up and finally let her hair grow out. Ironically, it was only then that it had sufficient body for some semblance of manageability.

Brigitte leaned into the mirror, so close that her breath fogged the glass. She knew that her eyes were the essence of her attractiveness, but even then, she didn't understand why people found them so appealing. They were like large, veined marbles that caught every light and complemented every color. People called them hazel because of how they would change with each outfit she wore, but up close they really were no color, or rather a kaleidoscope of colored slivers. Little Antonio's eyes had a similar effect and whenever they were out together, strangers would invariably stop them on the street and, to the envy of Maria and especially Sophie, would ask to take their photograph. In general Brigitte didn't understand the allure of eyes, why people said they were the windows to the soul. Eyes lied, as did every other part of the body.

When Brigitte turned from the sink, she caught her full reflection in profile: a blaze of red. She had just come from a walk and was still wearing the wool swagger coat Pia and Carmela had bought her for her first winter on Elba. They each had one—Carmela's was gray; Pia's, navy; and Brigitte's, bright crimson. Both Pia and Carmela had forsaken theirs after their pregnancies but Brigitte continued to wear hers year after year, from the first day of autumn well into spring. With its voluminous sleeves and wide, loose hem, it complemented any outfit. Two years prior, Pia and Carmela had given her a new coat for Christmas, but Brigitte took it back, insisting that she wasn't ready to give up her swagger. She bantered in defense, saying that for her it represented the sanguine love and florid generosity of her adopted family and besides, it had become her signature. The truth was it also enveloped her body. Every day she wasn't wearing the coat, she struggled for an outfit in which she could hide. Summer was unbearable with its sheer linen and scantily clad activities, like swimming, in which she refused to participate. Fashion was both cover and shield.

In contrast to her outmoded winter wear, Brigitte wore the latest styles from May to September. With each extravagant purchase, Brigitte would imagine Madeleine's contrary reactions, the pride of her influence negated by the hit to her bank account. The thought of Madeleine's certain quandary fueled Brigitte's addiction, and though her designer tastes were similar to her mother's, there were two fundamental differences. One was form—specifically Brigitte's predilection for less revealing cuts of more flamboyant prints and colors—and the other, function. Fashion became an obsession that Brigitte nurtured not to bring attention to herself, but to her clothes. A sideways leer admired the skirt, not her legs. A comment of how she looked in a designer's blouse was a comment of the blouse, not her breasts. Brigitte learned to desensualize each glance and remark until the skies grayed and air chilled and she once again donned her swagger. Or this year, until Donovan.

Brigitte had rationalized Donovan's initial attraction as that of a sweet boy who felt sorry for a young widow. During the first few days of the ninety-nine *99s* wager, she wore a different fashionable outfit to the café each day—Balmain, Fath, Laroche, Hermès. But there was no amount of false logic that could disguise the fact that Donovan's interest was not bound by Brigitte's clothes. With this realization, she would have ended the bet had it not been for the fact that though Donovan's interest went beyond Brigitte's clothes, it did not discard them. His flirtations kept all mental buttons buttoned and imaginary zippers zipped. During the slow courtship, he remained the utmost gentleman, until Padua, in that horrible theater, where he had suddenly changed.

Brigitte reached over and turned off the light. She shuddered as she removed her coat and then took her time unlacing her blouse, allowing herself to adjust to the sensual acuity of darkness.

Sitting with her legs outstretched in the empty tub, Brigitte explored her body. She forced herself to stay present as she touched places she had barely looked at, flinching as her fingertips probed the moist recess of her vagina. She turned on the faucets. The water was too hot for direct contact, painful at first, but she knew it would cool with the tub's fill. Brigitte reveled in the water's initial scald, reclaiming the instant access of hot water that as a child she had taken for granted. She gripped the shower handle, another unthinkable invention. The cold porcelain sent a violent contraction through Brigitte's body as she leaned against it and spread her legs as wide as she could manage in the narrow tub. She imagined Donovan touching her as she had touched herself. Fantasy replaced the present as she finally allowed mental buttons to be unbuttoned and imaginary zippers to unzip.

After her bath, Brigitte stood naked before the mirror, water pooling at her feet. While she did not have an orgasm or even enjoy herself in the physical sense, she did remember the entire experience and that in itself was a step in the right direction. She again leaned into the mirror. Her hair was a soggy matted mess that, regardless, still stuck out from her head in all directions. Upstairs, the familiar muffled voices began to speak. Brigitte smiled as she reached for her brush.

28

Portoferraio, December 7, 1958

Brigitte rose early and after breakfast with Doda, woke Sophie to see if she wanted to visit the Vigliettis.

Even at nine, Sophie had yet to abandon her cherubic swaddle and each night somehow managed to wrap herself tightly in her blanket so that only her head stuck out from a cocoon of spun wool. She yawned. "It's only eight o'clock. They'll still be asleep."

"Then we'll take the long way. It's a beautiful morning."

They walked up and over Fort Stella, out a partially concealed door in the fort's outer wall to a footpath that hugged the cliff. Donovan had shown Brigitte the path once when he convinced her to rise before dawn and come with him to watch the sunrise.

"Wow, Mother, this is amazing." Sophie gawked at the unobscured view of the mainland.

"Promise me you'll never come up here alone or with Antonio and Maria. In fact, promise you won't even tell them. You know how Antonio is. This can be our little secret."

Brigitte held Sophie's hand as they followed the narrow path around the fort's wall.

"I promise, but . . . " The sun's early light lit up Sophie's face and revealed a dubious grin.

"But what?"

"It's weird—we've never had a secret before and I would have *never* thought we could have a secret like this."

"Like what?"

"I don't know—adventurous, maybe."

"What, does everyone think I'm incapable of spontaneity?"

Sophie didn't answer. They turned the corner of the wall to the north side of the island. Just off the shore, the islet of Lo Scoglietto was a dot on the sea. The beacon from its tiny lighthouse blinked its warning.

Brigitte prodded, "Oh, I'm a overprotective bore, is that it?

"Well, yeah."

"Am I really that bad?"

"Mom, you never let me leave the house alone, and since your trip to Padua, you've not done much going out yourself."

Brigitte stopped. The path ahead had been washed out and though there appeared to be a newly forged detour around the eroded section, it was far too treacherous to attempt with Sophie. Beneath them, the Mediterranean's gentle waves lapped against the rocks.

"Looks like we have to turn back."

Mother and daughter retraced their steps in silence and thirty minutes later arrived at the Vigliettis' just as Carmela was putting breakfast on the table. Upon Brigitte's knock, Antonio rushed from the kitchen to change from his pajamas.

Carmela opened the door, wiping her hands on her apron before bestowing her welcoming kisses. "Well, this is certainly a surprise."

Sophie yawned, "*Buon gioooooorno*, Sig.ra Viglietti," and nodded toward Brigitte. "I told her it was too early, but you know Mom."

After ushering them inside, Carmela took their coats. "It is never too early for you two."

Antonio called from his room, "Mom, where's my Elvis Presley shirt?" Ever since Mr. Presley had set foot on European soil, Antonio had been fixated on the American singer. In the last few weeks, all he could talk about was a rumor that the American army was going to air an Elvis Presley Christmas concert that would be televised across Europe. Brigitte had one of her favorite clothing boutiques in Paris find the T-shirt and ship it all the way from California. Antonio had been enthralled by the gift and had worn it every day since.

Carmela rolled her eyes. "Hanging on the clothesline," she called back before returning her attention to her guests. "Would you like breakfast?"

"Not for me, I've already eaten, but I'm sure Sophie would."

"Yes, please."

After Carmela had served the children, she joined Brigitte on the terrace. Brigitte stared out into the tiered rows of young olive trees that Ugo had planted over the summer.

"I love the grove, what a wonderful idea."

"It was Antonio's doing—you know how he gets when he locks onto something. This summer it was an olive garden, now it's Elvis Presley."

"Well, it's beautiful."

Carmela turned to Brigitte. "Speaking of beautiful, have you done something to your hair?"

"No, I've just decided to let it go, quit fighting the constant battle to control it. It's a mess, no?"

"Actually no, it's stunning. I never realized it was so full. And there's something else: you look—I don't know—you look different."

"Different how?"

"I can't put my finger on it but whatever it is, it suits you."

"Hmm, well I guess I'll keep it up then." Under her breath, she added, "whatever it is," blushing as she thought of her bathtub episode the day before.

When the two women returned, Antonio and Sophie had already finished breakfast. Their empty bowls were by the sink and their conspiring voices echoed from the back of the house. Brigitte turned on the water and began to wash the dishes while Carmela manned the drying rack. It was an act of shared responsibility so unassuming that it was as if Brigitte had never moved out. Handing Carmela the first washed bowl, Brigitte said, "I think I'd like to have a New Year's party this year. I've lived here eight years now, and I realized this morning that I've never had a party. You and Pia always throw the birthday parties and invite me over for every celebration, but I've never reciprocated."

"Oh Brigitte, you don't have to—"

"I know, I know, it's just that I want to have a party. We Crémieux are known for our party throwing. What do you think?" It was the first time since she had moved to Elba that Brigitte had insinuated a broader connection to her family.

"I think it's a lovely idea."

29

Portoferraio, March, 21, 1959

March was unseasonably warm. Brigitte had already shed her swagger, and had begun her annual shopping spree. She had most of her clothing shipped from Paris, but there were three of four Elban stores she frequented. One, a small boutique in Marina di Campo, carried most of the French designers Brigitte wore. The bus ride from Portoferraio was at least twice as long as by car, but Brigitte had never learned to drive and didn't mind the local route that wound along the hilly terrain of Elba's northern coast. Nor did she mind the short walk from the bus stop to the boutique. It was nice to see unfamiliar faces of other Elbans who, like she, mostly stayed close to home. And then finally, the boutique itself, owned by another French exile who couldn't live without French fashion. It was always a pleasure to chat with her whenever she was there. Today she wasn't, and so Brigitte bypassed the sales clerk and appraised the shop's inventory. This year, the excess fabric dictated by the "New Look" had lost ground to more revealing styles. One, a royal blue belted A-line, was skimpier than most of Brigitte's nightgowns. She fingered the scalloped edges of the dress's cleavage.

"Brigitte, is that you?"

Again, Arianna wore white, another pantsuit even more severe in its cut than the one she had worn the night they'd met. The shock of seeing Donovan's mother was so sudden that Brigitte didn't have time to fluster. "*Buon giorno*, Sig.ra Gazzetta."

Arianna walked over to the rack where Brigitte stood and flicked through its dresses. "I must say that I'm surprised you could spare time away from your family to come all the way over here to shop."

In the past few months, Donovan had written Brigitte about his mother's manic attempts to find him a fiancée before his May graduation, after which he would return to Elba and she would lose her control over him. Brigitte lifted the blue dress from the rack and held it against her body.

"They're supportive of my little habit."

Arianna plucked a cream blouse from its hanger and walked over to the full-length mirror by the changing room. "I guess we mothers do long to feel single and attractive, don't we?" The mirror reflected Arianna's theatric chagrin. "I'm sorry. Of course, you, dear, are both single and attractive."

"*Grazie.*" Brigitte crossed behind Arianna to the dressing room, closed the curtain, and slipped out of her dress.

The curtain's thin cotton was sufficiently transparent to see Arianna's distorted shadow rippling between its folds before vanishing. Sadly, her voice remained audible. "Not all of us mothers have such fortune. After all, we have our husbands to consider."

Brigitte removed her brassiere. The dress was made to be worn without support but by a much smaller-chested woman. Fortunately, though she wore a D-cup, she was in less need of support than most women her size.

Arianna's voice was closer again. Her shadow again danced upon the curtain. "Donovan tells me that you and he have been writing one another. How sweet."

Brigitte pulled back the curtain. The dress's scalloped hem fluttered like a flag in a parade. Standing in the mirror elbow to elbow with Arianna, Brigitte replied. "Yes, in fact, I'm looking forward to his graduation. He's told me about all the crazy antics that his friends and family are supposed to put him through." Brigitte twisted to both sides to check out her figure in the mirror and after unquestionable approval, turned to look Arianna straight in the eye. "Aren't you?"

Arianna held Brigitte's stance and stare. The only muscles that moved on her face were her razor-thin lips. "Absolutely. I'm sure you're also looking forward to meeting Regina." Now it was Arianna who contorted herself in the mirror to model the dress she held to her body. "Although you've probably heard all about her from Donovan." Arianna nudged Brigitte over to get more of the mirror's reflection. "She's certainly a headstrong girl, insisting the wedding be in Paris just because she wants her Sorbonne friends to attend. I can tell you, her parents aren't too pleased about that. Though, how often does one get married? And at Notre Dame, no less."

Arianna returned the dress to the rack. "You are going to attend the wedding, I hope. If so, I would certainly love to meet your mother."

Arianna bid adieu to the boutique attendant, who obviously knew and feared her, and then stopped in the doorway, turning back to Brigitte. "Oh, one piece of advice: if you're buying that dress for Donovan's graduation, you should know that while the traditional graduation antics to which you refer are all fun and games, the actual ceremony is a conservative affair. I wouldn't want you feeling foolish or out of place."

When Donovan called later that night, Brigitte refused to speak with him and had Sophie tell him not to call or write her ever again. He complied. A few weeks afterward, Donovan ran into Ugo and asked him if he thought that Brigitte would ever forgive him. Ugo told Donovan to give it a year or so—that all wounds healed in time. Seven months later, when Donovan's bride and son died in childbirth, Ugo sent flowers on the pretext of offering his condolences. Brigitte guessed his hidden agenda.

"Your condolences or our condolences?" she asked.

Ugo did not deny her accusation but looked Brigitte square in the eye and said, "Bri, don't you think he's suffered enough? You don't have to forgive him to pity the man's grief."

Ugo's paternal conviction was his undoing. Like Arianna, Brigitte held his stare. "You are right. One doesn't need to forgive if one can eradicate the pain."

She had him strike her name from the card.

30

Portoferraio, September 28, 1969 - Afternoon

It was a day of celebration. This year the party was at Doda's because she no longer left her apartment. It wasn't just the stairs—Ugo and Angelo would have gladly carried her wheelchair down—but Brigitte had grown terrified of taking Doda outside. Even with constant surveillance, there had been accidents. The final one was nothing really, just Doda wheeling herself a foot or two nearer to the dock's edge. Brigitte had been helping Sophie off the Vigliettis' boat after Antonio had taken her and Maria out for a New Year's spin around the island. She'd taken her hand off the wheelchair for only a few seconds and Doda had slipped away. Even though Doda stopped herself and possibly grasped both the circumstances and the potential danger (she had mumbled something about her voyage across the sea), Brigitte was horrified and said for days afterward that she kept having phantom visions of Doda, strapped in her wheelchair, sinking into the water's depths. Doda didn't seem to care one way or the other, so Brigitte decided not to risk any further outings.

Doda's dining room table fit six comfortably, eight with its leaf added, but nine was a squeeze. The children—though at nineteen, they were hardly children—had to share two spaces. Brigitte knew that Sophie didn't mind being so near to Antonio, although recently she had stopped gloating about him and would go silent whenever Brigitte asked. Watching the three of them together, Brigitte now understood why. Antonio had a crush of his own—on Maria.

Ugo interrupted the party's chatter. "I have an announcement." He stood, but everyone kept talking, even after he clinked his fork upon his wine glass. "*Silenzio!*" he shouted. Finally, Carmela intermediated with her shrill whistle. Doda ducked, which redoubled the laughter in the room, including Doda's own maniacal cackle. In her old age, her lip had permanently curled over her snaggletooth and the effect produced an appearance that emphasized her dementia.

Carmela stood up and joined her husband, sweeping an arm in his direction then out again as if she were introducing him to a crowd of strangers. "Let's give our dear Ugo a little respect while he toasts Doda's and Brigitte's birthdays." Under her breath, but loud enough for everyone to hear, she also said, "I'm sure he'll also have a word or two to say about the new Don Camillo film—"

Angelo commentated, "*Mamma mia!* Is he ever going to grow up? A man has just walked on the moon, and all he can talk about—"

Pia smacked Angelo with her napkin. "Let her finish."

Angelo thrust his chin toward Carmela. "Who's not letting who finish?"

Carmela raised her voice, "And, the impending completion of the Ansóphia." Everyone cheered and again, Doda ducked, giggling as she went. Ugo remained standing with his glass in the air until the room had finally quieted.

"Why thank you, dear Carmela. It is true that I would like to toast to *La Bella Figura*, so aptly represented by the lovely Crémieux girls, without whom our lives would be void of light." Though his glass was raised to Doda, he winked over his shoulder at Sophie. "And to *Il Bel Paese*, which, as to your aside, has never been nor will ever be more accurately portrayed than by the master himself. And yes, my sources tell me that filming for Guareschi's final and best novel, *Don Camillo e i giovani d'oggi*, is slated to begin next spring." Ugo was a huge fan of Giovannino Guareschi (Carmela said that Ugo had always seen himself as the ideological embodiment of Peppone, Guareschi's celebrated nemesis of Don Camillo) and had still not recovered from his death over a year earlier. He crossed himself upon the author's mention. "But my dear

Carmela, the loveliest of women, misspoke when she asserted that I wanted to toast the *impending completion* of the Ansóphia." Ugo paused to milk everyone's sudden attention. "It is actually its completion I want to toast. So raise your glasses a hand higher to *La Bella Barca* and its maiden voyage at six o'clock today."

For a moment the room fell silent. The Ansóphia was three years behind schedule. At seventy-five feet, it would be the largest production fiberglass boat in the world and would catapult Le Voci into one of the top three sailboat manufacturers in Europe. Its design and subsequent redesigns had nearly bankrupted the company and almost destroyed Ugo and Angelo's friendship. Finally, Carmela and Pia had intervened and forced Ugo to a set of compromises that saved the company, their friendship, and at least one of their marriages.

Angelo leapt up from his chair. "I thought the rudder system had another month of testing."

Ugo reached his glass across the table and clinked Angelo's. "Initial tests were so positive that we've been approved for open water. Just heard this morning."

Angelo threw his empty wine glass to the floor, sending shards of glass everywhere. Doda squealed with either delight or fear—it was often difficult to discern between the two. "Sorry, Doda, but if this doesn't call for a good glass smashing, I don't know what does."

Ignoring Brigitte's command to stay put still until she cleaned up the glass, Angelo walked around the table and lifted Ugo off the ground with a bear hug.

31

Portoferraio, September 28, 1969 - Mid-afternoon

Brigitte and Sophie stood side by side at the kitchen sink. Brigitte washed dishes and Sophie held a stack of dirty cake saucers, waiting for Brigitte to take the plates as if there were no room on the counter to set them down. Sophie towered over Brigitte. She was nineteen, and though she had matured into her size, she would always be large, or, as Doda once remarked in one of her dementia-induced Yiddish throwbacks, "of *zaftig* proportion."

"*Chérie*, you don't need to help me clean up. Go on with the others and enjoy the send-off."

"That's okay, I don't think I'm wanted anyway."

Brigitte took the dishes from Sophie and put them in the water. "Oh dear, you know that's not true. For goodness sake, they named the boat Ansóphia after the three of you—I think that says something, don't you?"

"That's not what I mean." With Sophie's angst, the room closed in on them. Doda's kitchen was the same footprint as Brigitte's, but Doda had opted to put a large baker's table in the one empty corner, which made the small space feel cramped when there was more than one person working in it, and especially when there was tension in the air.

Brigitte picked up another soapy dish. She wore yellow latex gloves— *the newest thing in hand preservation*—that had been incessantly advertised over the past year or so, both in magazines and on TV. Brigitte took on the coy tone she often used to lift Sophie's spirits. "And, when you think about it, you have the most letters." She looked over her shoulder at her daughter and gave her a you-didn't-think-of-that-now-did-you eyebrow raise. "*And,*" Brigitte attempted to pinch Sophie's profiled cheek with her clumsy gloved fingers, leaving a smudge of suds on Sophie's chin. "It's *your* letters, not Maria's, that are next to Antonio's."

Sophie turned to face her mother. She was over six feet tall, by far the tallest girl in her entire school, including the nuns. The taller she grew, the shier she became, as if through modesty she could offset her physical presence. But in times of joy or anger, when an emotional surge matched her height, she dominated a room.

"What do you know about it?"

Brigitte reached to wipe the suds from Sophie's face but Sophie stopped her. "I'm not a child anymore, Mother. And can't you for once leave the dishes for Donata? She *is* the maid. Why do you always have to be doing something?"

When Brigitte retracted her arm, red marks from Sophie's grip encircled her wrist. "I didn't mean to—"

Sophie wiped the suds from her face with her sleeve. "What *did* you mean? What do you know about relationships? You just walk away."

"That's not fair."

"Not fair? I'll tell you what's not fair. Not telling a child anything about her father or keeping her from her grandparents, after she's begged over and over to meet them."

"Sophie, I didn't want them to hurt you. They—"

Sophie's checks were flush and her fists balled at her side. Sophie was slow to anger but when she arrived there, she arrived. "They what? They didn't want to acknowledge that I existed. They *exiled* you here because you were pregnant with me. You've told me a thousand times, Mother, I know—it was all my fault."

"*Chérie*, I never said that."

"You didn't need to say anything, Mother. You implied it every time you denied me even the tiniest scrap of information about them."

Brigitte had witnessed Sophie's ire a few times in her life but never directed at her. She silently turned and walked away. Sophie's voice calmed but her words still projected her discontent. "Look, Mother, I know your childhood was painful. I can't imagine what it was like to live through a war, to be interned in a concentration camp, to see your home ruined . . ." Sophie's hesitation was slight. "To discover your father . . ."

Brigitte stopped in the doorway but did not turn back to face her daughter. She raised her yellow hand to the door's frame for support. Sudsy water trickled from the glove down her forearm.

Brigitte remained facing away while Sophie spoke deliberate words with practiced modulation. "Mother, I'm sorry. I know it's painful but it's painful for them too. It's been almost twenty years now. Can't you just forgive them?"

Brigitte spun around.

"What are you saying?"

"I've talked with them, Mother. I got their address from Doda and I wrote them."

"When?"

"The first time was a year ago."

Brigitte's face drained of expression and color.

"Mother, they want to meet me and I want to meet them. I'm going to Paris to visit them and there's nothing you can do to stop me."

32

Portoferraio, September 28, 1969 - Evening

Sophie's pronouncement had left Brigitte stunned. As she methodically finished cleaning up after the party, Brigitte wrote the letter in her head. She chose each word with great care. After bathing Doda and propping her on the couch in front of the television, Brigitte sat down at her desk and began to write.

"She's right, you know."

Brigitte looked up, cocking her head, an unconscious gesture to orient her ears for better hearing. If Doda had indeed spoken, it would be her first intelligible sentence in over a year.

"You can't protect her her whole life. The war's over, it's time to move on."

Doda was no longer watching TV but looking directly at Brigitte, eyes as clear as the day she moved to Elba. Brigitte walked over, sat on the couch beside her and took her hand, still warm from the bath.

"Throwing a child's party is all well and good, but you have to realize she's a young lady now."

"Oh, Doda." Brigitte raised Doda's hand and held it to her cheek.

"Madeleine, I don't know what you and Christophe have told her but you need to tell her the truth—the absolute truth."

"Doda, it's me, Brigitte."

"One day she will understand."

Brigitte pulled Doda to her, hugged her tightly. *"Mamour, arête s'il te plaît, c'est moi, Brigitte."*

Doda's head rested on Brigitte's shoulder, her response a mere whisper. "But if you don't tell her now, she'll never forgive you."

It was after midnight before Brigitte completed the letter. On paper, her words seemed childish and vengeful. Over four hours of revision and she was finally satisfied that she'd made all of her points to ensure the invitation's retraction. She reread the letter one last time. She sounded content, if not happy, and willing to go to any measure to protect Sophie. She was addressing the envelope when the children burst into the room. Antonio was in a fury and Maria was sobbing. Sophie, still in her nightgown, was also crying, her arms wrapped around Maria.

Antonio's voice shook with dread. "They're gone. No one can find them."

Brigitte asked Antonio three times to slow down before she learned the full story. The Ansóphia had not returned at eight as planned. At ten, Antonio and Maria called Sal, Le Voci's radio operator, who met them at Le Voci's offices and attempted to contact the Ansóphia's radio. After an hour with no answer, he tried to console the children. He said that they shouldn't worry—that the electronics had probably failed. They'd probably motored out too far and had to sail back in, and would certainly be back by morning. Antonio argued to no avail and even called the police, who agreed with Sal but said to call back if they weren't back by dawn. Furious, Antonio decided to take one of Le Voci's boats and search for them on his own, but Maria had broken down into hysterics and convinced him not to go.

Brigitte reminded Antonio and Maria that their parents were experienced sailors who had been on overnight excursions before. Sal and the police were surely correct, and the Ansóphia would return safe and sound by dawn. Maria asked if they could pray together. Brigitte led the children downstairs to her flat, lit some candles on the dresser in the guest bedroom, and the four of them knelt together and prayed. It was the first time she had actually prayed since Drancy. The physicality of the act was far more hopeless than the prayer of her dreams. When she pressed her hands together, her stomach retched.

After Brigitte was certain everyone was asleep, she rose, dressed quietly, and walked down to the harbor. Again, she prayed and again her stomach rebelled. Nonetheless, she stayed for over an hour. On her way back, she passed a jewelry store by which she had walked almost every day without ever glancing at the display. Tonight, she stopped. From a headless mannequin bust in the window hung a silver St. Anthony medallion. She stared at it for some time. The next day, when initial search results yielded nothing, she would buy it, intending to tie it around the main mast of the Ansóphia.

When Brigitte returned to the flat, she heard Maria's muffled crying from the guest bedroom. She stopped at the door and debated whether she should knock. The sounds that followed were unmistakable. The pit in Brigitte's stomach returned and grew until it consumed her. She still believed the Ansóphia would be found, and therefore her anguish was neither her own nor compassion for Antonio and Maria. It was rather a deep maternal empathy for her daughter, who could certainly hear through the walls as the boy whom she adored made love to her best friend. Brigitte made her way to her bedroom in the darkness. Standing at her bedside table, she groped until she found the letter left on its edge. She picked it up and ripped it in two.

Brigitte rose before dawn and found Antonio dressed, just as he was about to leave. Neither of them spoke as Brigitte made him breakfast and packed a lunch for his journey. When he left, Brigitte collapsed onto the couch. Ugo, Carmela, Pia and Angelo were her parents, friends, teachers and guardians. Everything she had learned, everything she believed, everything she was, was because of them. They had to be alive. She crawled from the couch down to the floor, and prayed. Kneeling in the center of the room with her face turned upward and her hands lifted in supplication, it looked as if she were praying to the portrait of her father carrying the lamb to slaughter. She wasn't, but if she'd thought he could have intervened, she would have called even on him. An hour later, she awoke to Sophie standing above her, silent tears streaming down her face. Brigitte rose, took Sophie in her arms and without saying a word, rocked her, stroking her hair until her tears had dried.

Exactly one week later, Antonio finally returned in the middle of the night, dehydrated and barely conscious from exhaustion. Sophie and Maria were asleep, but Brigitte was up waiting. As before, they didn't speak as she fed him. Afterward, they stood before one another in front of the guestroom door, sounds from Maria's disturbed sleep emanating from within. From around her neck, Brigitte took the St. Anthony medallion and hung it around his. "You are my son now."

THE ASSUMPTION

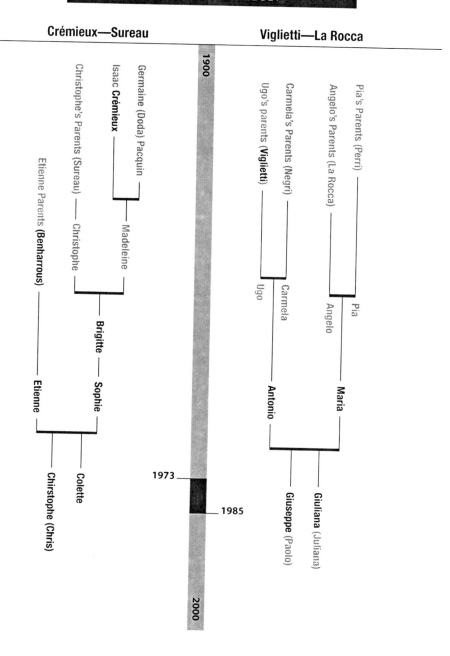

33

Bologna, Centrale Railway Station, January 31, 2000

"Sorpresa!"

Brigitte bolted awake, disoriented by her surroundings. Everything was still, even the train. Images from her dream dissipated into the reality before her, but its emotional intensity lingered.

In the aisle outside Brigitte's compartment was a stalled queue of grumbling passengers. Brigitte opened her door into a young college student with a backpack slung across her shoulder. Brigitte asked, *"Siamo a Roma?"*

The young girl smiled and, brushing her long hair from her face, replied. "No, Bologna. I'm afraid you still have a good three-hour ride ahead of you."

"Grazie." Before shutting the door, Brigitte noticed the family in the neighboring compartment. It appeared to be a surprise reunion of sorts, with everyone clamoring around a young man who, by the looks of his unstowed luggage, had just boarded the train. He basked in the attention, but he still managed to catch Brigitte's eye, returning her curious appraisal with a playful wink.

Brigitte returned to her seat thinking about her own reunion with Maria in a few hours. When the passengers began to file off the train, the girl in front of Brigitte's compartment waited for the line to disperse so she could relocate the backpack from her shoulder to her back. A gruff voice somewhere in the line behind her yelled, *"Per favore!"* The girl looked over at Brigitte in female camaraderie, shook her head, and rolled her eyes, taking her time to adjust the backpack's placement before finally making her way down the aisle. Brigitte didn't see the indignant man who had shouted his disapproval of the girl's delay because by the time he passed Brigitte's compartment, she had again drifted back to the past. Whether it was the girl's self-possessed verve or the family melodrama that Brigitte could still hear playing out in the neighboring compartment—or simply the need for her conscious mind to pick up where her subconscious had left off—Brigitte no longer reflected upon the reunion that lay ahead, but upon another that was almost thirty years before.

34

Portoferraio, October 2, 1973 - Early Evening

"Sorpresa!"

In her three years away at university, Sophie had become a woman. She had grown her hair long and was wearing a black beret. While she hadn't adopted the more casual style of the times, she had adopted style. Whether it was Rome's influence or Madeleine's genetic marker, Sophie had an eye for what worked on her large frame and, unlike her mother, she didn't limit her selection to French designers. Over time, Sophie would tend toward the conservative (in particular, the skirtsuit and designers who perfected it), but in the seventies she was still experimenting. On every visit, she had a different look. This afternoon's outfit was a bell bottom and halter one piece. The fabric's large print lay somewhere between polka dots and paisley.

"What on earth are you doing home?" Brigitte knew the answer but thought that, without Doda, this year's birthday celebration was going to be low key. "Don't you have a Civil Procedure exam Friday?"

"You know me, I was ready last week." Sophie had selected the Sapienza University primarily because of its size, and also because it was in Rome. Brigitte was worried because until Antonio and Maria married, Sophie had never shown much interest in school and had certainly never mentioned attending university. But after the accident, everyone had chosen a different escape. Brigitte knew that she, of all people, couldn't judge. She helped Maria plan her wedding and Sophie complete university applications. Brigitte assumed both diversions would be short-lived and continued to be surprised as Antonio and Maria's happiness grew and Sophie became more and more the student. After enrolling in humanities, Sophie had switched during her second term to law and had worked hard to complete the requirements she had missed. Civil Procedure was the final prerequisite and then she would be at the same level as the other law students.

Even though it was a small party, Bartolo had closed the café. He said it was because it was off-season and that there were never many customers on a Tuesday. Maria teased Brigitte that it was because Bartolo had a crush on her. Brigitte played along until Maria said, "He's old enough to be your father." Fortunately, that was right before Sophie's surprise entrance, so the impact of Maria's Freudian slip was averted. Brigitte spent most of the party catching up with Sophie, who was planning to catch the last ferry out.

"You can't even stay the night? You'll get into Rome so late."

"I'm not going back to Rome. I'm going to meet Etienne in Porto-Vecchio. His uncle has a place there."

"You're going to Corsica tonight? Couldn't he have come here?"

"Mother, please don't." Sophie took off her beret and swept her long hair over to one side. "He told me to tell you happy birthday, by the way."

"Yes, well, tell him I said next time, maybe he can tell me to my face."

"*Mother.*"

"*Ma puce,* I'm kidding. I just wish you could stay longer."

Brigitte wasn't kidding. She didn't much like Etienne, though she had only met him once in the two years Sophie had been dating him. Even during that visit, he'd convinced Sophie to stay on the other side of the island where some friends were meeting them for a spring break vacation. But at twenty-three, Sophie was too old to be babied.

A few minutes later, Brigitte stood at the bar, saying goodbye to the Oberndorf sisters, who had been so helpful during Doda's final years. Though Brigitte asked several times, Doda never adequately explained why she hadn't introduced her Jewish friends earlier. It was only after

Doda got sick that Brigitte had come to know the seven women with whom Doda spent every Saturday afternoon.

Behind her, Bartolo's voice boomed, "*Mi è sembrato di vedere un gatto.*"

When Brigitte turned around, Sophie was standing with another surprise guest.

"*Buon Compleanno!*"

"Hello, Donovan."

35

Portoferraio, October 2, 1973 - Evening

Donovan waited for Brigitte outside her apartment building, for she had refused his offer to help carry the presents to her flat. Within five minutes, she reappeared with freshly applied lipstick. While her expression was conciliatory, her tone was formal.

"First, let me say thank you for all that you did for Doda."

"What do you mean?" They walked across and out of the square to the harbor.

"One day, Dr. Murillo knows nothing about Alzheimer's Disease, and the week after you start in his practice, he's suddenly an expert."

"It was the least I could do."

There was a light wind. Docked boats creaked against their piers.

Donovan continued, "Brigitte, please let me tell you my side of the story. I know it's painful and it may not make any difference, but I need to tell you."

Brigitte didn't respond, but neither did her body language command him to stop.

"I never lied to you—I didn't love Regina. Everything I told you about my pity for her and going with her that weekend to talk her parents into transferring her back to Paris was true. What I left out was that she was so nervous the night before we went, she came over to practice what we were going to say. She brought a bottle of vodka; she said it would help us learn how to lie. I don't remember anything about how the night ended, but we woke up together in my bed the next morning. I felt terrible about it, but I didn't tell you because it meant nothing. Three months later, when Regina wrote to tell me she was pregnant, I was beside myself. My mother swept in and made all the decisions and arrangements for the wedding. I was working on a letter to you—I didn't have the guts to tell you in person—when Mother ran into you."

"Yes, she was delighted to convey the news, especially that you were planning to have the wedding in Paris."

"*Dio mio!* Brigitte, I swear that is not true."

The wind picked up, halyards rattled upon their masts.

"I know it doesn't make any difference, but I'm almost certain now that the baby was not mine. Regina died in labor. I knew the baby was premature, but what I didn't know was how premature. Three months. Had I been the father, the baby would have only been one month premature. It is horrible what happened to her, but I swear to you, I was not the father."

They strolled the harbor's length and were now at the entrance to Fort Falcone. Fifteen years ago they had trodden the fort's path and Brigitte had allowed Donovan to kiss her. It had been their first kiss. Brigitte shivered as she turned around to walk back. "Donovan, I'm sorry. But you're right, this makes no difference."

Donovan stopped and turned to face Brigitte. He had aged. He was only thirty-eight and yet his face was that of a much older man. "Brigitte, give me another chance. Look, I'm finally moving out. I'm quitting medicine and moving to Portoferraio. I never really wanted to be a doctor. That was Mother's idea."

"What will you do instead?"

"You're going to laugh." When Donovan smiled, his eyes twinkled and the lines of his forehead smoothed, transforming him into the boy who had won her heart. "I bought a hotel. Remember when I researched hotels for your trip to Padua? Even though you didn't end up staying there, I was intrigued by a business where your entire goal is to make people happy.

Medicine certainly isn't like that. Anyway, I've saved all my money and just last week, bought the Crystal Hotel over on via Cairoli."

Brigitte did indeed laugh "You're not serious." The wind billowed her dress and hair about her. It carried her laughter so that it came out more joyous than she felt, as if the elements conspired to lighten the mood and heal old wounds.

"Absolutely." Caught up in Brigitte's mood shift or the story itself, Donovan became animated, waving his arms while he talked, like he used to whenever he got excited. "Mom is so angry. Even though the contract has been signed and the money transferred, she's putting the Lombardis—the current owners—through hell. You can't imagine."

The wind died. "Yes, I can."

Donovan took both of her hands. "Of course you can. God, Brigitte, I'm sorry. I know that I will never be able to make it up to you, but I will swear that if you give me another chance, I'll never let anyone get in the way again."

"Donovan, I don't know what to say. I need time to think. Please just walk me home."

On the way back, Donovan continued to hold Brigitte's hand. She did not pull away. They cut in from the harbor and took an interior route. It was a new moon so they stuck to the lit streets, bypassing many of the dark alleys they had walked in their youth. Neither spoke until they arrived at Brigitte's door.

Donovan spoke first, though he dared not push his gain. "Can I call you tomorrow?"

"Please do," Brigitte replied as she released her hand from his.

Inside her apartment building, Brigitte went to bolt the door. She was forever forgetting that she'd removed the building's exterior lock years before. Nevertheless, she remained at the threshold and listened to the stillness until she heard the gravel crunch of Donovan's receding footsteps.

36

Portoferraio, October 2, 1973 - Nighttime

Brigitte sat at the kitchen table with her journal, registering each gift and who had given it to her. She did this not only to remind herself to write thank you cards, but also as a way to record special occasions. After dinner parties, she would recreate the menu. For special religious ceremonies (after the Ansóphia incident, Brigitte had started attending mass), she would note the sermon. For birthdays, Christmas, and other gift-giving holidays, she would itemize the gifts. Although Donovan had shown up at the party empty-handed, she included his name. She paused for a minute and then wrote beside it: *a second chance.*

Brigitte turned Maria and Antonio's gift over in her hands. Maria had been unusually secretive about it and had even asked Brigitte not to open it until she was home. Given its dimensions and weight, it was certainly a book, and by the paper and string wrapping, Brigitte guessed it was a new journal from Franco's shop. Pia had always encouraged Brigitte's journaling, and after her parents' death, Maria had taken up her mother's cause. But when Brigitte unwrapped the gift, she was surprised to find a coffee table book on modern art. Given Brigitte's well-known aesthetics, it was a strange choice, an oddity she considered for a moment before she opened the card that was taped to the book's cover.

Happy Birthday Brigitte,

Antonio was flipping through *La Stampa* while at the dentist last month and came across an article that was a shock to us both. We wanted to be sure, so we had Franco order this book where there's a larger image. See the clipped article that marks the page in the book. It may or may not be as much of a surprise to you as it was to us, but just in case, we wanted you to open this while you were alone.

Bacioni,
Maria and Antonio

Brigitte pondered the book's cover photo, a replication of a painting that was a single square of color, various shades of orange. She would never understand modern art, even though many critics contended that only in abstraction did one have the faculty for transcendence. She turned to the marked page expecting an article on her mother or maybe a photo of some painting she had. Instead, there was a picture of a piece of sculpture, modernist but still figurative: a man holding a large amorphous object, maybe a child. It looked vaguely familiar. Maria had folded the magazine article she referenced and used it as a bookmark. When Brigitte unclipped it and it fell from its place, she let out a small gasp. On the book's facing page was a sketch of the sculpture. The man held not a child but a lamb. She looked from the book's image to the sketch above her mantel. There was no doubt that they were drawn by the same hand. She picked up the magazine article where there was a smaller image of the similar sketch as well as a photo of Tío Piquot. He was older than she remembered him but there was no denying the photo was of Tío Piquot.

The article was titled: "Picasso's Sentinel." It began, "*After 1943, whether friends or foes entered Picasso's atelier, they were greeted by* The Man with a Lamb." The article continued by comparing the sculpture to Picasso's famous Guernica. The author asserted that, in a similar allegorical construct as Guernica's representation of the utter desolation caused by the Spanish Civil War, *The Man with a Lamb* represented the Holocaust's slaughter of innocent Jews.

It had never occurred to Brigitte that *Tío* was Spanish for *Uncle*. *Piquot* must be short for *Picasso*. Maybe it was a nickname he used with close friends. Or maybe it was a pet name that, like Doda, was derived from a young Brigitte's puerile attempt to say his name. Regardless, Tío Piquot was the painter Pablo Picasso—whose name even she knew—and according to this article, he had turned her sketch into a sculpture that was being heralded as one of his most significant works.

Brigitte flipped back to the beginning of the section, read Picasso's bio, and then flipped through the pages one by one, examining each replication of his work to see if it held any significance for her. On the next to last page of the section, there was a painting entitled *Night Fishing in Antibes*. This was one of the few plates that were in color, with bold cubist blocks of blues and greens and reds. Near the center was a child formed of two opposing yellow triangles, one inverted atop the other, like an ill-drawn hourglass. The child was turned away from the scene of a fisherman who was spearing his catch. The child's mouth, if it could be called a mouth, gaped open as if she were screaming.

Brigitte looked at this image for a long while before closing the book and placing it on the mantel beneath the framed sketch. Sitting back down on the sofa, she tore a page from her journal.

> *Dear Donovan,*
>
> *I can't tell you how happy I am that you are following your dream. Know that I am your friend and will support you in whatever way I can, but as far as anything beyond a friendship, I can't open that door again. Let's put the past in the past—both the good and the bad—and focus on the present and the future.*
>
> *-Brigitte*

The next morning Brigitte rose and made tea. While the water was heating, she reviewed the list of guests and the gifts they had brought. The teapot's whistle began to sing. Before she laid the journal aside, she crossed out Donovan's name.

37

Brigitte watched the children play in the sand. It was amazing how much they were both like and unlike their parents. Little Giuseppe and Giuliana were each a blend of Antonio and Maria. Giuseppe had inherited Antonio's inquisitiveness but Maria's caution. Giuliana was quiet but with Antonio's self-assuredness and Maria's will. Giuliana always got her way. As for their appearance, they both had Maria's contrasting light skin and dark features except that Giuliana had Antonio's light eyes. Colette and Christophe, on the other hand, were like clones of Sophie and Etienne, except in reverse: Colette was dark, brooding and selfish like her father, and Christophe was the spitting image of Sophie when she was his age.

Brigitte had finally come to terms with Etienne's last toss of salt in the familial wound: Christophe had been his name choice, not Sophie's. Etienne claimed the name was in his family as well—a distant uncle so distant that Sophie had never met him. More likely, Etienne was kissing up to the rich in-laws. He'd called Brigitte from the hospital to gloat about finding a name worthy of honor in both families. Brigitte held her tongue. She had already lost too many years harboring ill will. Sophie and Etienne had been married a decade, and she had spent much of that time feuding with them. First, it was the Paris wedding (which, of course, she didn't attend), then the subsequent move to Paris (to flee Italy's political unrest, which, after Moro's assassination, of course, she couldn't argue), and finally, it was the inclusion of Madeleine and Christophe in their lives. Every Sunday they had dinner together—every Sunday.

This last betrayal was incomprehensible, but Brigitte had taken the blow without grievance. She and Sophie had developed a truce of sorts, where Brigitte wouldn't ask and Sophie wouldn't tell. Whenever the subject was unavoidable, Brigitte chose her words carefully. So when Etienne chose to name their son Christophe, Brigitte conveyed her well wishes, remarking to Sophie, "Your grandfather must be so proud," and left it at that. It infuriated Etienne that Brigitte called him by the English diminutive Chris, which stuck. Now Chris had insisted his parents no longer refer to him as Christophe. Brigitte smiled at her small victory.

The children got along well enough, though Brigitte could already tell that there was no bond that would endure. It had less to do with their personalities than with their disparate cultural proclivities. Giuseppe and Giuliana were of the island; their pleasures were simple: the sand and the sea. Colette and Chris were Parisian. Even now during their last ten minutes of play, most of their attention was on not mussing their clothes. Brigitte heard Sophie and Etienne approach. They were still fighting.

Etienne huffed, "You see, the ferry's not even docked yet—we have plenty of time."

"If you don't mind, I would like to say a proper farewell to my mother without having to rush. *Nom de Dieu,* they sell cigarettes on the boat."

As Etienne turned downwind from them to light his cigarette, he chided, "Did I say you had to go with me?"

After seeing the ferry off, Brigitte began to walk Giuseppe and Giuliana home, but the children had other plans and convinced her to go for an ice cream first. Like Doda, she was the only grandparent these children had and though she was not blood kin, it certainly did not stop her from indulgences warranted by the position.

Another ferry had just docked and was loaded with passengers. It seemed like every year August drew more and more foreigners. Families and teenagers shot past them to secure their accommodations so they could get a full day on the beach before tonight's *Ferragosto* celebration.

38

Portoferraio, August 15, 1985 - Mid-afternoon

After Brigitte dropped off the children, she visited a while with Maria, and was on her way home when she saw Antonio from afar. As usual, he was in his own world and didn't notice Brigitte's wave. He carried his toolbox, so he must have been returning home from a job. A young man who appeared to be following him thought Brigitte was waving at him and waved back.

"*Mi scusi,*" a deep voice boomed from behind her. Brigitte spun around, startled, but quickly composed herself to address the middle-aged man who stood before her with a map in his hand.

"*Sì.*"

"I'm sorry, I didn't mean to scare you."

Brigitte adjusted her scarf. "There's no need to apologize. I was just waving to someone and didn't hear you."

"Yes, I saw you."

He had an accent that Brigitte couldn't place, Sicilian maybe.

"And?" she asked, matter-of-factly.

"And what?"

"Do you need help finding something?"

He seemed to have forgotten his purpose, but then said, "Oh yes, I'm sorry. Do you know where the Hotel Crystal is?"

"Yes, it's up a few blocks on via Cairoli."

"Are you going that way?"

"In fact, I am."

"Can I walk with you?"

Brigitte saw no harm in the request. "Of course."

"My name is Alessandro Perri."

"Brigitte Crémieux."

After Brigitte pointed Alessandro down via Cairoli, she took her time walking back. Usually Brigitte hated the rude summer tourists who'd begun frequenting the island, but today she enjoyed the cacophony of languages, just as she did the cool sea breeze that had picked up throughout the day. Instead of going straight home, Brigitte stopped at the beachside park and sat in one of the swings, trying to remember the last time she'd been on a swing set. She kicked off her shoes and, firmly gripping the chains, she swung her legs back and forth, but she had trouble building momentum. One of the teenagers who were playing football on the beach came up and asked, "Would you like some help?"

"Please. It appears I have forgotten how to get it going."

With a few pushes, Brigitte's swing glided through the air in a wide arc. She was self-conscious of her skirt blowing up, but she managed to pin it between her knees, thereby restraining it to a pleasant flutter against her ankles. Her hair was going to be a knotted snarl.

"Tell me when to stop," the boy said.

"You're so sweet, but you don't need to push me. Go back to your friends."

His voice wavered in frequency with the swing. "It's no problem Sig.ra Cremiù. It's nice to see you smile again."

Brigitte smiled at his pronunciation of her name. It brought back memories of Antonio and Maria when they were little. "And you are?"

"Benito, Dr. Murillo's son."

"My goodness, I didn't recognize you. You're all grown up."

"Well, the last time we talked, I was five. I hope I've changed since then."

"I guess that's true. Thank you, Benito. I think that's quite enough."

"Certainly, any time."

Benito came from behind the swing and nodded a farewell before running back to his friends. Brigitte enjoyed the swing's slowing motion as she watched Benito rejoin the game. Counting back the years, she realized that he must be almost eighteen by now. She rose from the swing feeling a little unsteady. As she was putting back on her shoes, Benito waved. Brigitte waved back.

She arrived home just in time to catch the phone. It was Maria. "Hi Brigitte, I know we're meeting up later, but is there anyway you can come for dinner beforehand?"

"I would, but I promised Patrizia I'd try out another one of her recipes. She's bound and determined to get that business of hers off the ground. Is there anything wrong?"

"Antonio's done it again. He's invited a houseful of strangers to stay with us—*American* college kids, no less. What am I going to talk about with American college kids? Please, you're so good with strangers. And they don't speak Italian! You know how bad my English is."

"Oh, Maria, it will be good for you. I'd rather not cancel on Patrizia, but I will if you want me to."

"No, no, that's okay. I can manage." Maria's voice became distant. "Wait, I think one of them has just come in from the beach. I'll be back in a second."

Brigitte heard awkward introductions in English. When Maria returned, she whispered into the receiver. "Brigitte, I've got to go, but can you believe there's a girl with them? Or I should say *at least* one. I thought they were all boys. What am I supposed to do—let them sleep together? What will the children think?"

Brigitte sympathized. "Oh dear."

Maria sighed, but when she spoke, the exasperation had faded from her voice. "I'll figure something out. At least Antonio asked them to pay, unlike most of the other stragglers he's brought home. See you at nine in front of the church."

39

Portoferraio, August 15, 1985 - Early Evening

This year's Virgin was spectacular. Each year, the school children made a *papier-mâché* statue, and most years that was just what it looked like: a *papier-mâché* statue made by school children. But this year's was almost lifelike, and the rich colors that they had chosen for the robes added to her brilliance, like one of Brigitte's colorful scarves, such as the orange and gold one she wore tonight. The statue's face did not reflect the ecstasy of her heavenly assumption, but was instead the doleful countenance of a mother who has lost an only child.

Maria approached with a tall beautiful girl by her side. The girl was clearly a hit with the children. She had one arm draped over Giuseppe's shoulder and, at her other side, Giuliana clung to her skirt. If it weren't for their unmistakable resemblance to Maria, a stranger may have thought the girl was the children's mother. Brigitte waved them over.

The girl thrust out her free hand. "*Bona sara.* I'm sorry, that's about the extent of my Italian."

Brigitte shook the girl's hand. When Sophie was in third grade, the school had added English as a requirement, and Brigitte learned it by association and spoke it far better than most of Sophie's classmates, including Antonio and Maria. She understood more than she spoke, and though her accent was an odd mix of French and Italian and she often confused words, she usually got her point across.

"Ello, mi nahm es Brigitte."

"Nice to met you. I'm Miriam."

Brigitte was charmed by Miriam's casual *savoir-faire*. "Air you amusing?"

Miriam's smile covered a good half of her face. She had big white American teeth. "Yes, we're having a wonderful time, thanks to Maria here. If she hadn't opened her house, I don't know what we'd have done."

Brigitte could tell by Maria's expression that she liked Miriam. It wasn't quite a smile, but then Maria was not prone to frivolous gestures. "Where's Antonio?"

Maria rolled her eyes. "Where do you think?"

"Fishing?"

"If that's what you call it."

The procession started and they found their place along its edge, a few meters away from the group that lifted the Virgin high above the crowd.

"Hello again. It must be my lucky day." It was Alessandro, who had again surprised Brigitte from behind.

He was overdressed for the occasion, and at least a decade out of style, in a navy pinstripe three-piece suit complete with a watch chain that dangled from his vest pocket. He was of medium build, a little thick through the middle, and though he was probably in his mid-forties, he looked older because his once-handsome face sagged from either ill health or heartache. It was dispiriting to see a man with such a confident disposition appear so beaten down. Something about his stature reminded her of Ugo, although maybe it was just his bushy mustache. Brigitte wondered if Maria noticed the resemblance.

Brigitte was surprised when he shifted to perfect English and started talking to Miriam about New York City, a conversation that continued uninterrupted through the rest of the procession. When Giuliana asked Miriam to put her on her shoulders so she could see the final ceremony, Alessandro returned his attention to Brigitte.

Brigitte smiled. "So you're American?"

"And you're French."

"I was born in France." Brigitte looked to Maria for support, but she had stopped to address, with Miriam's assistance, another English-speaking tourist who had asked her to explain the meaning of *Ferragosto*. Brigitte continued walking with Alessandro.

"I was born in Sicily."

"Oh, I see."

In silence, Alessandro and Brigitte watched the Virgin's final descent into the sea. When the crowd dispersed, he asked her to his hotel for a nightcap. Brigitte politely refused.

40

Portoferraio, August 15, 1985 - Late Evening

"Why didn't you have a drink with him?" Giuseppe and Giuliana were sleeping over at a friend's, and the house was empty except for Miriam, who had moved her pallet to the living room. Having discovered that Miriam was traveling with her fiancé, Maria said that it would be fine if they slept together, but in deference, Miriam had insisted they sleep apart. Brigitte knew that it would not be fine with Maria if an unmarried couple shared a bed in her home, and that Miriam's persistence was one of the things that warmed Maria to her. Maria took the unfinished bottle of wine from dinner and Brigitte followed her to the master bedroom, waiting until the door was closed before she answered Maria's question.

"Oh, Maria, he's too young for me. And besides, he told me his wife died less than a year—"

"Wait, shhhhhh." Maria tiptoed to the bedroom door and peeked out. One of the other Americans had just arrived and was stumbling down the hallway. Maria went and turned on the hallway light, calling out, "*Buona notte*," before returning to the bedroom and shutting the door behind her.

The young man stumbled again, this time more likely a result of his inebriation than the darkness. "*Bona notay*," he whispered through the closed door.

"*Americani*," Maria said, rolling her eyes. She poured the wine and continued her teasing. "Brigitte, come on, you always have some excuse. I saw the way you two looked at each other."

Brigitte sipped her wine before replying, "Should I have a one-night stand? I think not. After all, he's staying at the Crystal." Of course, this mention evoked the same old argument about how Brigitte should give Donovan another chance. Brigitte spent the next hour defending her position while Maria readied herself for bed. Fully clothed, Brigitte crawled under the sheets with her, and the two women continued their pillow talk by the light of the moon that shone through the small bedroom window. As Maria drifted off, Brigitte's voice softened and slowed like a mother lulling a child, until all was quiet except Maria's deepening breath.

Quietly, Brigitte swiveled herself off the bed. When she bent over to put on her shoes, she saw Antonio through the window, at the edge of the grove behind the house. He stood naked with his legs wide apart and his head thrown back. His wet body shimmered in the moonlight. Kneeling in front of Antonio was the young man Brigitte had seen following him earlier in the day. Brigitte didn't need to be told what was happening; she had seen it before. It was a memory buried deep in her subconscious.

Maria slurred, "Can you pull the curtain shut before you leave? The moon is like a spotlight when it's full."

"*Certamente,*" Brigitte whispered in reply.

Brigitte waited until she was certain Maria was fast asleep and then slipped out of the house quietly. As she walked away, she heard the insistent grunting of two men defiling nature.

41

Portoferraio, August 15, 1985 - Nighttime

Brigitte found the dress in the back of the closet. It was still in the original garment sack; she had never worn it. When she pulled it from the bag, its scalloped edges fluttered. She went to the bathroom and held it against herself in the mirror. Its style was timeless.

Ten minutes earlier, when Brigitte had arrived at her flat, she couldn't remember the walk home because she was a tangle of emotions. Antonio had always attracted people to him. He had a mesmerizing effect that was irresistible to everyone, regardless of gender or age. But she would have never believed that he could be unfaithful. Not only unfaithful, but vile! It was a shock that brought with it another.

It had been years since she'd had the Antibes dream. Now it had once again thrust itself upon her, but this time not as a disjointed maze of surreal images, but as a memory, complete and intact. The memory started like the dream: Brigitte was five or six years old, and she and her mother were sitting on the shore, waiting for Christophe. Madeleine was reading a copy of *Vogue,* and Brigitte repeatedly asked her why Christophe hadn't yet arisen from bed and joined them at the beach. But instead of him not coming, or magically showing up, Madeleine responded, "If you're careful and walk straight to the house, you can go get him. I'm sure he's ready by now."

Brigitte slowly made her way up the sandy path to Tío Piquot's house. She went in. The foyer was nearly black. All the shades had been pulled and the only illumination was from a faint band of light under the parlor door, beyond which she heard muffled animal sounds—sounds that the adult Brigitte now realized were moaning. *"Il y a quelqu'un?"* she called out. Nothing. Whispers emanated from the library. In the darkness, she felt like she was snooping but was drawn forward by the hushed voices. She tiptoed to the parlor door and pushed it open. The room had no windows and was lit by a single reading lamp that cast an eerie green light on two men—one with his pants around his ankles and the other kneeling in front of him.

She called out a second time. *"Papa, es tu là?"*

"Nom d'un chien, Brigitte. Qu'est ce que tu fais ici?"

The end of the memory was cloaked in sensory fragments. The images dissipated but the sounds filled her head: the yelling of her father, her own crying, and the high-pitched laughter of the other man.

42

Portoferraio, August 15, 1985 - Midnight

When Brigitte arrived at the Hotel Crystal, Donovan was sitting alone at the desk, reading. In his distraction, she had a few moments to observe him unawares. He was deep in concentration, as if he were a student studying for an exam. She had never seen him wear glasses, and she watched as he unconsciously stroked one of the earpieces while he read. Brigitte had always wondered why an island hotel would have a lobby so dark and formal. It had seemed so out of place before, and yet tonight, it seemed nothing of the sort. It was she who felt out of place, and time. The dress she wore was meant for a much younger woman, one who was trying to impress her beau.

"Hello, Donovan."

Donovan looked up from his book. "*Gesú*! Brigitte . . . you, uh, look amazing."

Brigitte's reply was tentative. "*Grazie.*"

Though trivial, the dialogue that followed reflected the palpable disconnect between Donovan and Brigitte. Donovan's words were tinged with optimism and hers with a confusing assimilation of shame, regret, and liberation. At last, Brigitte brought the pleasantry to an abrupt close.

"Donovan, can you ring the room of Alessandro Perri?"

"Brigitte, it's midnight."

"I know. Just tell him it's me."

Donovan took off his glasses and picked up the phone.

Alessandro opened the door still wearing his suit, or rather, rewearing it—Brigitte could tell he'd quickly put it back on after he'd received Donovan's call. No words were spoken, but everything was communicated. She undressed first and watched as he nervously took off his suit, his hands shaking. At one point he turned off the light, but she walked over and switched it back on. As she passed, he embraced her. How he managed to disrobe she wasn't sure because from that point on, his arms never left her. In bed, she climbed on top and when she slid him into her, there was a wince of pain, but then it was gone and her body took over. She held his eyes and they were indeed windows into his soul. They shone with his desire and his pain. They also revealed, though she didn't have the experience to physically realize it, his inability to complete the act.

The next morning, he admitted that his children had sent him on this trip because they were worried about him. After his wife died, he'd given up on life. He whispered in Brigitte's ear that she had done what his children hadn't been able to do, what this trip couldn't accomplish: she made him want to live again. With Alessandro's confession, she felt his erection rising into her. She knew that with her back to him, he might be imagining his wife, but it didn't matter—Brigitte had her own fantasy, one in which, at long last, she allowed herself to fully indulge. Afterward, she finally understood.

Donovan wasn't at the front desk when they went downstairs but, just in case, Brigitte told Alessandro to meet her at the café across the street after he'd finished checking out. During breakfast, he talked about his children, his life in New York, and his little grocery store that his wife helped him open. He became headstrong and chatty and Brigitte could imagine him haggling with his customers in a good-humored way. Brigitte shared Alessandro's post-coital glow but was deprived the essence of its bliss. And though she enjoyed his stories, each one stoked what felt like a cinder burning in the pit of her stomach. At one point, she thought she would be nauseous, but then it passed.

At the ferry station, Brigitte felt indecent in her skimpy dress. It didn't matter that the August heat was oppressive, and most passengers were dressed in shorts and tank tops. Some were even in their bathing suits. Still, Brigitte shielded herself with clutched arms while she waited for the boat to set sail. Alessandro stood upon the bow and waved as the ferry pulled from the dock. She waved back, keeping one arm wrapped around her. Miriam was also on the bow waving, but it took a moment for Brigitte to recognize her. When she did, she smiled and returned the wave until she noticed the young man who stood at Miriam's side. Brigitte's hand dropped mid-wave. As she walked home, Brigitte could not get the man's face out of her mind, though she had seen it fully only twice from afar and once in profile. But then it had cast by the moonlight, hidden mostly in shadow.

RECONCILIATION AND DISSILLUSION

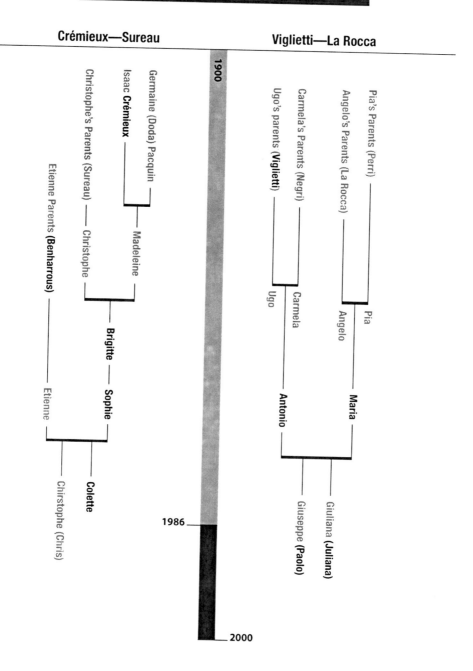

Crémieux—Sureau

Viglietti—La Rocca

1900

Germaine (Doda) Pacquin

Isaac **Crémieux**

Christophe's Parents (Sureau)

Etienne Parents (**Benharrous**)

Madeleine

Christophe

Brigitte

Sophie

Etienne

Colette

Chirstophe (Chris)

Ugo's parents (**Viglietti**)

Carmela's Parents (Negri)

Angelo's Parents (La Rocca)

Pia's Parents (Perri)

Ugo

Carmela

Angelo

Pia

Antonio

Maria

Giuseppe (**Paolo**)

Giuliana (**Juliana**)

1986

2000

43

Train from Padua to Rome, January 31, 2000

Brigitte looked out the window. She had heard of Tuscany's burgeoning popularity and had expected the modern development that Elba had experienced in its more touristy cities. But from the train, all she could see was open space—a pastoral beauty that, given other circumstances, would have calmed her. Yet the nearer she got to Rome, the more claustrophobic the landscape became. The mountains that rose on both sides of the track occluded the horizon, and storm clouds bathed the valley in shadow. Since Brigitte had moved to Elba, she had never spent this much time away from the sea. It was always there, an endless vista. And yet it was the sea that had taken everyone she loved. It had taken Carmela and Ugo, Pia and Angelo, and in their wake, Antonio. In a way, it had taken Maria as well.

After the final tragedy, Maria despised the sea. Her last few weeks on Elba, she couldn't even look at it. On the day the she left, they had to sedate her to get her on the ferry, and although she moved to yet another island, according to Paolo, she had never once seen the water surrounding New York.

If only Antonio could have let matters be, everything could have been different. If only he had let go. But he couldn't, or didn't. He knew that the mysterious circumstance of the Ansóphia's disappearance plagued Maria, and so, for over fifteen years, he spent every available night and weekend searching for its remains.

Brigitte stared out the window at one of the many medieval hilltop towns that dotted the Tuscan countryside. It began to rain; the storm was moving south. Brigitte watched the raindrops sweep across the window and recalled the tragic resolution of Antonio's search. In his obsession to slay Maria's demons, he had propagated them tenfold.

44

Portoferraio, May 1986

When the Ansóphia still had not returned the morning after her maiden voyage—the morning after Antonio had been convinced not to go search for her, the morning after he first made love to Maria—he swore he'd find her. He had combed, as had several rescue boats, all chartered waterways around Elba. It was two weeks before the *Capitaneria di Porto* gave up the search. There were rumors that the Vigliettis and La Roccas had fled to escape the debt incurred by the Ansóphia's delays, but the only person who said such a thing within earshot of Antonio found himself in the emergency room with a broken nose. It made no sense: there was not one splinter of debris from the Ansóphia's sinking. Antonio bought and studied every nautical chart he could find. He risked his personal safety— and once Giuseppe's as well—exploring the unpredictable current streams and innavigable craggy inlets of the Mediterranean's darker corners. After the near accident with Giuseppe, Antonio had promised Maria that he would give up his search. It was month later, when a Pianosa prison guard discovered a lifejacket from the Ansóphia, that Antonio began his "fishing" excursions. Maria questioned him, but he refused to answer and after repeated attempts to stop him, she gave up. For over fifteen years he searched, until one beautiful spring day in 1986, when his search came to an end.

Antonio's sailboat was discovered by another fisherman in a quiet bay on the south side of Montecristo. His body was located floating just above the seafloor, facedown at the ledge of a deep ravine. The man who found him said it looked as though he was still searching.

When the police arrived to inform Maria of Antonio's death, she was sitting in the middle of the living room. She had insisted that Giuseppe and Giuliana go to school and had returned home to wait, leaving the front door standing open so she wouldn't have to get up when they came. This was Antonio's room, where he sat every night and watched the news. Occasionally, she joined him and whenever she did, she sat on the sofa with her cross-stitch. But that day, she sat in the middle of the room, in a hardback chair she'd pulled from the kitchen and positioned so it sat facing his well-worn armchair. It was as if she were waiting for him to return to finish a discussion. When they told her that he didn't suffer the struggle of a typical drowning, that it appeared to be a sudden death, she didn't look at them. Instead, she stared into Antonio's empty chair. She asked one question: was he still wearing his St. Anthony medallion? No one knew.

45

Portoferraio, June 1986

When Sophie heard about Antonio's death, she dropped everything and left immediately for Elba. She was in the final week of the most important case of her career. Even though she spent hours each day on the phone with her associate, walking him through her litigation strategy (and ultimately won the case), her sudden departure resulted in a perception of "dedication issues" that delayed her promotion to partner by at least a year. Sophie's stalwart demeanor evaporated as soon as she saw Brigitte from the ferry, standing alone at the dock, wearing a mismatched skirt and blouse without one of her scarves to accent the dull ensemble or catch the wind of the blustery day. Her hair was an untamed frenzy capped by a yarmulke of undisguised gray. Sophie broke down in tears as she collapsed into her mother's embrace. Brigitte whispered in her ear, *"Chérie,* I need you to be strong." Sophie pulled away, still convulsing with sobs, and looked into her mother's eyes, bloodshot from sleep deprivation. Brigitte's face was void of any expression, without lines, as if she had never laughed, smiled, or cried. Their absence made her old beyond her years. When she spoke, her lips barely moved. "For the first time in my life, I have no idea what to do."

"I'll take care of Maria," Sophie said as she picked up her bag and led her mother from the ferry landing.

"I'm not sure she's going to make it," Brigitte said.

"She'll make it," Sophie replied. "She has to. She has her children to consider."

Brigitte had moved in and taken over caring for of Giuseppe and Giuliana the best she could, but they needed their mother's consolation, and Maria was nearly comatose. She hadn't said a word in three days, nor had she showered or eaten or arisen from bed. The night before, after one of her nightmares, she had wet the bed and Brigitte couldn't move her to change the sheets. Brigitte had threatened to call Bartolo and even Donovan for help. Maria finally responded with a glare that forced Brigitte to reconsider. Brigitte knew that if anyone could will herself to die, Maria could.

Sophie succeeded where Brigitte hadn't. She walked into Maria's bedroom, and shut the door behind her. An hour later, Maria was bathed and the children were packed. Sophie suggested that they all stay at Brigitte's, that she and Maria sleep upstairs in Doda's old flat, and that Brigitte keep the children downstairs. Over the course of the next two days, Maria began talking and even making decisions about the funeral. The Peratas, the new owners of Le Voci, sensed an opportunity to undo bad will from their takeover of the company after the Ansóphia affair. They offered to pay for everything and suggested a public memorial service to honor Antonio and all that the Vigliettis and La Roccas had done for Portoferraio. Maria refused. She insisted the funeral be kept private, simple, and most adamantly, that the casket remain closed.

The night of the funeral, everyone was quiet. Giuseppe and Giuliana had cried themselves to sleep, and Brigitte, Sophie and Maria all sat in Brigitte's living room. It was too somber to put on a movie, so they left the television on a news station to fill the silence. One story was about the erection of a new skyscraper in New York. America's President Reagan was at the building site for the christening and gave a short speech. It was a trivial news segment of American pomp that would on any other occasion have been ridiculed, or at best, ignored, but no one had the energy for either. Everyone watched and listened.

The inauguration of 7 World Trade Center is a momentous occasion for New York, America, and indeed the rest of the world. Since its 1966 groundbreaking, the World Trade Center has become a beacon for America's strength, imagination, and global leadership. At times in our past, we have been accused of being isolationist. But the World Trade Center is an iconic symbol of the opposite: it pays homage to The American Dream and its accessibility, regardless of race, class, creed or nationality. 7 World Trade Center completes the complex and when its doors open next Monday, it will not just be to one of New York's financial powerhouses— investment banking firm Drexel Burnham Lambert—but it will commemorate yet another of America's pioneering steps toward global democracy and freedom.

"We're moving to New York."

The channel had switched to a commercial and the increased volume drowned out Maria's comment.

Sophie turned down the TV and asked, "What about New York?"

Maria responded, "We're moving there—me, Giuseppe, and Giuliana."

Brigitte put her hand on top of Maria's. "You can't just run away."

Maria pulled her hand free. "You did."

Two weeks later, Brigitte again stood at the ferry landing and waved goodbye. When she'd called Alessandro and asked for his help, it was a far less awkward conversation than she had imagined it would be. Except for his initial inquiry, to which, though baffling, she responded without hesitation.

"This is Brigitte Crémieux from Elba. Do you remember me?"

"Is the pope Catholic?"

"Yes."

Alessandro's laugh blared over the receiver. "I'm sorry—I meant, of course I remember you. How could I not remember you?"

It felt good to hear laughter, even over a transatlantic phone line. Alessandro swept into action and called back the next day, having arranged a short-term lease of a small apartment in Little Italy. He assured Brigitte that it was safe, bragging that he was part of a tight Sicilian community who looked after their own. "Believe me, they'll be watched over."

"You know they hardly speak any English," Brigitte said.

Alessandro replied, "Don't worry, Little Italy really is a little slice of Italy. You can go all day without speaking a word of English." He then added flirtatiously, "Does this mean you might be visiting soon?"

Brigitte let his question hang, unanswered. Instead, she replied, "Thank you for helping my friends."

Alessandro switched tact. "How long do you think they'll stay? Two weeks? Three?"

Brigitte thought about how excited Sophie was to see Maria with a purpose, packing as if she were going to actually move. The day before Sophie left, all of them were at the house, in the kitchen, boxing up Maria's dishes. When Maria went to get more paper, Sophie had asked Brigitte, "How long do you think she'll stay? Two weeks? Three?"

"Brigitte, are you there?"

"Yes, I'm sorry. To be honest, I'm not sure how long they'll stay."

"You don't believe that she'll really move here, do you?"

"Yes, I do."

Long after the ferry sailed away, Brigitte remained at the landing, staring out to sea in a state of dissociation, a psychological seawall of sorts, hastily built to replace the foundational piers that had been swept away. It held for six years.

46

Portoferraio, July-October 1986

The year that Maria moved to New York, Brigitte was issued more invitations to celebrate her birthday than she had ever received before. And yet it was the first birthday she'd ever spent alone.

Her first invitation was from Bartolo, who had taken Brigitte's recent solitude as an opportunity to make known the extent of his infatuation with her, to which he had only insinuated before. Brigitte was too dispirited for flirtation but was too lonely to say no. Still, she eluded him for a week, waiting for divine intervention, which came in the form of Patrizia. When Brigitte confided her dilemma, Patrizia was aghast at Bartolo's presumption.

"There is time for courtship later," she said. "Why don't I host a party? You can invite Bartolo if you want, but at least I'll be there to keep my eye on him." Brigitte tried to refuse, but Patrizia was adamant that a party was just what Brigitte needed. Relieved, Brigitte returned home where she was presented with yet another quandary. In her mail was a letter from Sophie saying she had purchased tickets for both of them to go to New York for Brigitte's birthday. Sophie had attempted on several occasions to convince Brigitte to travel abroad, or even to the mainland, but Brigitte always made some excuse. Brigitte told herself she didn't want to spend any more time with Etienne than she had to. This was true, but not *the* truth. The underlying reasons for her disinterest were so deeply buried that Brigitte dared not question them. Rather, she nurtured her isolation as one does the comfort of any preference. Moreover, she was terrified by the prospect of leaving Elba, even for a weekend. She was therefore stunned when Sophie's offer produced a positive effect.

While Patrizia was disappointed to cancel her party, she was thrilled with Brigitte's decision to go to New York. She even convinced Brigitte to buy a new outfit for the occasion (it was Brigitte's refrain from shopping which had caused Patrizia the most concern over the previous few months. She believed that Brigitte's waning interest in clothes was a sure sign of a deep depression).

The night before her departure, Brigitte had her first-ever dream of flying. The airplane was the double-decker *Deux Ponts*, the same plane Madeleine had flown to America. In fact, it was that very journey of which Brigitte dreamt. As in many of Brigitte's other dreams, Madeleine was dressed in her black tuxedo dress, reading *Vogue*, while Brigitte sat beside her by the window, gazing out to wing's massive twin propellers beyond which puffy clouds that floated by like boats in a harbor. Sitting across the compartment from Brigitte was an older woman, knitting. The clack of the woman's needles and the slight rustle of Madeleine's occasional page turn were the only sounds to be heard—no motors, no voices, no rush of air. Brigitte was studying the clouds for various shapes when she felt her first contraction.

Madeleine looked up from her *Vogue* and said, "*Chérie*, there are some things you must know."

Brigitte couldn't remember the rest of the dream, but she awoke in such a state of dread that she called Sophie and canceled the trip. She told neither Patrizia nor Bartolo of this decision and made up her mind to spend her birthday by herself. When the day came, Brigitte awoke to flowers upon her doorstep—a gift from Donovan. She tried to muster some sentiment but could not even bring herself to call and thank him, and ignored the phone that rang on and off throughout the day. She finally opened the card that accompanied Donovan's flowers. It read: "Never hesitate to call if you need anything. *Tuo per sempre*." She chided herself for her self-pity, donned her new dress, and hired a car to take her to a newly acclaimed restaurant in Porto Azzurro. The food was delicious but there was no joy in the meal. She told her driver on the ride back an abbreviated story of why was celebrating her birthday alone. After hearing that Maria's recent move to New York had left Brigitte with no remaining family on Elba, the driver asked, "Why then do you stay?" Brigitte didn't respond, and they rode the rest of the way in silence.

47

Portoferraio, Summer 1992

Brigitte had spent weeks planning for her granddaughter's visit, and yet she was wholly unprepared for Colette's ennui. She had never been able to communicate with the child. When Colette walked off the ferry with eyes blackened by heavy mascara, spiky pink hair, and a jean skirt short enough to be irrelevant, Brigitte tried to keep a straight face. Their forty-year generational gap felt more like an unbridgeable schism. Colette descended the plank alone, as though the other ferry passengers were keeping their distance.

After Colette's disaffected greeting, Brigitte asked, "So, what should we do?"

Colette didn't respond but dropped her bags at Brigitte's feet and walked ahead, apparently to find a bathroom in one of the harbor shops. God knows why she couldn't have gone on the boat. Brigitte picked up the bags and followed her. "Well, I guess we have all summer."

It had not been Colette's choice to spend the summer in Portoferraio. It was Sophie's. Etienne had refused at first, but after Colette was arrested for shoplifting a box of condoms, he finally gave in. Though Brigitte longed to once again be surrounded by family, a summer with Colette would not have been her first choice. Colette had been trouble since she could walk, and with puberty, things had only gotten worse. She had been kicked out of school, and her parents had spent a fortune to enroll her in a private academy. Within a year, she'd already been suspended twice.

One more time and she would be expelled from there as well. Brigitte had no idea what she was supposed to do with such an unruly adolescent, granddaughter or not. Sophie had simply instructed, "Give her what you gave us. I'm obviously failing miserably."

Colette had not packed light, yet that didn't stop her from letting her grandmother struggle with both bags. Fortunately, the luggage was the latest pilot-style design, compact and with built-in wheels, although the wheels didn't roll so well over Portoferraio's cobblestone streets.

After settling into the guest bedroom, Colette went to take a shower, complaining about having to share a bathroom. When, after an hour, she still hadn't reemerged, Brigitte asked through the closed door, "*Ma chérie, do you want an ice cream?*"

The door unexpectedly swung open, almost causing Brigitte to fall inward. Colette stood unapologetically naked, brushing her hair and mocked, "*Non, ma chérie.*" She then straddled the bidet and began to trim her pubic hair. "Why can't I stay upstairs? There's nobody else living there."

Brigitte reached in the bathroom and, pulling the door shut, replied, "*Parce que je l'ai dit.*"

The first month, Brigitte and Colette barely interacted, except at mealtimes or to express mutual disdain for each other's interests. As far as Brigitte could tell, Colette's were limited to tanning, television, and poorly applied makeup. Colette, on the other hand, scoffed at Brigitte's *comportement de vieille*, ridiculing her antiquated tastes and her mundane hobbies of knitting and playing solitaire. Not only was Colette disrespectful to Brigitte, she was rude to all of Brigitte's friends. Patrizia refused to come over and Bartolo said, "If she were my grandchild, I'd have her bussing the tables to pay her keep."

Bartolo had finally learned to dissemble his amorous feelings for Brigitte and in turn, he'd adopted her as his best friend. They had a late dinner every Wednesday after he closed the café. Brigitte had asked if he minded Colette joining them for this weekly date, but after the first two disastrous dinners together, Brigitte had told Colette that if she couldn't display basic table manners or engage in simple polite conversation, she should stay home. "Fine by me," Colette responded. "Do you think I want to sit through an hour of such utter *vacuité*?"

When Brigitte told Bartolo, she laughed, "She actually used the word *vacuity*. At least I know she's learning something in school."

One morning, Brigitte was running errands and happened to see Colette sitting in a small café. Brigitte hurried past and ducked into the florist across the street. From the florist's window, she watched the waiter approach Colette's table. Colette appeared to be polite and even charming. She had combed her hair and now Brigitte could see that the dyed pink streaks were not random but intended to frame her face. When Colette smiled at the young waiter, he smiled back, and before leaving the table, he gave her a flirtatious wink. It could have been the window's glare, but Brigitte was almost certain that Colette blushed in response.

"*Posso aiutarla?*"

Brigitte turned to the shop attendant. "*Violette, per favore.*"

When Colette arrived home for lunch, her ill humor had returned. "Who died?"

Brigitte replied, "I thought it would be nice to have flowers."

Colette flung her beach bag on the kitchen table, almost knocking over the vase. "Smells like great-grandmother."

Brigitte stripped off her apron and threw it on the floor. She had recently developed a mild case of rosacea, which flushed bright red whenever she was angry or experienced menopausal hot flashes. She was currently overtaken by both. Her face radiated her internal swelter and beads of sweat rose on her brow. "Colette, you are my guest and my granddaughter. Neither position gives you the right to be *une chienne*. Like it or not, we have two more months together and I say we make the best of it, don't you?"

Colette's eyes widened in surprise, but she maintained an embittered tone. "What do you mean?"

"What I mean is why don't we call a truce? I will stop being a boring old lady if you stop being an insufferable bitch?"

"I think that's a little strong."

"Think what you may, but I will not be subjected to your pathetic displays, nor will I allow my friends to be."

"Why don't you send me home then?"

"Because your parents don't want you there. They're hoping that a summer on Elba will miraculously transform you from a selfish brat into someone who can at least finish school without getting kicked out."

"I can't believe that you, of all people, are saying this to me. You have no idea what my life is like. You have *never* visited us in Paris. We always have to come to you—to this stupid island. Just because—"

"Colette, don't you dare."

"You started it. What's it been—fifty years stuck on this hellhole? You call me selfish? You can't even set aside your own shame to visit your family. But you certainly force them to spend every vacation with you. And you talk about what I've put my parents through. You, who refuse to talk to yours, even though they've paid for your pampered life."

Colette's blow had found its target.

"What—is that surprise I see? Didn't think I knew that all this time you've been nothing but a daddy's—."

Brigitte slapped her. She had never hit anyone before and she was more stunned than Colette.

"I didn't know you had it in you." Colette grabbed her bag from the table, went to her room, and slammed the door.

48

Portoferraio, July 17, 1992

"Sleep well?" Brigitte knew that Colette had locked herself in her room waiting for Brigitte to either apologize or leave. Brigitte did neither. She made lunch, watched TV, made dinner, washed the dishes, went to bed late, arose early, made coffee, read, and finally—*voilà*, Colette emerged.

"One doesn't sleep well after being abused."

Brigitte ignored her. "Would you like some coffee?"

"I'll get my own."

"Fine, but today I'd like you to run some errands with me."

"You're kidding, right?"

"No, I am not kidding. If you're to live here the rest of the summer, you will help me with a few things."

"I don't—"

"You will."

"I will what?"

"You will come with me on my errands—period."

Colette took her time showering and dressing while Brigitte waited patiently in the living room and read.

When Colette finally emerged from the bathroom, she was resigned. "What errands?"

Brigitte looked up from her book. "First, you're going to help me not be such a boring old lady."

"Excuse me?"

"You heard me. You're going to go clothes shopping with me and advise me on what to wear to be less of an old-fashioned *shnock*."

Colette rolled her eyes. "Are you for real?"

"*Pour de vrai.*" Brigitte inwardly cringed as she heard the phrase come out of her mouth, certain that it was at least a decade out of vogue. Regardless, she continued with her forced bravado. "I may not take your advice, but I'll keep an open mind. You can huff all you want. Tomorrow, it's your turn. Let's see if we can find something that makes it appear as if you actually care how you look."

Four hours and seven outfits later, they stood again in Brigitte's foyer, each carrying her share of shopping bags. Brigitte motioned toward her bedroom. "One more favor and then you're free for the rest of the day. Would you mind helping me put these away?"

Colette shrugged. "Sure."

In the bedroom, Brigitte surveyed her overstuffed wardrobe while Colette sat on the bed and de-pinned Brigitte's new clothes. As Brigitte searched for available hangers, she attempted small talk. "You know, I used to be such a fashion plate. Every spring I would go out and buy the latest styles. But after everybody died or moved away, there didn't seem to be any purpose for it." Colette didn't respond, and the two went about their respective tasks in silence.

The final two dresses that Colette unbagged were the day's most extravagant purchases. The first was a retro Pucci print, with a skirt length that Brigitte thought she could only barely pull off with perfect lighting and a sufficient quantity of wine. It was Colette's first recommendation, so Brigitte hadn't been able to say no. The other was a black evening gown that plunged down the back. Brigitte had difficulty imagining an Elban occasion that would call for such formal attire, but the dress had elicited from her such an emotional response that she bought it anyway, if only as a reminder of unfettered joy.

"*Bah alors,* I need to get rid of some of, what did you call them—potato sacks?"

Colette protested. "Come on, I didn't say all your clothes were bad."

"That's only because you haven't seen the rest." When Brigitte turned around, Colette was smiling as she had in the café. "Can you put these on the bed while I tackle the back of the closet?"

As they sorted through Brigitte's old clothes, Colette said, "I know I can be difficult." Before Brigitte could sympathize, Colette quickly added, "Not a bitch mind you, but a little difficult."

Brigitte couldn't help but snicker, which caused Colette to respond in kind. Their laughter escalated, until finally, Brigitte laughed so hard that she had to go to the bathroom to keep from wetting herself. When she returned, Colette asked, "Who was Giovanni?"

The sales clerk at the second store had been decidedly effeminate and declared that everything Brigitte tried on looked *meraviglioso*. Upon checking out, he gave her a card with his name imprinted on it: Claudio Moretti. Brigitte asked, "You wouldn't by chance know a Giovanni Ferrari Bravo, would you?" Claudio was exuberant in his response, exclaiming that he and Giovanni had been friends since university. When Brigitte asked how Giovanni was, Claudio told her that he had passed away five years ago. Brigitte had never again seen Giovanni after her Padua trip. He had written her once, but she hadn't responded. After Claudio told Brigitte that Giovanni had died, she said, "But he was so young." Claudio responded, "A lot of us have died young."

"Nobody, just a man I met years ago on a train." Brigitte pulled the next dress from the closet.

"Mom would love that one."

Brigitte was holding a cellophane-wrapped pink skirtsuit that was at least twenty years old. Brigitte held it out in front of her as if examining its size. "Do you miss your mom?"

Colette's reply was sudden. The bitterness in her voice had returned. "God, no. I mean, why would I miss her? I never see her when I'm there."

Brigitte self-edited her maternal defense and instead asked, "What about your father?"

"What, do I miss him? Are you kidding? Come on, you know Dad—Mister I-could-give-a-damn. I barely know him. How could I miss him?"

"Well, I guess I assumed you spent more time with him, since he works from home. And no, I don't really know your father. He's never—how do I say it—shown any interest in getting to know me."

"Join the club." Colette was assessing the clothes that Brigitte had piled on the bed. "What are you going to do with all these?"

"Take them down to the church. They are always sending relief packages to Libya, Serbia, or wherever the latest crisis is."

Colette pulled one dress out of the pile. "*Ah bah oui,* I'm certain that all that's needed for peace in Croatia is *haute couture.*"

Brigitte cringed but then couldn't help but smile as she turned to see Colette holding one of Brigitte's old dresses against her body. "Do you like that one?"

"Actually, yes. It's sort of retro-modern."

"Try it on."

"You've got to be kidding—me in a dress like that?"

"Why not? Tomorrow's your day. Let's start early."

After Colette went to the bathroom to change, Brigitte flashed back to the two occasions she had worn the dress. She saw herself standing at Portoferraio's ferry landing, waving goodbye to the only man with whom, as an adult woman, she'd ever had intercourse. She then recalled her mirrored reflection twenty-five years prior, when she was a vulnerable young woman choosing a dress to impress the only man she'd ever loved.

When Colette opened the bathroom door, the dress's scalloped edges fluttering in its wake. "What do you think?" she asked sheepishly.

Brigitte gasped. "*Oh la la,* Colette, you look stunning."

49

"Don't sell it. Why don't you run it yourself?" Colette and Brigitte had just come from the lawyer's office and were sitting at the counter in Caffè Roma. A week after their two-day shopping spree, Bartolo had fallen dead of a heart attack. Adding to the shock of his death was the discovery that he had willed Brigitte the café. All of the plans that Brigitte had made to show Colette the rest of the island were now compromised. She had been researching a trip to Rome—which would have been a first for both of them—to explore the city and see the university where Sophie had graduated.

"Why me? Why would he leave it to me?" Brigitte pondered out loud. "I know nothing about business."

"Obviously you were special to him, and as far as business goes, aren't you the woman who moved here when she was thirteen and figured out how to buy a house?"

Brigitte looked up. "I was fourteen and I had help."

"Look, I'll help you, and maybe I can come back next summer to help out as well."

Brigitte felt a dry burning behind her eyes. "You would do that?"

"Sure, it'll be fun. God knows, I need to learn *some* skill."

They kept Caffè Roma closed for a month. Brigitte tackled the books, vendor management, and minor décor changes, while Colette talked with the staff about what else could be improved upon. When one of the waiters told her that Caffè Isla was the primary competition, Colette spent a day there in surveillance, plopped upon a bar stool, over-caffeinating herself. She'd pretended to write letters while flirting with Luigi, the owner, to ferret out his management secrets.

"Beach food," Colette reported back. "It's all about having food and drink that is refreshing and not too filling. Oh, and the TV channel— during the summer months and weekend nights, Luigi plays music videos."

"Music videos?"

"Oh, come on, Grandma, you're not that old. Anyway, with all the German tourists, I say we play VIVA instead of MTV. I'll find out how much it costs to get a satellite connection. And then, we'll up the ante."

"Up the ante?" Brigitte was wary, unsure of what to expect from Colette's newfound zeal.

Colette's eyes gleamed. "We'll have theme nights."

On opening night, Colette surprised Brigitte by ensuring that the regulars were there. She had asked each of the waiters about his favorite customers and used the phone book to locate them. One by one, she went to their homes and told them that her grandmother was now running Caffè Roma and that it would be even better than before. She left a handmade flyer giving them a discount on the first drink and a free *antipasto* with every dinner. Brigitte had decided to try her hand in the kitchen, but she was not prepared for the onslaught of diners (after all, the café had never been known for its food). She and the cook managed through the evening to mostly good review.

The next night, an entirely different crowd showed up: teenagers dressed in the evening's thematic attire. Colette had scoffed when Brigitte said she'd never heard of *The Rocky Horror Picture Show*, a musical with which apparently many young people were obsessed, including Colette. Colette had convinced her that a *Rocky Horror* showing would draw hordes of youth, even on Elba. Initially Brigitte balked at the idea, but Colette's enthusiasm was impossible to deny. Colette was right—the bar was more crowded than Brigitte had ever seen it. At one point, Brigitte stopped and took it all in: the costumes, the energy, the youth. Colette was helping the barman and chatting with every customer. She was definitely in her element, dressed in a skimpy multi-colored sequin outfit from the movie. There was one customer in particular—the waiter from the café who Brigitte had spied Colette flirting with—to whom Colette paid special attention. In return, he stationed himself at the bar for much of the evening.

"Hey, Sig.ra Cremiù!" a young voice called from behind Brigitte.

Startled, Brigitte turned to see Benito Murillo dressed in lace panties and a black leather corset.

"*Buona sera*, Benito," she managed.

"Rad idea. So retro," Benito exclaimed excitedly.

Benito also wore blood red lipstick and eye shadow so dark that Brigitte had trouble looking him in the eyes. But then, looking at any other part of him certainly wasn't an option. She almost asked, "'Retro' from when?" but she thought better of it.

"Yes, isn't it?" she agreed.

The following week, Colette returned to Paris. This time she carried her own bags to the ferry landing. She wore one of the dresses from her shopping day, an orange and brown baby doll dress that connoted lighthearted gaiety, though Brigitte certainly hadn't described the dress as such when she convinced Colette to buy it.

"Colette, I don't know what to say. It certainly wasn't the summer I imagined we'd have."

Colette pursed her lips as if readying them for a smart aleck remark, but then simply said, "*Moi, non plus.*"

"How am I going to run the café without you?"

"Oh please, you've got the staff. You don't need me."

"Yes, I do."

"Well, like I said, maybe I can come back next year for summer break."

"And maybe I can come visit you for Christmas this year."

Colette was stunned. "*Vraiment?*"

"Yes, really."

In early December, two weeks before Brigitte's Christmas trip to Paris (a surprise visit to which only Colette was privy), she received a call from Sophie whose voice was so mechanical and tinny that Brigitte could barely recognize it. Sophie told her, in short precise sentences, that Colette was pregnant and that Etienne blamed Brigitte's lack of supervision.

Brigitte didn't know what to say. "May I speak to Colette?"

"She has nothing to say to you." It was the first time Sophie had ever ended a call without saying, "*Je t'aime.*"

When Brigitte hung up the phone, she called Air France and canceled her flight.

50

Portoferraio, May 26, 1999

Brigitte wiped the bar's counters and then walked to each table to check its stability. It was always the last thing she did before she locked up for the night. Without fail, there was at least one table that had been tipped off balance over the course of the day and needed a little extra lift under one leg, or sometimes two. Brigitte carried with her a box of cardboard pieces folded into various widths that she could use to rebalance even the most off-kilter table.

Over the past seven years, she had mastered the ropes. The café was doing a decent business, a small steady profit year-over-year. She'd given up on cooking and was now the barmaid. At first the regulars had a difficult time adjusting to a woman *barista*, but over time, Brigitte's efficiency and dedication overshadowed her gender. She was just one of the guys. So much so that, with the exception of sports debates, she was often pulled in to settle their frequent disputes: Weren't the Bianchis splitting up? Didn't Bruno beat his wife? How many Elbans died in Operation Brassard? As for the regulars, there were some from the Bartolo days, but there were new ones as well. One or two had real crushes on her but, for most of them, the strutting was for show, affording the type of relentless bragging and teasing that fueled the conversations of old men. Brigitte went along, acting the part, flashing a seductive smile on cue and ignoring the heckling of the audience. Every now and then, Donovan dropped by, though he was never very comfortable interacting with her at the café. Brigitte speculated that this was because their role reversal in the café was too emblematic of the failure of their courtship. Although, perhaps he had simply lost interest.

Tourists occasionally ventured in, but Brigitte had long ceased trying to establish Caffè Roma as a "destination." Saturday theme nights were short-lived because the regulars grumbled. Brigitte knew that while a night's double bar intake was hard to forgo, continued patronage was her bread and butter, and keeping pace with fickle teenagers was well beyond her grasp.

Brigitte worked her way from the back of the café to the front. The last table she checked was always the one where she, Sophie, Antonio, and Maria had sat every day eating their *99* ice cream cones during that first summer after she met Donovan. Some nights she skipped it because, when she was alone in the café, the memories it triggered were too painful. Tonight, it was just another table. She knelt before it, exchanging one cardboard footing for another. Satisfied with her choice, she stood, put one hand on each side of the table and shifted her weight between them. It remained steady. She took one last inventory of the room, pausing briefly to look out the front door to the harbor beyond, and then took the box back to the storeroom.

Back in her flat, Brigitte began her nightly routine: she put on a pot of tea and sat at the kitchen table to open her mail. One letter's return address stopped her cold. She waited for the teapot's whistle, and then poured her tea before opening the letter.

> *Sig.ra Crémieux,*
>
> *I know I haven't written you since I was a boy, but Mom keeps me and Juliana up to date (in case Mom hasn't told you, Juliana now spells her name with a J and I go by Paolo—Mom's attempt to tone down our ethnicity). Mom says you can speak English pretty well and I hope that you can read enough to understand this letter because my*

Italian is terrible. Mom also tells me you now own Caffè Roma. I remember going there as a boy—at least I think I do. Didn't you used to say it was your second kitchen? I guess now it really is. Anyway, it is part of the reason that I'm writing you. Don't tell Mom, but I've been thinking about coming to Elba. I've just finished college and I am considering spending the summer there. Before I tell Mom, I thought I would see if I could stay with you and maybe work at the café to pay for my room and board. If it doesn't work out, let me know if there's anybody else in Portoferraio who may have a room and where you would recommend that I look for a summer job. I can't wait to see you again. I have such good memories of my childhood there.

Ciao,
Paolo (aka Giuseppe) Viglietti

PS In case you threw away the envelope, my address is: #301 Freeborn Hall, 2650 Durant Avenue, Berkeley, CA 94720, USA. The phone number at my dorm is 510.578.3245 (my roommate's name is Cliff in case he answers), but I also just got one of those new mobile phones that everybody in California has. I'm not sure if it works overseas (or what the charges are) but, just in case, the number is 510.448.2895.

51

Portoferraio, December 24, 1999

"Merry Christmas." Brigitte stood in the doorway holding a two-foot Christmas tree draped by tiny strings of popcorn.

To Brigitte's delight, Paolo had extended his Elban summer to fall and now winter, and when his flight home for Christmas was cancelled due to bad weather in New York, Brigitte was secretly overjoyed. "This is my first Christmas tree and I must tell you, finding popcorn on this island was a Herculean task. Not to mention this miniature tree stand. Cute, no?"

"Not as cute as your holiday cheer." Taking both the tree and her coat, Paolo ushered Brigitte in the door of Doda's flat where he was staying. When he first arrived on Elba, Brigitte had been taken aback by his beauty. She'd seen photographs but they did not portray the elegant precision of his features. He wore long dark curls that Maria told her he intentionally grew out to match the photo he kept in his wallet of Antonio. Both his desire to resemble his father and his success at doing so unnerved Maria, but she had learned never to discuss Antonio with Paolo for his insatiable curiosity was too much for her to bear.

With Giuseppe's return to Elba (Brigitte still couldn't get used to calling him Paolo), Brigitte's life had taken another turn. While Brigitte's café devotees loved her in their own way (and she them), they were not family. Giuseppe's return was the return of the prodigal son, except that it was Brigitte who was the prodigal one, not Paolo. She refurbished Doda's flat with excess. She kept much of Doda's rococo furnishings but updated all the appliances, including trading out Doda's old Grammont for a much smaller and thinner version with a flat screen that the salesman convinced her was the future of television. She paid extra to ensure that everything was delivered and installed before Paolo arrived. The result was a mélange of old and new, a fusion of style that Patrizia swore was the latest craze in Milan.

"Aunt Brigitte, you're the best. You didn't need to do anything special for me. I'm happy to just spend Christmas here with you." Paolo moved a stack of magazines from the coffee table and placed the tree in its center. When he went to hang her coat, Brigitte rotated the tree to its best viewing angle.

Brigitte downplayed her enthusiasm. "You are a sweet boy, but I know you miss your mother and your sister. I'm sorry your flights didn't work out. By the way, I've been meaning to tell you, your Italian is impeccable. I can't believe how much you've improved, especially over the last month. Thank goodness, because if we had to rely on my English, I'm afraid we would have little to discuss."

"*Grazie zia, sei un ottima maestro.* And stop apologizing. I really did want to stay here for the holidays. I think the flight cancellation was a sign. I remember one time when I was a kid when we all spent Christmas together, and Mom tells me that before that, you all sometimes used to have Christmas dinner in this very apartment, at your grandmother's."

Brigitte looked around the flat. "Yes, that was a lifetime ago." As Paolo busied himself in the kitchen, she asked, "Can I help with something?"

"No, no, just go sit in the living room and pour yourself some wine. You know I'm a one-man chef." Brigitte complied, went to the living room and settled into the couch. Within a matter of minutes, smells and sounds of sautéing onions filled the flat.

Paolo raised his voice to make himself heard from the kitchen. "Tell me about it. What was Elba like fifty years ago?"

Maria hadn't been joking about his incessant curiosity. "To begin with, fifty years ago I had just moved here and your parents weren't yet born. Both of your grandmothers were pregnant, and so was I, and we spent

Christmas furiously preparing for the imminent growth spurt in our little family."

"And then?"

"Then one, two, three—Antonio, Maria, and Sophie."

"No, I mean, tell me about Christmases over the years. What did you do? How did you celebrate?"

Brigitte picked up one of Paolo's magazines and thumbed through it. "Well, your grandparents were *comunisti* and didn't celebrate Christmas in the early days. They did have a large dinner for all of the Le Voci employees and their families. And your grandmothers started a tradition where we took the ferry to Piombino on Christmas Day and brought cakes and jams to the children in the hospital there."

"Wait, I think I remember going with you once." Paolo was rapt. "Tell me more," he urged as he rushed from the kitchen with two plates of steak Roquefort abed a beautiful medley of winter squash. At some point along the way, Paolo had picked up a more refined culinary palate than his mother, unless Maria's had shifted as well.

"Hold on, let me get our silverware first." Paolo raced into the kitchen and was back moments later. He jumped over the arm of the sofa and landed at Brigitte's side, her knife, fork and napkin in his hand.

"Okay, shoot." Paolo's deep obsidian eyes were his mother's, and when he fixed his gaze, it was captivating, like the intense gaze of his father.

Brigitte placed her utensils on the coffee table and spread her napkin across her lap. Such casual dining was new to her. "Do you also remember that when you were really little, you didn't get presents for Christmas? You got them in January?"

"I don't think so. Why January?"

"You don't remember Zia Patrizia dressing up as La Befana?"

Paolo's hands shot up from his plate to his forehead, fortunately holding neither his wine glass nor his knife. "Wait, I remember—the New Year's witch? God, I haven't thought about that in years. What was that about?"

Paolo's fervor always rubbed off on Brigitte. She loved reliving their past together, especially when she was allowed to edit. "It is an old tradition that, since we didn't celebrate Christmas, your grandparents took hold of with their usual gusto."

"*Gesú*! I remember now. Juliana was so scared of her and would cry even as she wolfed down her *panettone*."

"That was one of the reasons your mother wanted to celebrate Christmas. Well, that and she rebelled against your grandparents' atheism by insisting that you be raised in the church."

"Mom was religious? You've got to be kidding."

"At first she was quiet about it. I remember she bought this little hand carved *presepe* and put it on the windowsill. Your father was adamantly opposed to the church and did not want any religious icons around the house. But your mother fought back and won."

"How come I don't remember any of this?"

"You were young, and after your father's accident, she stopped going to church. I think she blamed God."

"This I know."

They sat quietly for a few minutes until Paolo asked, "What was Dad like during Christmas?"

Since Paolo had arrived on Elba, every conversation eventually turned to an inquiry about his father: what he was like as a child, how he came to be a carpenter, how he and his mother went from friends to lovers (Brigitte skirted the answer to that one).

"Oh, he was the same way he always was—intent. I remember one Christmas when he and Maria saved and saved to buy you a bicycle that you'd begged them for all year."

"The BMX." Paolo almost spat out his bite of steak. Brigitte had gotten accustomed to his American manners.

"Yes, that's right."

"Anyway, something on it was either broken or difficult to assemble, and he worked on it for hours. He didn't eat dinner and barely talked to anyone all of Christmas Eve. In fact, I think he stayed up the entire night getting it ready for you."

"Man, I remember that Christmas so well. I walked right by the bike and opened up my other presents. No one said a word until I practically tripped over it while going to the bathroom. I was so blown away because they had said it was too expensive."

"If I recall correctly, your father worked nights and weekends that summer and fall so he and your mother could afford it."

Paolo ate his food with the fury of a starving man. "God, Brigitte, I wish I remembered more about him. I try and I try but for some reason, I seem to block him out."

"Dear, memory is a tricky thing. Sometimes the most wonderful times in our lives are the ones we remember the least. Maybe during our best experiences our brains are too busy being in the present. Maybe it's like a vacation where you're enjoying yourself too much to take pictures. How many pictures have you taken during your six months here?"

"I'm not one to take pictures. Juliana's the photographer of the family. On that note, are you sure you're okay with us watching *Life is Beautiful*? When I rented it, I had completely forgotten that you were interned. Mom just reminded me. It was a camp just outside of Paris, right?"

Before replying, Brigitte took a moment to swallow her food. "Yes, dear, that was a long time ago."

Paolo's hesitation was more considered. "Do you mind my asking how your family escaped?"

Brigitte picked up her napkin and wiped the corners of her mouth before responding. "We were fortunate, my mother's family, including my grandmother that your mother has told you about—"

"Doda." Paolo smiled as if he remembered her. Though Maria had refused to tell the children much about their father, it appeared that she made up for the omission with stories of Doda.

"Yes, Doda. Well, she and my grandfather were visiting friends in England in the early forties, right after France was invaded, when my grandfather became ill and was forced into a hospital. When things got bad, they were still there and stayed throughout the war. In fact, Grandmother didn't return until after Grandfather died in 1947. That's when I first really got to know her, and I never knew any of her or my grandfather's extended family. I'm sure they were affected, though I don't know any details."

"How did they get out of France if they were Jewish?"

Brigitte spread her napkin back across her lap. "You know, I've never really thought about it. It does seem odd, now that you ask. They must have left early in the Occupation, when foreign travel wasn't as restricted."

"Lucky them. Well, at least lucky for Doda."

"Strange that I've never considered that—Doda's good fortune, that is."

"What about your parents? How did you guys manage to avoid the Germans for so long?"

Brigitte set her plate on the coffee table. "Because we weren't Jewish. My father is Catholic and I imagine that my mother converted when she married him, although we didn't go to church when I was growing up. The only reason I know anything about Judaism is because of Doda. When she moved back to Paris, she secretly taught me about Jewish customs and tradition."

"Why *secretly* if the war was over?"

"I don't think my parents wanted her to influence me."

"Are your parents still alive?" In asking the question, Paolo's voice slowed and his tone was cautious. Maria must have shared other stories as well.

"Yes, they are still in Paris, but I haven't spoken to them in years."

Knowing that he'd overstepped a boundary, Paolo backtracked. "Wait, if you were Catholic, why were you interned then?"

"I'm not sure. It was late in the war and, ironically, we got picked up when we were leaving the first and only mass I ever attended as a child. I guess my mother's Jewish heritage was discovered somehow. Anyway, they took us to this holding camp called Drancy where we spent about a month before Liberation."

Paolo got excited, as he did whenever he surfaced a forgotten detail or coincidence from the past. "That is so weird. I went to school with a girl whose grandparents were both interned at Drancy. Her grandmother told her how evil the warden was and how the only reason she escaped was because someone sabotaged the buses that were supposed to take them to the train station."

"Yes, thankfully, we arrived at Drancy just after the last deportation train had left. The camp was practically empty until a couple of days later when others began to arrive."

"According to her, the entire camp was supposed to be transported to Auschwitz a few days before Drancy was liberated. She said that hundreds of people were saved, all thanks to that anonymous saboteur. I wonder if he ever knew what a hero he was."

"I wonder." Brigitte looked away as she smoothed her scarf across her shoulder.

"God, Aunt Brigitte, I'm sorry. You obviously didn't know that."

Brigitte picked up her wine glass and held it before her as though admiring its sanguine color. "No, no . . . as I said, it's been a long time. It's nice to be reminded that there was also was some goodness back then."

"Are you sure? We really don't have to see this movie. I mean, it is Christmas Eve. I'm sure we can find a million other movies to watch."

After a sip of wine, Brigitte resumed eating. "No, I've heard it's a wonderful movie. It won an award, yes?"

"Yeah, many, including an Oscar for Best Actor." Paolo pressed *Play* on the remote and Brigitte had to admit, the clarity of the new TV's screen was impressive.

During the movie's title sequence, the soundtrack was silent, with no music to underscore the impending drama. Paolo whispered, "Let me at least share some good news before the movie starts." Brigitte raised a practiced eyebrow and on cue, Paolo revealed his surprise. "I think I've just about talked Mom into flying to Italy for her birthday. She won't come to Elba, but I've convinced her that maybe we could meet in Milan or Rome."

Now it was Brigitte who almost spit out her food. "Oh dear, that is wonderful news. Are you serious? She is actually considering it?"

"So she says." Paolo moved the little Christmas tree to one side of the coffee table, though it remained in Brigitte's peripheral vision.

"God, what a joy that would be."

The movie began and somehow the charismatic actor managed to capture Brigitte's distracted attention. As he charmed his way through the farcical opening scenes, Brigitte couldn't help but wonder how, as a Jew in the Holocaust, his life was going to turn out beautiful.

52

Portoferraio, January 26, 2000 - Midmorning

"*C R E. Accent aigu. M I E U X.*"

"Wait, that was *C*—the second letter was an *R*, right?"

"Yes, *C Are-uh.*"

"And did you say *A* next?

In the course of six months, Brigitte's regimented life had been turned topsy-turvy. Paolo had taken to Elba as if he had never left it. Within a week of his arrival, as many people greeted him on the streets and in the shops as greeted Brigitte. Most of this familiarity was from old family friends who adopted him as though he had never left, but there was also the broader Le Voci legend. In addition to the company's long history and the mysterious disappearance of its founders, Le Voci had recently been sold to Scaccia Navi for what was rumored to be a substantial amount of money. The lore's combination of nostalgia, tragedy and fortune was irresistible and, given the garrulous nature of Caffè Roma's regulars, everyone had heard of Paolo's link to it. Fanning the flame was the rumor of Maria's impending visit. Brigitte's unbridled anticipation overflowed into her every conversation. Even though Maria insisted she would not come to Elba, it didn't matter—she was returning to the Motherland.

"No, *E*." With her finger, Brigitte drew the letter *E* on the desk, topping it with a flick of her fingernail. "With a *accent aigu.*"

"I don't know how to do accents, let's try it without. What's next, *M* and then *E*?"

Like Colette, Paolo had adopted the café as a pet project. He too sought to attract a younger crowd, but with more subtlety: expanding the beer list to include imports, convincing Brigitte to install a sound system and to play music in the front room, and adding a computer with an Internet connection. The computer had turned out to be too much trouble and they had tucked it into a corner, until Paolo befriended Grey, an American who favored Robert Redford and who was an expert in both computers and home renovation. Grey was unusually generous with his time and had offered to help them renovate the Vigliettis' home that, since Maria had moved to New York, had been abused through fifteen years of seasonal renters. Brigitte had overcome her initial mistrust of Grey, although his effusive interest in Paolo remained unsettling.

"No, *I*." Brigitte reached over Grey's hands to the keyboard and typed the rest of her name. "I do not understand why in English, *Es* are *Is* and *Is* are *Es*."

"You know the English."

Brigitte didn't acknowledge the joke, and Grey continued. "Now, if you wanted to search on a full name, *Grey Tigrett*, for example, you would put the entire name in double quotes. Otherwise, it would search for all references of *Grey* and all references for *Tigrett* as opposed to just searching for *Grey Tigrett*. Does that make sense? Do you want to search for *Brigitte Crémieux*?"

"*Non.*" Brigitte's response was instant, but she immediately corrected herself. "Yes, I think I am to understand but let us only to explore *Crémieux*."

"As you wish. Let's see what we find." Grey pressed the *Enter* key.

Grey was a tourist, a lost soul who had come to Elba to escape his hectic life in America. Paolo had met him just before the holidays and the two had struck an odd friendship that Brigitte didn't quite understand, or for that matter, trust. She told herself that she was being overprotective, but there was something about Grey's instant familiarity that made her uneasy. Still, that didn't stop her from availing herself of his goodwill. When she learned that his renovated Manhattan flat had been featured in

Metropolitan Home, she got the brilliant idea to see if he would help her refurbish Maria's old house. Grey not only agreed to do it, but he also said he would upgrade the café's computer and teach them both how to maintain it. Brigitte told him that she had never used a computer and doubted that she could maintain one, but he insisted and said he'd teach her.

"Wow, looks like you've a pretty popular name. There's a model named Madeleine Crémieux who appears all over the place, as well as a couple of links to an Adolphe Crémieux. Know either of them?"

Before Brigitte could answer, Paolo called out from the bar, "Grey, can you show me again which ovens you decided on?"

"You mean, *you* decided on. I'm only making recommendations." Grey winked at Brigitte as he stood up. "You saw how I did it before. Click on any of those blue underlined words to read the whole article."

Five minutes later, as Brigitte was putting on her coat, Grey and Paolo had moved on to refrigerators. "Does this one really cool better?" Paolo asked.

Grey replied, "It's not about cooling, it's about perception. With a SMEG you can tack another fifty dollars a week on to the rental price. Wait, Brigitte, are you leaving? How was your first time surfing the Web?"

"It's all gibberish to me, I'll leave it to the young."

53

Portoferraio, January 26, 2000 - Midnight

It was midnight. Brigitte waited until she was sure Paolo was asleep. He had turned off his TV around eleven and she gave it another hour before she sneaked out of the building and crossed the square to the café. Inside, Brigitte didn't switch on any lights for fear of Paolo waking up and noticing the lit café from his window. It didn't matter, for she knew the café layout by heart and the small lights of the computer equipment sufficed to show her the way. Sitting in the fancy chair that Grey had purchased for the new Internet station, Brigitte pushed the power button and waited for the computer to come to life.

When Brigitte typed *Cremieux* into the browser, it produced the same list of articles as it had when Grey had typed it earlier. She started with the two articles on Adolphe Crémieux. Brigitte was astonished. Both Madeleine and Doda had talked about their esteemed forefather, but to read of his impressive career was another thing entirely. Brigitte took her time, clicking on the various links within the article to learn about this campaign or that decree. Moreover, reading about her great-great-great-grandfather gave her time to work up to Madeleine.

The first article she read about her mother was on Christian Dior's "New Look".

> *The "New Look" revolutionized women's dress and*
> *reestablished Paris as the center of the fashion world after*

World War II. Dior's designs were more voluptuous than the boxy, fabric-conserving shapes of the recent World War II styles. He was a master at creating shapes and silhouettes. Dior is quoted as saying, "I have designed flower women." Among the many New York models, Dior's favorite was Madeleine Crémieux. "Madeleine embodies both the beauty and hope of the new world. She is the perfect wife, hostess, mother and Dior model."

Brigitte studied Dior's photo. She vaguely remembered the car ride to the airport when her mother went to America. Brigitte had shared the backseat with Mr. Dior, but she could not remember what he looked like. His bald head and large nose reminded her of Picasso, but that was probably because she had recently seen Picasso's photo in the art book that Maria and Antonio had given her. In searching on *Picasso*, Brigitte found hundreds of articles on him. One essay analyzed both the *Man with a Lamb* and *Night Fishing at Antibes*, but none referenced any connection to Madeleine or Christophe.

After Brigitte typed *Christophe Sureau*, she hesitated. When she finally pressed *Enter*, it produced only two links. The first was a memorial service for a René Carmille at which Christophe had given the eulogy. The article said that M. Carmille, who was head of Service National des Statistiques from 1940-1941, had been responsible for saving thousands of lives by instructing his staff to falsify data that was used to identify Jews. While not Jewish himself, he was arrested, tortured and then deported to Dachau, where he died a prisoner of war. Brigitte hadn't thought of her father's profession in years. He had never discussed his work. As far as she was aware, he had worked his whole life as a cartographer for the SNS, but she only knew this because Doda had told her.

The second link was to a *Le Monde* article titled "Reconciliation." When she clicked on it, it took some time for the article to appear and Brigitte drifted to a memory of herself as a little girl spying on her father through the study door he'd left ajar. She had been mesmerized by his intensity as he pored over various maps. When the article finally came up, she remembered it immediately and hit the *Backspace* key, but again the browser was slow in its transition. The article remained on the screen long enough for her to see (or recall) its last words.

Journalist: *"You have obviously inherited your mother's looks and sense of style. Anything else?"*

Brigitte: *"The love of my father."*

54

Portoferraio, January 27, 2000

In under a month, Grey had transformed Maria's former Elban home from a renter-abused sty to a showplace worthy of publication in one of Brigitte's design magazines.

"*Mon Dieu, c'est incroyable,*" Brigitte declared.

Grey had just given Brigitte the tour of the renovation, and was pouring the champagne she'd brought to celebrate its completion. While preparing a tray, he continued talking to Brigitte from the kitchen, an easy thing to do in the remodeled home's open floor plan.

"You like it?"

Brigitte sat on the couch and surveyed the room. It was hard to believe this was Maria's house. "I can to speak it in French or Italian, but I do not to speak English to speak it well."

"I think *inquoiahbla* is almost the same in English."

"In Italian, we are more close: *incredibile.*"

There were elements of Grey's design that were truly inspired, the most innovative being the sheer room dividers that could be lit and adjusted for varying degrees of transparency. At the lowest setting, the dividers were practically invisible and the dining room would open into the living room. Brigitte was stunned. Only weeks before, she had been proud of her modest renovation of Doda's apartment. Now she realized that she was dealing with a master.

Grey came in from the kitchen carrying the tray of cocktail accoutrements of the same vintage style as the furniture. He had thought of every detail. "If I stay here long enough, I'll be trilingual."

"I am here for fifty years and I speak only two."

Handing Brigitte a flute of champagne, Grey said, "Come on, your English is great and what's important, you understand what I say. For example, I don't even think *trilingual*'s a word and you were able to figure out what I meant."

Brigitte tipped her flute in his direction.

He tipped his back. "To the international language of champagne."

"This style—" Brigitte swept her free hand out in front of her. "—it is familiar."

Grey joined Brigitte on the couch. "Yes, fifties modern—it's all the rage. Everything old is new again."

Brigitte raised her glass a second time. "*Je l'espère.*"

Though he understood the literal translation of Brigitte's reply, Grey didn't catch her play on words. "I bet you've seen some of this furniture before."

Brigitte placed her glass down on the circular chrome side table that sat next to the couch. "The table is designed by Eileen Gray, yes?"

"You know your designers."

"My mother is fifties modern in the forties. You can to see in my flat that I ... regressed." Brigitte paused and then asked, "Is *regress* a word?"

"Yes, *regress* is a perfect word choice. And I love your taste. It's so warm, so inviting." He picked up the bottle of champagne from the tray. "I'm going to put his outside to keep it cold."

Grey got up and walked out to the terrace, continuing the conversation over his shoulder as he went. "Can you believe that table is the one piece that I actually found on the island?"

Brigitte rose from the couch and followed him. As she formulated a response in her head, she watched as Grey searched the terrace wall for a flat stone on which to set the bottle. Before he found one, he stopped and stared out into the olive grove. Finally, she said, "There are people here whose tastes are more cold."

Grey turned around, surprised by Brigitte's presence on the terrace, but at the same time, unfazed by it. When he spoke, his voice was distant, almost sad. "I'm sorry, what did you say? I was thinking of something else."

Brigitte wondered about this mysterious American. Ostensibly, he had everything: good looks, money, and a life partner (if that's what homosexuals called it these days). He even had a modest degree of fame, and yet at times he seemed so utterly distracted and melancholic.

She replied, "It is of no importance. Of what do you think?"

"It's nothing really. A friend recently asked me if I knew anybody else with the name *Grey*. I didn't think of Eileen."

"*Grey* is not a usual name in America?"

"No, it isn't." Grey took a sip of champagne and turned from her to again look out over the olive grove. "Speaking of strange names, why did Paolo's grandparents name their company *Le Voci*? It means *the voices*, right?"

Brigitte was still unaccustomed to Grey's candor regarding subjects that no Italian would think to ask of a new acquaintance. But then, the degree to which Grey had offered his time, skills and resources went beyond mere acquaintanceship. Not only had he designed and managed the renovation, he had also taken care of all of the logistics for Maria's upcoming fiftieth birthday party in Rome. Brigitte was eminently grateful. Still, she couldn't shake the feeling that his motivations were not as virtuous as they seemed.

"That is what it means, yes. But it is also . . . " Whenever Brigitte struggled with an English word, Brigitte resorted to French, as she knew Grey understood French better than Italian. " . . . *une assimilation* of their names. The first and last letters are from Viglietti, and the middle two letters are from La Rocca. I never asked, but I suppose the name is also a—I am sorry, how does one to say *double entendre*?"

"We actually use the same French phrase: *double entendre*. Literally, it means a double meaning."

"Ah yes, a double meaning—possibly to relate with their political convictions."

"That's right, they were socialists. How clever! I can't remember—was Paolo's father a socialist as well?"

In previous conversations, Brigitte had used subtlety in an attempt to steer Grey away from topics that were too personal. This time, she responded with an unequivocal admonition. "It is a question I never ask, and I would advise that you do not ask this question when you meet Maria. I do not think that she likes to visit the past."

Although he appeared to take heed, Grey inadvertently switched to another subject that was equally personal in nature. "Yes, of course. That reminds me of another odd name. I'm supposed to give you Donovan Gazzetta's regards. I guess you two go way back."

"If you are to mean, do I know him for a long time, then yes. We know each other for many years. But I regret—why is Donovan Gazzetta a odd name?"

"Well, I don't think of Donovan as an Italian name."

Brigitte wrapped her arms around her to fend off the chill. "Oh, yes—the family of his mother is Celtic."

"There you have it."

"Have what?"

"It's just an expression. Anyway, he says hello, and hopes you'll come around, now that his leg is better."

In the summer, Donovan had broken his leg in a nasty accident when the handle of one of the guest's suitcases broke while he was carrying it up the stairs. He lost his balance and fell back against the stair railing, which gave way and sent him crashing to the lobby floor below. Though it was only a meter or so, his leg landed under him and literally snapped in two. Brigitte had visited him in the hospital and taken care of both proprietor and property while they were on the mend. As he healed, her visits became less and less frequent.

"Tell him I'll come when he hires a bellboy."

"Funny, he said you'd say that." Grey's smirk was that of a prescient observer.

Brigitte tried to hold Grey's gaze but couldn't. His eyes darted like those of a caged animal. "Grey, thank you for all you've done."

"Sure, it's been my pleasure—a wonderful diversion."

"I never see Paolo so happy. You do not know how important this is. You show to him the house tomorrow, yes?"

"Yes. I'm making dinner, though I must admit, I'm no great chef."

"I can to assist if you need."

Grey walked to the edge of the terrace wall and bent down to pick something up, a stone or a broken olive branch. The moon hovered over the grove. The bare tree limbs created a snarl of shadows on the ground. "I just may take you up on that, especially because I'm making an Italian dish that I've only made once before. It's probably a bad idea for a *gringo* who can't cook to make pasta for an Italian."

"*Gringo?*"

"It's a word Mexicans use to refer to Americans. I think it means foreigner. How would you say *foreigner* in French?" When he lifted his head, the moonlight caught his face in profile and Brigitte suddenly knew where she had seen him before—fifteen years ago on this very terrace, naked, kneeling before Antonio in the moonlight.

"*Étranger.*"

55

"Why must I go in person? I've given you my *codice fiscale*. Isn't that sufficient?"

Brigitte paced the salon with the receiver in her hand. Paolo had just replaced her old telephone with a cordless, but she still traipsed back and forth across the floor as she used to when she was limited by the cord's reach. Her turmoil was aggravated by the fact that she hadn't slept. She'd stayed up all night trying to figure out what to do.

She stopped in front of the salon windows and looked out across the piazza. It was nearing lunchtime and people walked to and fro on their daily errands. "Can't they give me any information?"

Maria was arriving in Rome in three days and she would be greeted by the man who had seduced her husband. Brigitte played all of her conversations with Grey over word by word and realized that it was Antonio he had been after all along. Poor Paolo! He had no idea.

"It's impossible for me to come by the bank Monday morning. I have to be in Roma Monday by two o'clock."

Dawn had brought with it two revelations. The first was Maria's present. Brigitte hadn't the vaguest notion what to give her and ended up enlarging and framing an old photo of her, Antonio, and Sophie when they were children. When Paolo found out about Brigitte's gift, he'd told her that Maria refused to display photos of Antonio. Nevertheless, the idea struck a chord because he and Juliana decided to restore Maria and

Antonio's wedding photos. Brigitte didn't want the entire birthday to be a painful memorializing of Antonio, so she had to think of something else. It had come to her as she sat on the couch in the darkness, watching the sun's first rays illuminate the room into view. In the morning light, the choice was obvious.

"There is absolutely no way they will tell me over the phone?"

The second revelation was more of a hunch—one that if true, would be nothing short of miraculous, a far better gift than the first. In perseverating over Grey's motives, Brigitte remembered a comment he had made at Paolo's New Year's Eve party. It was during her initial conversation with him, when he'd asked about Paolo's inheritance. Straining to recall the specifics of the dialogue, it had suddenly occurred to Brigitte that there may indeed be an inheritance after all. She had spent the entire morning on the phone and all indication so far was that she might be, at least to some degree, right.

"Yes, yes, I understand. Excuse me, there's someone at my door. I need to call you back."

Brigitte decided to forget about her hunch for now. If she was right, Maria could fly back and go find out the details herself. She would definitely be able to afford to fly back.

"Oh, Grey, good morning." Now that she had recognized Grey from the past, Brigitte saw him for who he was. She knew that she must confront him in order to prevent any inquisitive meddling in Rome—or worse, guilt-laden apologies. Maria would be devastated. But as of yet, Brigitte had no plan for how to preempt such a disaster.

"Brigitte, I'm sorry. Did I wake you?"

Brigitte had not yet dressed or even run a brush through her hair. She was hopeful that the disarray masked her disdain.

"No, I am waked—I am not prepared, that is all."

"I'm sorry, it's just that you offered to help me with dinner tonight."

"Oh, yes."

"If you don't mind, I need some time alone, so I'll just wing it by myself."

"Wing it?"

"I'm sorry. I keep using slang phrases. Well, it means to do something that you aren't prepared to do."

"I see."

After Grey left, Brigitte placed another phone call.

"Patrizia, *buon giorno*. I have a strange question for you. You go to the mainland a lot, right? Is it at all possible for me to get to Padua today before four o'clock?"

56

Train from Piombino to Padua, January 28, 2000 - Morning

Patrizia had arranged everything while Brigitte hurried to shower and change in order to make the ten o'clock ferry. Unfortunately, the train was a half-hour late, but the conductor said he'd make up the time en route to Padua. If it arrived on schedule, she would have only twenty minutes to get from the train station to the bank.

Another passenger peered into her compartment. Brigitte had laid her coat across the seat facing hers. "*Occupato?*" the man asked.

"Yes, I'm afraid so."

The train wasn't full, so Brigitte didn't mind lying. She couldn't abide a conversation with a stranger. After settling into her seat, she looked about her. This train, with its synthetic interior of plastics and laminates, was as different from the last train she had taken to Padua as the reasons were for the two journeys, over forty years apart. Brigitte thought back to her first trip to Padua. Rather than immediately jumping to its unsavory conclusion, she allowed herself to relive some of the more positive memories of the trip. Thus, with a wistful smile, she recalled Giovanni's secret mission and his infallible linguistic ear. Brigitte welcomed the distraction and watched from the train's window as the Italian countryside sped by.

When the train pulled into the Padua railway station, it was a quarter to four. By the time she got her luggage and caught a taxi, it was five till.

"*Banca Antonveneta, presto per favore.*"

"What branch?"

"Whichever is closest?"

One-way streets added a few minutes to the ride, and when Brigitte arrived at five after four, the bank's doors were closed. She pounded her fists against the glass. She was ignored for ten minutes until a woman finally came to the door and shook her head, mouthing, "*Siamo chiusi.*"

Brigitte mouthed back, "*Per favore*, I need to talk to the manager."

The woman held up eight fingers and mouthed, "*Lunedì mattina. Alle otto.*"

There was no way Brigitte could stay until Monday. She would not miss Maria's arrival, especially since Grey would be there. She had to intervene. Her plan foiled, Brigitte walked slowly down the bank steps dragging her luggage behind her. She searched the streets for another taxi but there were none to be found. In her survey, she didn't notice a familiar site: the Palazzo Bo. Across its grand façade draped a banner that hailed, *Teatro Anatomico—più di cinquecento anni di progresso scientifico.*

After checking into the hotel, Brigitte collapsed onto her bed, reviewing the sequence of events that had led to this fiasco. It was a crazy idea, one that she hadn't thought all the way through. She picked up the phone and called the front desk. "Yes, can you help me place a long distance call?" Brigitte waited on the phone and looked about the room while the receptionist dialed the number she had given him. This was the hotel that Donovan had booked for her before Ugo colluded with Professor Ferrari Bravo to put her up for the weekend. It wasn't difficult to visualize how it would have looked back then because with its peeling wallpaper and Art Deco flourishes, it was unlikely that the hotel had ever been renovated. Out of her window, she followed the line of the canal that stretched from the train station down to the stone gate and bridge across which she, Donovan, and Giovanni had walked.

"Paolo, it's me, Brigitte. Yes, I'm okay. Did you get my note? I know, but I had to leave suddenly. I'm not going to be able to go with you to Rome. No, of course I'm coming, but I'm going to have to meet you there. Yes, at the terminal. Oh it's nothing, I'll tell you Monday." When Paolo asked about the renovation, Brigitte tried to sound excited. "I saw it last night but I'm not going to spoil the surprise. Yes, he certainly is something." Brigitte found it difficult to suppress the animosity she felt toward Grey, and was glad when Paolo quickly changed the subject to Maria and Juliana. "I can't wait to see them either. She said what? So, she's a comedian, is she? Goodness, I can't wait to see her all grown up. She was barely talking when you moved. Okay, I love you too. Now, go have a good time. You're going to be amazed by what he's done."

Brigitte hung up the phone and called downstairs.

"This is Brigitte Crémieux from room three-twelve. I'm not sure you can help me but I have an eight thirty train to Rome tomorrow morning and I want to find out if there is another train that leaves Monday morning after eight thirty that will get me to Rome in time to be at Fiumicino Airport by two o'clock. Yes, I'm willing to cut it close, as close as I need to."

57

Padua, January 28, 2000 - Evening

"How was the zabaglione?"

Brigitte exaggerated. "Wonderful."

When the hotel receptionist recommended Caffè Pedrocchi, Brigitte had smiled and said she knew where it was. The food was mediocre and the zabaglione too sweet, probably the result of recipe changes over the years to appeal to the tourist crowd. The eclectic interiors looked the same, although for whatever reason, they appeared to be a kitschy remake of the authentic nineteenth-century neoclassicism that she remembered.

After paying her check, Brigitte walked around the corner and, like a moth to a flame, found herself standing before the Libreria Draghi. It too looked the same except that its window was a veritable bulletin board of announcements and flyers organized into groupings of "staff picks." It was amazing how much this city had to offer, and Brigitte found herself wondering what it would be like to live in an urban center again. In the bottom corner of the window, the "Avidly Recommended" section, was a flyer for a lecture that had already come and gone:

SEXUALITY AND VIOLENCE IN CINEMA

Associazione culturale Antonio Rosmini will host University of Southern California's Professore Christine Panushka in a discussion of how shifting cultural attitudes of sexuality and

*violence have shaped 20ᵗʰ century cinema. As a case study,
Professore Panushka will dissect how the various sexual and
violent undercurrents of Vladimir Nabokov's classic Lolita
were cinematically conveyed in Stanley Kubrick's 1962
depiction versus Adrian Lynne's more recent 1997 release.
January 10, 2 P.M. Palazzo Bo, Aula Magna*

Before Brigitte had time to think about the last time *Lolita* was avidly recommended to her by this bookstore staff, another flyer distracted her. It was a dance performance, and the promotion had been translated into both English and German. It was the German translation that caught her eye:

*Zaven Bozigian, Volkstänze tanzt Tänze der armenischen
Diaspora. Herr Bozigian, der in Paris geboren war und nun
in San Francisco, Kalifornien left, ist um die ganze Welt
gereist, um Armenien und die Armenier durch Musik,
Sprache, und Tanz darzustellen. 28 bis 31 Januar 2000.
Teatro Verdi, um 20 Uhr.*

*Zaven Bozigian, Folk Dances of the Armenian Diaspora. Mr.
Bozigian, born in Paris, France but now living in San
Francisco, California, has traveled the world representing
Armenia and her people through his music, language, and
dance. 28-31 January 2000. Teatro Verdi, 8 P.M.*

"*Herr Bozigian.*" Brigitte mouthed the name. She felt her heart begin to race as she glanced at her watch. It was nine thirty; it was possible the performance had not yet ended. The map on the flyer showed the theater to be near her hotel. If she walked fast she could get there in ten minutes. A peal of thunder resounded above. There had been predictions of a storm, but the clouds had yet to break. Suddenly, the exhaustion of her day vanished and instinct took over.

When Brigitte arrived at the theater, she had to take a moment to catch her breath before she asked the doorman. "Is the show over?"

"No, it runs until ten."

"Where do I buy a ticket?"

He looked at his watch. "There's only twenty minutes left."

"I know."

"Don't worry about the ticket. If you go over to those far side doors and don't mind standing in the back, you can see the rest of the show for free."

"*Grazie mille.*"

Brigitte stood quietly behind the last row of seats. The audience was sparse so she could have sat, although it didn't cross her mind. Nor did the grandeur of the theater, which thirty minutes earlier would have fed her fantasies of urban living. Instead, she was focused on the dancer, not the music nor the dance, but the man.

After the show, Brigitte was the only one waiting at the stage door. When Herr Bozigian finally appeared. he was dressed in an overcoat, scarf and a fur-lined hat, as if he were prepared for a winter night in Russia, not Italy.

"*Grazie per lo spettacolo, è stato meraviglioso.*"

"I'm sorry I don't speak Italian. Do you speak English?"

"I do not speak English good, but I will try. Thank you for your wonderful dance."

"No, it is I who should thank you. It's been a long time since a beautiful woman waited at my stage door. Are you Armenian?"

"No, French."

"And how did such a beautiful French woman become interested in Armenian folkdance?"

"I know of your name for a long time. You are a borned in Paris, yes?"

Herr Bozigian replied with more regard than suspicion, "You've certainly done your homework."

"I read it in *la publicité. Vous parlez Français?*" Brigitte hesitated before adding, "*Ou Allemand?*"

"Sorry, but no, only English and Armenian."

Brigitte didn't reply, but stared at him as though awaiting a subsequent proposition."

"Well, thank you again for making my night. Finally, I can let my wife know that her jealousy of my solo tour was warranted."

"Can I to ask you a question?"

"If you don't mind walking with me. I'm heading back to my hotel. It's just down the street."

"I stay at a near hotel also—*l'Hotel Grand'Italia.*"

"When worlds collide."

"*Pardon?*"

"We're at the same hotel. Now, I definitely can't tell the wife that. But please, ask your question."

"I was borned in Paris also. I needed to leave when I was a child. I never return for many reasons."

"I understand."

"You do?"

"Yes, I am Armenian."

"So you must to leave Paris also. I do not comprehend."

Mr. Bozigian took off his hat and tucked it under his arm. "I'm sorry, what I meant was that I understand being forced to flee one's home. We Armenians are exiles without a land. It's not that we can't go home, but rather, there is no home to go to. After the genocide, we scattered with the wind, all over the world."

"Genocide?"

"Yes, World War I. In many ways it was genocide far worse than the Holocaust because it almost wiped out an entire race and culture. Ask an Armenian of his homeland and he will often reply with the sadness of an orphaned child."

"I regret."

"It's an old tale, one that I've devoted my life to. I no longer yearn for Armenia's past. Instead, I promote our future. And now, we've arrived at our hotel and you still haven't asked me your question."

"It is no more important."

"Your accent is as charming as you are but now I must bid you good night and go call my wife so that my last thought tonight is of *her* beautiful face, not yours."

Back in her room, Brigitte sat with her suitcase on the bed, the lining torn open. She hadn't mended it. By the time she had decided to give Maria the sketch, it was too late to ship it to Rome. The frame wouldn't fit in Brigitte's suitcase, so Brigitte had to extract the sketch and bring it alone. Besides, it seemed only fitting that it should resume its old travel sleeve.

Brigitte removed the sketch and unfolded it. When she turned it over, the eyebrow pencil had faded, but her writing underneath it was still clear:

Sprechen sie keines. Gerte es klein Herr Pozigian
They do not speak. Switch it small, Herr Pozigian.

She hadn't thought of the phrase in years and as she folded and replaced the sketch in the lining, she felt her conversation with Mr. Bozigian had given her the perspective to finally extinguish any remaining desire to discover its meaning. Come Monday, she would be proven wrong.

L'Agneau Sacrificiel

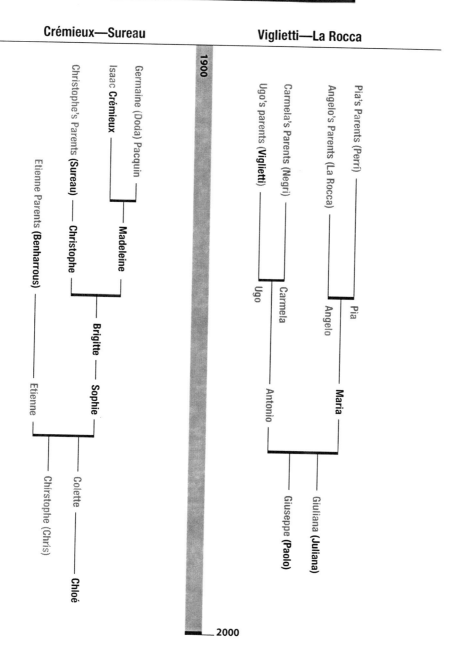

58

Rome, Termini Railway Station, January 31, 2000

Termini Station teemed with life. Brigitte had never seen anything like it. She checked her watch: one twenty—she had forty minutes to get to the airport. Though hurried, she collected herself and watched from her window as the exiting passengers assimilated into the horde of other commuters on the platform. At the end of the track, a fashionably dressed elderly woman caught her eye. The woman stood immobile amidst the crowd, appraising all who passed. Brigitte thought of all the times she had waited at the Portoferraio ferry station for loved ones to arrive, and to leave.

Brigitte was suddenly paralyzed by anxiety. If Maria recognized Grey, what memories would it stir? She thought back to the days and weeks after witnessing Antonio and Grey's indiscretion. She had struggled with whether or not she should tell Maria. She'd pried into Maria and Antonio's relationship. She found subtle ways to ask Maria about everything from their shared interests to their sex life. Maria, as always, had been discreet. Finally, Brigitte decided that it was Antonio whom she should confront. She planned a surprise encounter one afternoon at her friend Patrizia's house, where he was installing new kitchen cabinets. Brigitte had intentionally stopped by at a time when she knew Patrizia would not be home, and she'd asked Antonio if she could see the progress.

Antonio was opening the new pantry to showcase its craftsmanship when Brigitte blurted, "So tell me about what you do on your fishing expeditions?"

The St. Anthony's medal Brigitte had given Antonio hung from his neck. Its chain was exposed, but the medallion itself was tucked just below the neckline of his T-shirt. "I think you know what I do."

Stunned by his implied confession, Brigitte demanded, "Why then do you continue if you know how much it hurts her?"

Antonio slammed the pantry door shut so hard that he would have to replace one of its hinges. "I will find them, Brigitte. I don't care how long it takes, I will find them. She will know what happened and she will finally sleep in peace." He was so impassioned in his conviction that Brigitte couldn't bring herself to question him further.

That day, Brigitte decided to lock away Antonio's infidelity in the mental vault she had constructed for her own unresolved past. She never told anyone, and now after all of these years, she would face the repercussions of that decision.

In the train aisle, the family from the neighboring compartment collected their luggage from the overhead bins. The young man whose surprise boarding in Bologna had awakened Brigitte laughed as he handed the bags, one by one, to an older man whom Brigitte guessed was his father. Brigitte composed herself, opened her suitcase and placed Maria's envelope on top. Before zipping the suitcase closed, she dug out the checkered yellow and blue scarf that Maria had given her the Christmas before she left for New York. It was a bit garish against the orange pantsuit Brigitte wore. Outside swarmed a sophisticated urban spectrum of wintry blacks and blues—not a swatch of color to be seen. She was rethinking her decision when she looked up and found the young man watching her. He raised his hand to his cheek and gave it a mock pinch-twist—a flirtatious gesture usually bestowed upon women far younger than she. Brigitte nodded in gratitude and tied the scarf around her neck.

Finally ready to disembark, Brigitte surveyed the empty compartment and noticed the violet posy she'd purchased from gypsy girl at the Padua train station. It was on the floor, ruined. She must have trampled it when repacking her suitcase. She picked up the mangled flowers and held them to her nose. The crushed petals excreted a stronger scent than before. Brigitte dropped the posy into her purse, making a mental note to discard it as soon as she came across a trashcan.

59

"Where's Grey?" Brigitte had arrived just before two. Fortunately, Maria's flight was ten minutes late, which gave Brigitte time to collect herself after the frantic cab ride from the train station.

Paolo's response was piqued, his voice giddy with excitement. "He left a day early and said he'd meet us here."

Brigitte was suspicious, but she hoped Grey's absence would provide her the opportunity to forewarn Maria of his past. How she'd do this, she still hadn't figured out. Nor did she know if Maria could withstand such a shock. Brigitte thought maybe she should appeal to Grey instead. She could expose his duplicity, insist that he use a different name and make him deny that he'd ever been to Elba before.

"What do you think of the renovation?" she asked.

"It's beyond incredible! I can't wait to tell Mom. Maybe you can talk her into coming to Elba to see it, or maybe Grey can. He's pretty amazing, that one. There's something about him that is so completely disarming."

"That is true." In her thoughts, Brigitte added, *for both father and son.*

To avoid further discussion, Brigitte began thumbing through her magazine. She had enough to worry about. Paolo was an adult; he could take care of himself.

"Brigitte, here they come."

Maria and Juliana walked arm in arm down the terminal. The last time Brigitte had seen them, despondency had overshadowed Maria's beauty and her face bore the blotches and shadows of her bitter despair. Now, fifteen years later, Maria had reclaimed the ivory-skinned radiance of her youth. Her quiet intensity preceded her, as did Juliana's brash exuberance, a far cry from her reticence as a child.

Paolo ran to them while Brigitte stayed back and observed the family homecoming. Afterward, Maria walked from her children to Brigitte. The two women hugged. Neither said a word; they just held one another.

"What am I, chopped liver?" Juliana asked, her arms akimbo in mock anger. While Paolo had his father's frame, Juliana's resemblance to Antonio was breathtaking. She was dressed head to toe in black, which drew all attention to her face and made the likeness more severe. Of the three Vigliettis, she was the shortest in stature but unless you thought about it, you may have sworn she was the tallest, even while they stood side by side.

Brigitte did not catch Juliana's comment. She had assumed they would be speaking Italian and it took her a moment to adjust to English. "Dear, I am not able to believe I am seeing you. Do you remember me?"

Juliana looped her arm through Brigitte's. "I remember a beautiful and fashionable aunt who spoiled us with gifts and ice cream. I see your fashion sense hasn't changed. Let's hope the spoiling hasn't either."

"For God's sake, Sis, let her catch her breath before you start in. Ah, here he is, our gracious host for the weekend."

Brigitte's concern resurfaced as Grey approached. She looked to Maria—there appeared to be no immediate recognition when Grey introduced himself. As for Grey, he was the perfect actor, charming yet reserved, as one would be upon a first meeting. When he suggested they get a bite to eat at the airport café, Juliana leapt at the idea. "Thank God, an eater—a man after my own heart."

After they ordered lunch, Paolo bragged about the renovation and tried to convince his mother to come to Elba. When Maria refused, she was decided but not adamant. The unexpected possibility stirred Brigitte, and for a moment her fears of Maria's remembering Grey were allayed. "Maria, you need to come to see it—it is fabulous. It is the only house similar on the island. I am sure that people will rent it all season. I know you have bad reminders but much has changed. I don't mean to—"

Brigitte stopped mid-sentence, interrupted by an unmistakable scent that vanquished her words. She felt faint, and the sights and sounds of the airport terminal were transposed by others from her past. Already forgotten images from her morning's dream crystallized as the familiar perfume overwhelmed her.

"*Mamie!*"

"What are you—" Brigitte looked down in utter confusion at her great-granddaughter, Chloé, who had seemingly materialized from nowhere.

Brigitte was paralyzed with shock. A perfectly formed teardrop, the first she had shed in fifty years, eluded her lash and fell upon the cover of the magazine she held, blurring its ink into an unsightly stain. Brigitte dropped the magazine, but in the commotion of the reunion, no one noticed.

"Surprise!" Beside Chloé stood Sophie, tears streaming down her face. Grey had secretly orchestrated Sophie's invitation to Maria's party, but not even he had known that Sophie was bringing a surprise of her own. Accompanying Sophie and Chloé were Christophe and Madeleine. As Brigitte turned to face her parents, faded memories from her childhood rose from their subliminal depths, dragging with them scenes yet unplayed. A stream of tears supplanted the first. Though no one at this reunion but her parents had ever seen Brigitte cry, only Grey assumed that her weeping had sprung from the joy of the occasion.

60

Rome, Fiumicino Airport, January 31, 2000 - Afternoon

In the cheerless aftermath of the surprise, Grey took charge and motioned the waiter over.

"Could we have a bottle of Chianti and a lemonade for the young lady?"

Chloé suddenly perked up. "I can drink wine, can't I, *Mamour?*"

Sophie shook her head. "You can have a sip of wine, but if you would like to join us in a drink, I think a lemonade will suffice. Or would you like something else?"

Chloé smiled at Grey. "No, you are right, a lemonade will suffice."

Grey chuckled good-naturedly at Chloé's precocious compromise.

Fully aware of the extent of Brigitte's shock, Sophie and Maria sidled up to her for support. For the next hour, Brigitte passively interacted with the group via rote etiquette: her responses were formal and movements autonomic.

When Juliana's naïve probing forced Sophie to divulge why she had invited Christophe and Madeleine, she preceded her awkward explanation with yet another. Sophie had never told Maria of Colette's pregnancy, and was therefore evasive when she introduced Chloé, leaving it unclear as to who exactly Chloé was. She then began prattling nervously about how well Colette was doing and how she had just secured a new job at a posh new Paris boutique (coincidentally named *Colette*), and—.

Noting Sophie's unease, Juliana interrupted with the likely intent of shifting the conversation to a less controversial topic. Little did she know she was doing just the opposite. With a wink at Madeleine and Christophe, she prodded, "Aunt Sophie, it's great to hear that Colette is doing so well, but you were about to tell us why you decided to cart along your entourage."

Sophie admitted that when Grey had called to see if she could come to Rome for Maria's birthday, she'd immediately said yes without checking her schedule. She later discovered that she was already committed for the weekend of the party, having promised months before that she would look after Chloé so Colette could attend the Foire de Paris. When Sophie asked her grandparents to babysit so she could come to Rome, Chloé had been listening in and had suggested, "Why don't we all go?"

Grey remarked, "Out of the mouths of babes."

Chloé took immediate offense. "What do you mean?"

Whether it was planned or not, Grey's interjection broke the tension. He followed it by introducing himself to Brigitte's parents, and then attempted to explain the idiom. Sophie smiled gratefully for the digression, whereas Chloé began an ardent rebuttal against his pronouncement of her as a "babe." For the remainder of their lunch, gratuitous pleasantries dominated the conversation, until finally, transportation logistics required the group to divide into its logical halves.

"Grey, can you fit Paolo, Maria, Juliana, and their luggage in your car?" Brigitte's plans to intervene between Maria and Grey were a distant consideration. Her attention was consumed by her parents who stood gracious and quiet by her side. Through careful ordination, Brigitte had managed to avoid any physical contact with them since their arrival, but when Madeleine leaned over to kiss Maria adieu, Brigitte felt her mother's skirt brush against her leg—coarse fabric. Every word took concentration, every thought was muddled.

"I think we can manage." True to breeding (or artifice), Grey remained the gentleman. He helped Sophie, Madeleine and Christophe into the taxi's backseat—Chloé refused his assistance and crawled into Madeleine's lap—and held the door for Brigitte who had opted to share the front seat with the driver.

The taxi was stifling. Although it wasn't very cold outside, the driver would not lower the heater, and it blasted a gale of hot dry air. They were all miserable, yet no one complained. To counter the evident discomfort between Brigitte and her parents, Sophie maintained her role as the conversational catalyst while Chloé's presence enforced the limits of discourse.

"So are you surprised by my outfit?" Sophie's mirth convinced no one.

Brigitte's glance to the backseat was cursory. Sophie wore a pink skirtsuit that looked vaguely familiar but Brigitte was in no mood for guessing games. "Should I be?"

"Don't you recognize it? When Colette brought it back years ago, I laughed. There was no way my tailor could alter it to fit me."

If Brigitte had any nostalgic recall, she didn't show it. "Well, someone did a beautiful job."

The austerity of Brigitte's tone mitigated the compliment, but Sophie continued, relentless in her enthusiasm. "Believe it or not, it was Colette. She's really serious about becoming a designer. This was one of her assignments in her seamstress class."

Chloé chimed in from the backseat. "Mommy's going to make me my first communion dress."

Sophie recited her next line as if she and Chloé had rehearsed it. "Yes and she asked us to ask your great-grandmother if she would come for the ceremony." When she addressed Brigitte directly, Sophie's voice was more apologetic than hopeful. "Colette said that you told her once that you would come visit us in Paris."

Chloé squealed. "*Oui, oui, s'il vous plaît, Mamie.*"

Brigitte did not reply but kept staring straight ahead. The passenger-side windshield visor was broken and hung down obscuring Brigitte's view, though this was not as disconcerting as the mirror in the visor that Brigitte attempted to ignore by fixating on the dashboard. But as the cab

239

took off, Brigitte looked up into the small mirror, not at her parents whose faces she could not yet fully regard even in reflection, but at the little girl who sat in Madeleine's lap. Madeleine had one arm around Chloé's waist and the other stretched across the seat, her hand clasped around Christophe's. Until this very moment, Brigitte had avoided even a desultory glimpse into her father's eyes, and when he looked away from the mirror, she realized he was avoiding hers as well.

"Mother, it's illegal to ride with a child in your lap. You should put her beside you and have her wear a seatbelt "

Madeleine did as she was told.

Sophie did not reassert her invitation, and for the rest of the cab ride, Chloé extolled what she had learned in her communion classes, parable by parable.

61

Rome, January 31, 2000 - Mid-afternoon

Sophie had booked two separate suites in the Hotel Hassler, which was at the top of the Spanish Steps, directly across from the flat that Grey had secured for Maria, Paolo and Juliana. The plan was that Sophie and Brigitte would share one room, and Madeleine, Christophe, and Chloé would stay in the other. Upon checking in, they were informed that there had been an accident in one of the suites and it would not be ready for another few hours. When Sophie inquired about the nature of the accident, the receptionist's voice took on an ominous tone and said he was not at liberty to discuss the matter. Misinterpreting Sophie's discontent, the receptionist excused himself to the manager's office. When he returned a few minutes later, he relayed that all standard rooms were reserved, but if the two parties were willing to stay together, he could offer them the three-bedroom *Suite Imperiale* at no extra charge. Sophie's nervous response was garbled and unintelligible.

Brigitte interceded. "That would be lovely. We are one family, after all."

Brigitte completed the registration, listing the room under *La Famille de Crémieux* and recording each of their names separately. After the bellman was called to retrieve their luggage, Madeleine had politely asked the attentive receptionist, "Could you change the surnames for Madeleine and Christophe to Sureau?"

"Certainly," the receptionist replied.

The bellman escorted them to the magnificent suite (the confines of the elevator were made just bearable by Chloé's chatter), and directed them to their respective rooms based on assumption: the room with twin beds for Sophie and Chloé; the master for Christophe and Madeleine; and Brigitte, the room off the salon, set apart from the others. Afterward, Brigitte stood in her lavish bedroom, in front of the window, looking out at the crowd that clustered on the Spanish Steps. It was a quintessential Roman vista. Across the street was Grey's flat—or rather, a friend's flat—where he, Maria, Paolo, and Juliana were staying. Brigitte knew exactly which one it was, because moments before, Juliana had rushed out to the flat's terrace and made quite a scene over the view. The commotion had escalated when Juliana saw Brigitte in the hotel window and shrieked loud enough to attract the attention of a good portion of the pedestrians three stories below.

The flat was ideally situated and appeared to be beautifully appointed. Its now vacant terrace boasted a beautiful arbor of tangled grape vines that stretched across its width. Beyond its barren vines, Brigitte could see through the sliding glass doors into the flat's living room, where Paolo, Juliana, and Grey now chatted. Brigitte felt a dull pang of concern for the potential heartache of the scene playing out before her, but it was a dull pang and nothing more. It was as if she were watching the second act of a play in which, before the intermission, she was terribly engrossed, but after, had somehow lost interest. Maria entered from stage left and joined the conversation.

Brigitte closed the blinds. Crossing the room to unpack her suitcase, she stopped in front of the dresser mirror and noted that her mascara had run. She leaned in and gently ran her fingertip over the corner of her right lower eyelid, pausing at the swollen protrusion of her tear duct. It was inflamed and tender. On the opposite side of the wall, she heard Chloé ask, "Can we please visit the Vatican? Last time we didn't get to see the Sistine Chapel because it was being restored. *Pleeeeeease!*"

It was Madeleine who replied. Though she was eighty-five, her voice remained tonally pure, unwithered by age. "Dear, this time we're not here to go sightseeing, but ask your grandmother. Maybe she'll have time to take you."

Brigitte took her purse and stormed from her bedroom, barely slowing to acknowledge Madeleine and Chloé as she passed. "I'll be back within the hour."

In the lobby, Brigitte dashed from the elevator toward the hotel's front door but came to a sudden stop in front of the registration desk. The receptionist asked, "Sig.ra Sureau, may I be of assistance?"

"No." Brigitte's response was shrill. She turned to face the tall thin older gentleman who looked more northern European than southern. She had been so distracted when checking in, she'd barely considered him. He had a high brow and sad, gentle eyes. They were eyes of someone who has seen much, and judged little. They were eyes that convinced Brigitte not to correct his misuse of her parents' surname.

"I mean yes. Can you call me a taxi?"

"Certainly, *signora*." The receptionist's diction was perfect, as was his elocution. His distinguished manner served the hotel well.

In the taxi, Brigitte requested the driver give her a tour of Rome.

"Should we start with the Vatican?" the driver asked.

Brigitte sighed. "Yes, that will be fine."

The driver sped off, exhilarated by either the prospective cab fare or the opportunity to showcase his city. The rosary hanging from the rearview mirror swung back and forth like a hypnotist's watch, its beads catching the occasional shard of light and revealing their opaque glass to be a deep teal—the color of the sea. Brigitte closed her eyes and listened to the driver's incessant commentary.

As the taxi maneuvered the perimeters of Castel Sant'Angelo, Brigitte did her best to focus on particulars of the tour. With every historical fact, she receded further from the present. After the Vatican, they hugged the Tiber toward Trastevere, a neighborhood that the driver proclaimed "the bowels of modern day Rome." Turning in from the river, he called Brigitte's attention to Isola Tiberina—"the smallest inhabited island in the world." It was upon this comment that Brigitte reopened her eyes.

From what she could tell, the island in question was just a little sliver of land covered with a cluster of buildings and a quaint bridge that crossed to its center. She asked the driver, "By 'inhabited,' do you mean that people still live there?"

"Actually, I'm not exactly sure, but I do know there's still a functioning hospital there, and a church, San Bartolomeo, I think. Maybe that counts as *inhabited*."

"I'm sorry, can you let me out—I'd love to walk around it."

With the driver's abrupt stop, the rosary's cross slammed into the windshield.

Outside, Brigitte clutched her shoulders. In her haste, she had forgotten her coat and scarf at the hotel and the light wind from the Tiber chilled her. She crossed the street and walked out to the center of the short bridge. The island was indeed tiny, with a wide concrete shoulder that encircled it. She was searching for the stairs down to the walkway when she noticed a cloaked woman coming out of one of the island's narrow alleys. Brigitte rushed across the bridge and followed the woman into a tiny *gelateria*.

"*Mi scusi,*" she said.

The woman turned around. Her cloak was not a cloak but a habit. The nun's face was crisscrossed with lines that all smiled when she did.

"*Sì?*"

"Oh." Again, Brigitte wrapped her arms around herself.

"Do you need help?" the nun asked.

"No, I was just wondering if you lived on the island."

"*Santo cielo,* no, but you might think I did, given how often I come here. It's my secret indulgence." The nun swept her arm over the glass case displaying select gelatos. There was no one behind the case or, for that matter, in the rest of the *gelateria*.

"Does anyone live on this island?"

The nun's wizened face constricted in contemplation until a large matronly woman emerged from the kitchen wiping her hands on an apron. "I don't think so—Sita, does anyone live on the island?"

The proprietress shrugged. "Some used to, but I don't think so anymore. Not since the great flood."

Brigitte thanked the two women and then spent the next ten minutes negotiating her way out of continued conversation. When she finally managed her leave, she hurried across the island, across a second bridge, to the other side of the river. She held a cone of spicy chocolate gelato that the nun had confided was "sinful." Ice cream in hand, Brigitte appeared to be a carefree tourist.

"*Signora*, may I help you?" A uniformed guard emerged from a glass kiosk and stood before Brigitte.

"No, thank you, I'm just wandering."

"I'm sorry, but you'll need to wander elsewhere. You can't loiter here."

"Excuse me?"

"I said you can't loiter here. If you want to visit the synagogue, you need to take one of the guided tours. Now, if you could please be on your way." The guard handed Brigitte a pamphlet and watched to ensure she picked up her pace. At the end of the block, Brigitte found a trashcan and went to discard the pamphlet, but before doing so, the title of an article at the bottom of the pamphlet caught her eye, and she threw away her ice cream instead.

The pamphlet, *A Self-Guided Walk through Rome's Jewish Ghetto*, explained the guard's rudeness. It noted that the synagogue had remained under surveillance since a PLO attack in the early eighties. Brigitte followed the guide's map around to the opposite side of the synagogue, to a small square in front of a cluster of fenced-off Roman ruins that memorialized the date when Nazi soldiers stormed Rome. The pamphlet told how many Jewish families escaped detection by converting to Catholicism and attending mass to make a public show of their new faith. Some, it said, were too proud to convert but sent their children to live with Christian friends. When the Germans came, the sequestered children were spared, though after the war, many reclaimed their Jewish faith. At the bottom of the pamphlet was the article that had caught Brigitte's eye. It was entitled "Coping with Exile," which, it explained, was the name of a monthly group meeting at the synagogue for descendents of these orphaned children. The last line of the article was the group's mantra: *Only in forgiveness can we truly be liberated.* For the second time in fifty years, Brigitte wept.

Brigitte retraced her steps back over the river to the Isola Tiberina for a better view of the synagogue. It was immense, of an eclectic architecture that didn't conform to the classical buildings surrounding it. Searching for a tissue to wipe her eyes, Brigitte opened her purse only to find the violet posy, wilted from its enclosure. She held the posy to her nose, but its reticent fragrance had withered like the flower itself. Brigitte dropped it over the bridge's ledge. It should have fallen upon the embankment, but a sudden wind caught the posy's canopy of leaves and carried it out to the water. Brigitte watched as the flowers floated downstream, finally lodging against the footing of a bridge remnant that was impossible to access since neither side was connected to its adjacent street. It was a massive stone arch jutting up in the middle of the river, a triumphant symbol of civilization's defiance of nature. In reality, such a comparison was ridiculous since the arch went unnoticed, too insignificant to be preserved from further ruin by a monument-conscious city. It was what it was: an ugly remnant of a bridge whose triumph over the river was fleeting at best.

On the cab ride back to the hotel, Brigitte discovered from her pamphlet that the bridge remnant was called *Ponte Rotto*, the Broken Bridge. It was the first masonry bridge ever built across the Tiber and was mostly destroyed in the flood of 1598. As the taxi neared the hotel, Brigitte wondered if that was the same flood that drove the last inhabitants from Isola Tiberina.

62

Rome, January 31, 2000 - Early Evening

"Would you like an aperitif? Blanc cassé, if I remember correctly?" Brigitte stood, with her back to Madeleine, at the fully stocked wet bar that separated the salon from the kitchen. The bar was white mahogany with Calacatta marble counters—impressive, even by Madeleine's standards.

Madeleine sat on the sofa waiting for Brigitte's full attention. *"Non, merci.* Also, we are not going to join you for dinner. Your father is tired. We'll stay here with Chloé so you and Sophie have some time to yourselves."

"I see," Brigitte said and turned to hand her mother her unsolicited cocktail.

Madeleine set the glass on the coffee table, where it remained untouched throughout the conversation. "Dear, I know that we must talk, but I can't tonight. Can we wait until tomorrow?"

"Father too?"

"No, I'd prefer if you and I talk first. He's not yet prepared."

Brigitte broke from her feigned indifference. "Not prepared—is fifty years not time enough to prepare?"

"Please, Brigitte, I want to talk with you first, alone. All I ask for is one hour."

"One hour?"

"Yes."

Brigitte sipped her kir. "Can I ask you one question tonight?"

"Brigitte, please." Madeleine's voice conveyed her exhaustion.

"You asked for one hour, I ask for one question. Fair is fair."

"Yes, alright." Madeleine's reply was practiced rather than resigned.

Brigitte sat by her mother, her rancor momentarily displaced by curiosity. "I have a memory of a cocktail party that you took me to. I was very young and there were books and candles everywhere."

"You remember that?"

"Yes, I remember that everyone was speaking German and I didn't understand anything and then Tío Piquot came over."

Madeleine smiled. She was still captivating, even at eighty-five. "Tío Piquot . . . I haven't thought of that name in years. Actually, that was the night we met Pablo. Uncle Max introduced us."

"Uncle Max?"

"Yes, Uncle Max. You must remember Uncle Max."

"I remember there was some man with Tío Piquot that night."

Madeleine's formality returned. "Brigitte, please, let's wait until tomorrow."

"I haven't asked my one question."

"Then *ask* it." The muscles of Madeleine's face tensed and her skin stretched taut across her perfect bone structure. Determination had always enhanced her beauty.

"At one point, you swept me into your arms and we left the party. We left Father there. Did that happen?"

"Yes."

"Do you remember why? Was it because of Tío Piquot's friend—who I guess was Uncle Max—was it because of something he said?"

"Yes, but I can't remember exactly what it was. The party was a birthday party for the author James Joyce. Uncle Max wanted to introduce me to Pablo and insisted that we go. He said I had a face that Pablo must paint. At the last minute, your grandmother fell ill and couldn't babysit, so we decided to take you with us. It was not a party for a young girl. Everyone was gossiping about Mr. Joyce's rumored anti-Semitism, and then Uncle Max made some terrible joke. Whatever Max said was so rude, it made me realize that I had made a mistake by bringing you. I took you home immediately, and your father met us there an hour later."

"All because of a joke?"

"Yes, two women were arguing over something, and Max ridiculed them."

"Do you remember what he said?"

"No, I remember the women were Gertrude Stein and her friend Alice Toklas. I'm sure you've heard of them."

"Yes, Elba is not wholly devoid of culture."

"I didn't mean to imply that it was."

"Nothing more? About that night, I mean."

"Not that I recall. I just remember that whatever he said was terribly vulgar."

"That's it?"

"Yes, I'm surprised you even remember it. You were so young." Madeleine stood. She had answered her one question.

Brigitte rose as well, and mother and daughter stood face to face. "Did Picasso ever paint you?"

Madeleine smirked. "Pablo wasn't the kind of man whom you told what to paint. He did say that he painted me, but then, given the way he paints, how could one ever tell?"

"Was it *Night Fishing at Antibes*?"

"As a matter of fact, it was." If she was surprised, Madeleine's detachment belied it.

"And me?"

"Brigitte, please. Let's finish this tomorrow?"

"Am I in that painting, Mother?"

"Darling, I never asked him. But why, of all things, would that matter?"

"I'm not sure. Does it?"

Sophie emerged from her bedroom, "Mother, are you ready to go?"

"Yes." Brigitte set her champagne flute on the coffee table beside her mother's.

Chloé bounded past Sophie and Brigitte and ran to Madeleine. "Can I order room service?"

Madeleine's attention turned to her great-great-grandchild. "Of course you can, dear."

Sophie was in the hall and Brigitte still in the open doorway when Madeleine called out, "Brigitte, did you say you remembered people speaking German at the party?"

"Yes, but I don't remember anything because I couldn't understand it."

Chloé had disappeared again into Madeleine's bedroom. Apparently Christophe wasn't too tired for her company. When Madeleine glanced at the bedroom door, any emotion underlying her expression was impossible to discern.

"That's because they weren't speaking German. Dear, Mr. Joyce is Irish. Everyone was speaking English."

63

Rome, January 31, 2000 - Evening

In the taxi, Brigitte finally lashed out at Sophie for inviting Madeleine and Christophe. "How dare you bring them!"

Alone with her mother, Sophie abandoned her convivial script. "I thought it was time you put your differences aside."

"You thought it was time?"

"It's not always about you, Mother."

"Yes, I know. In fact, I thought this weekend was about Maria."

Sophie began to cry. "Mother, Etienne and I are getting a divorce. Colette may finally be on a good track. Chris is moving away. And I need a little stability in my life. Is that too much to ask?"

Brigitte was too angry for sympathy. "I'm sorry to hear about you and Etienne, but I wish—"

"Mother, we need you."

"We?"

"Yes, me, Colette, Chloé . . . " Sophie's voice wavered but she managed to finish. " . . . and Grandmother."

"Dear, I highly doubt it. Madeleine Crémieux needs no one."

"Mother, Grandfather is dying."

The taxi stopped at the curb where Grey and Paolo stood waiting. Grey opened Brigitte's door. "*Bienvenue.*"

Neither Brigitte nor Sophie accepted Grey's escort and the three descended into the subterranean restaurant one by one. Maria and Juliana were inside, waiting at the bar.

Juliana raised her voiced above the din. "This place is so cool. How did you find it?"

Sophie replied, "I used to come here when I was in college. I met my husband right over there, third barstool in."

Throughout dinner, everyone played their roles: Maria was the reluctant heroine; Paolo, her doting son; Juliana, the comic interlude; Grey, the curious stranger; and Brigitte, the wise, elegant (albeit distracted) oracle. Sophie continued to narrate.

"Supposedly, it was some wealthy family's bomb shelter during the war. It was uncovered fully intact, with a cook's kitchen, and servants' quarters, which is now a private dining room that you can rent for special occasions."

"What happened to the owners?" Grey asked.

"They all died—the whole family was caught unawares and taken away in the middle of the night."

Although the plot devices were clearly spelled out, everyone followed separate storylines and the evening ended with many questions still unanswered.

Back at the hotel, Brigitte could not suppress her overwhelming sense of dread. As she began to undress, old feelings of self-destruction rose within her. There was no logic to it—her father was decrepit and dying, but still it was suffocating to think of him sleeping in the same hotel suite. Instead of going straight to bed, she decided to take a walk. As she exited the hotel, she saw Maria and Grey sitting alone midway up the Spanish Steps, just down from the hotel's entrance. Brigitte about-faced and returned to the lobby.

"May I help you?" At the registration desk stood the same receptionist as before.

"No, I was going for a walk but I changed my mind."

"There's tea in the library, if you'd like."

"Yes, I think I would."

"It is the door across the lobby on the left."

Brigitte walked over and looked in. It was a quaint room with a settee and two armchairs arranged around a fireplace. Three walls were lined with shelves of leather-bound books. It would have been a room worthy of a Victorian salon, were it not for the fourth wall that was shared by a desk and side table, both equipped for modern convenience.

Brigitte called back across the lobby, "Does the computer in here work?"

"Yes, it's free for all guests. Let me give you an access code."

Situated at the desk with a cup of chamomile tea, Brigitte typed *James Joyce* and the browser responded with several links to a variety of Jameses and Joyces. Brigitte clicked through some of the articles on James Joyce, the author, and found nothing. She then entered *"James Joyce" birthday,* and scanned the results looking for any reference to a birthday party in the late thirties or early forties. She stopped when she saw the link: *James Joyce and the Self-hating Jew.*

> *Most scholars agree that James Joyce was not anti-Semitic but then how, in his opus Ulysses, is one to take Leopold Bloom's reference to Judea as the "grey sunken cunt of the world?" Some suggest that Joyce's skepticism about Zionism is filtered through his exposure to the Austrian Zionist Otto Weininger, who has been described by many Jewish critics as a classic "self-hating Jew."*

If this had been the topic of conversation her mother had referenced, Brigitte could understand why Madeleine, regardless of her disaffiliation with her Jewish heritage, would have been uncomfortable with any such discussion. Nevertheless, Brigitte spent the next forty-five minutes searching for any mention of the party. She found nothing.

"Excuse me?" The receptionist stood in the library doorway.

Brigitte was startled. "Oh no, I'm sorry, have I been using the computer too long?"

"No *signora*, there's no maximum time limit if no one is waiting, but you'll need a new access code after an hour. Would you like me to provide you with a new one?"

"No, thank you. I should go to bed anyway."

After the receptionist left, Brigitte stared at the computer screen for a moment and then typed in one last search: *Max "Pablo Picasso."* The first link was an article entitled: *Gertrude, Alice, and the Lost Generation.*

> *After Gertrude Stein met Alice B. Toklas in 1907, they became inseparable. Alice was Gertrude's "Pussy," and Gertrude was "Lovey" to Alice. Alice cooked, typed manuscripts, fended off unwanted publicity, and hobnobbed with Stein's circle of literati that included <u>Ernest Hemingway</u>, <u>F. Scott Fitzgerald</u>, <u>T.S. Eliot</u>, <u>Guillaume Apollinaire</u>, <u>Jean Cocteau</u>, <u>Djuana Barnes</u>, <u>Sylvia Beach</u> (owner of the famous Shakespeare and Company Bookshop and Lending Library), <u>Ezra Pound</u>, <u>Paul Valery</u>, <u>Andre Gide</u>, and <u>Max Jacob</u> (who roomed with <u>Pablo Picasso</u> at the time). Though Stein coined her entourage a "lost generation," perhaps they were neither, in a personal nor artistic sense, a "lost" generation. They were instead wanderers and seekers.*

Brigitte clicked on *Max Jacob.*

> *Born in <u>Quimper</u>, <u>Brittany</u>, <u>France</u>, Max Jacob was enrolled in the <u>Paris</u> Colonial School, which he left in 1897 for an artistic career. On the Boulevard Voltaire, he shared a room with <u>Pablo Picasso</u>, who introduced him to <u>Guillaume Apollinaire</u>, who in turn introduced him to <u>Georges Braque</u>. He would become close friends with <u>Jean Cocteau</u>, <u>Christopher Wood</u> and <u>Amedeo Modigliani</u>, who painted his*

portrait in 1916. Jacob, who had <u>Jewish</u> origins, claimed to have had a vision of <u>Christ</u> in 1909, and converted to <u>Catholicism</u>. But, despite his hopes, his new religion could not rid him of his <u>homosexual</u> longings, about which he once said, "If heaven witnesses my regrets, heaven will pardon me for the pleasures which it knows are involuntary." On February 24, 1944 Max Jacob too was arrested by the—

The computer screen went blank and prompted her for a new access code. At the reception desk, a small placard read: *"Torno subito."* Brigitte decided not to wait.

That night Brigitte dreamt in English.

She was late and had just arrived at the restaurant, alone. She was pushing her way through the crowd to find Sophie when she spotted Madeleine sitting at the bar, on the third barstool in. Beside her stood Tío Piquot and Uncle Max. Uncle Max leaned into Madeleine and pointed his chin over her shoulder, toward Brigitte. When he spoke, all sound and motion stopped. Lights glared and mouths hung open. Out of his mouth, words fell like spittle. "Speaking of cunts, looks like Gertie's clawing her Pussy again."

His laughter carried Brigitte's repulsed subconscious back in time to its second offense, to the library in the Antibes house, where as a four-year-old child, Brigitte had just come in from the beach in search of her father.

64

The next morning, Brigitte hosted a continental breakfast at their suite in the Hotel Hassler. Throughout the hour-long affair, Brigitte was manic in her hospitality and it made everyone uncomfortable, except for Grey. He seemed to ignore the tension in the room as if he was accustomed to its coexistence. Brigitte's parents sat on the couch, holding hands like newlyweds. Madeleine was elegant and Christophe dapper, dressed in attire fit for a hunting party at a British country manor after which tea would immediately follow. Madeleine defied her age; one could still see the stunning beauty she once was. Conversely, Christophe looked every one of his eighty-seven years, more so because he wore the permanent expression of apprehension that comes with decrepitude. His only feature that was not aged was his hair. While it was stark white, its thickness and strong hairline were that of a twenty-year old. His eyes hid behind thick round wire-rimmed glasses, never seeming to focus on any one person or thing but rather on the negative space in between. He didn't speak the entire morning, nor did he let go of his wife's hand.

"Aren't you a bit young for first communion?" Grey was engaged in a conversation with Chloé, who had sequestered him from the moment he'd walked through the door.

Sophie answered for her granddaughter. "Don't get her started about the age of reason, which is the whole point of first communion, or so I'm told." From Chloé's beaming smile, it was certain who the source of this information had been. "When I first insisted that this was an arbitrary concept, which is why tradition has the parents deciding what age is appropriate, our little encyclopedia here found a reference to something called the Seven-Year Decree that at one point—"

Chloé interrupted. "1910."

Sophie rolled her eyes. "—that in 1910 dictated that all children should have their first communion at the age of seven." Sophie turned from Grey to address everyone in the room. "Children and their computers—is there no limit to what they can find these days?"

Paolo squatted and faced Chloé on her level. He squinched up his face as if he were studying her. "Certainly sounds to me like she's reached the age of reason." He stood and, twisting his body, stretched his arms toward the ceiling and said, "Come on Grey, let's tool around the city."

Juliana had pulled a kitchen chair over to the terrace windows and was slumped in it, basking in the midmorning sun that lit up the suite's salon. She appeared to be oblivious to all other sensory input, a false assumption because, upon hearing Paolo's suggestion, she immediately jumped up, eager to tag along.

"Me too!" Chloé exclaimed with exaggerated emphasis in an attempt to counteract her grandmother's certain rejection of the idea—a rejection that Sophie instantly issued.

"Remember you're going to go with me and *Tante* Maria to see where your grandmother went to university."

"But I want to go with Grey," Chloé whined. It was the first time she'd sounded her age.

"You'll see Grey later. Now, come back and tell your *Mamie* all about what you're learning in school this year."

Sophie turned to Grey and said, "You certainly have a way with children."

From the moment she had arisen from her fitful sleep, Brigitte had filled the morning with evasive busywork and resumed doing so after the party broke up. She took the dishes into the small kitchen and began washing them, even though the room service waiter had told her to call down and he would take care of everything.

Maria joined her at the sink. She took Brigitte's hands, ignoring their soggy clutch. "My God, Brigitte, how are you holding up?"

It was their first moment alone together, and Brigitte remembered her recrimination of Sophie the night before: this weekend was for Maria. "Better than expected. I guess I always knew I would have to face them one day. I just don't want them to ruin our time together. Maria, I've missed you so much. You have no idea how happy I am you're here."

Wrapping her arms around Brigitte's shoulders, Maria said, "For God's sake Brigitte, it's me! You have been there for me my whole life. Let me be here for you."

Maria fought Brigitte's desire to pull away from the embrace.

"Brigitte, please, I know how difficult it must be to . . . " Maria chose her next words carefully. She had never once in her entire life mentioned Brigitte's parents and did not want to make matters worse by tacitly acknowledging secrets unspoken. " . . . to be around them."

"Oh Maria, what do I do? He's dying and I still can't forgive him." Brigitte gave in and let herself be held. Again, her tears overcame their formerly unassailable dam, but this time there was no stopping them and the dam ruptured from their fury. Maria held Brigitte until she had depleted her tears. When at last the two women reemerged from the kitchen, Christophe and Madeleine had already retreated to their room and Sophie and Chloé had put on their coats.

"Maria, I don't mean to rush you but if we don't get Chloé outside in the next five minutes, I think she's going to implode."

Chloé looked up at her grandmother. "You're the one who said we needed to leave so they could talk."

Sophie shrugged her shoulders and repeated Grey's biblical aphorism. "Out of the mouths of babes."

Chloé folded her arms and groaned in protest, "*Mamour*, I didn't ask you what that meant so you could repeat it."

Sophie shook her head in defeat.

Before leaving, Chloé made yet another non sequitur to draw everyone's attention to her impending first communion. She begged Brigitte to come to Paris to attend the ceremony. *"Mamie,* please say yes."

Brigitte considered Chloé at length, and then turned to Sophie and said, "Yes, I will come. It's long past time I came home."

65

Rome, February 1, 2000 - Dusk

"Should we start with Max Jacob?" As with the previous night's confrontation, Brigitte's tone was strident.

The two women sat across from one another, Madeleine on the sofa facing the terrace and Brigitte in one of the armchairs. The setting sun spilled from the terrace window, softening the tint of everything in the room except Brigitte's manner. On the contrary, Madeleine relaxed into the stiff couch, the perfect complement to dusk's repose. "I thought you said you didn't remember Max."

"I too am capable of finding things via the computer."

"Brigitte, you gave me an hour. Can I ask that you give me half of that without interruption? I know that I have no right to propose such a request, but I get confused easily these days and, while I'm not making any excuses, I do believe it will be easier for both of us."

Madeleine's legs were crossed at the ankles. Brigitte crossed hers as well in an exaggerated pose meant to mock her mother's gentility. "Easier would be nice."

"Then yes, let's start with Max. Do you remember Antibes?"

"Am I allowed to answer?"

"Brigitte, let us be civil, at least for this hour."

"If you mean the library scene, yes, I remember. I've had a recurring dream ever since I was a child, and that dream involves Antibes. But I didn't remember the library incident until much later and I didn't realize that Max Jacob was the other man until last night."

"Dear, I know this will sound strange to you but back then your father and I were . . . experimental. We had what today you would call "an agreement." That weekend in Antibes, the agreement ended. But then soon afterward, the world fell apart." Madeleine turned from Brigitte. During her childhood, Brigitte had never seen her mother cry. Madeleine had been the perfect role model for Brigitte's self-possession. The thought of her breaking was as disorienting as the truth. When Madeleine turned back, her eyes were clear. "It was in Antibes that we met Ugo and Angelo."

Brigitte took this first blow with grace. "You knew Angelo and Ugo?"

"Yes dear. Not only did they save you, they saved us. They convinced us of the seriousness of Hitler's mania. They convinced me to send your grandparents away and persuaded your father to join them in their mission."

Brigitte's disbelief turned to anger. Ugo and Angelo were *her* friends, *her* family. "Join them in what mission?"

"To save as many as could be saved. In the early days, the waterways were the safest escape. Even in the end, if we could get families to the southern ports, Ugo and Angelo would risk La Royale because most of their coast guard fleet had been recruited into battle and was stationed in Normandy."

"Families?"

"There needed to be some filter. We couldn't save everyone. Your father focused on families with young children."

Brigitte's mind raced, unraveling years of intertwined conjecture. "Father helped save Jewish families?"

"Dear, your father saved our family, as well as thousands of others. He convinced his boss to ignore certain families' Jewish descent."

"Was his boss René Carmille?"

"How on earth do you remember René'? We were careful to never speak of your father's work in your presence."

"I don't remember him, but I recently read that Father gave the eulogy at his funeral."

"Yes, poor René paid with his life, one of the many regrets your father lives with."

Brigitte was in no mood for pity. "Was Doda another pawn?"

"I'm not sure what you mean." Madeleine appeared genuinely baffled by Brigitte's question.

"Did Doda choose to come to Elba or did you force her?"

Madeleine maintained her poise. "Dear, when you decided to stay, we were stunned. Your father was going to go and bring you back, but when Ugo and Angelo told us that you were eating well and were happy, we didn't want to risk your getting sick again. It may seem to you like an inconceivable decision, but we were convinced we were doing the right thing. And, to answer your question, Doda chose to move to Elba. After Father died, you became Doda's world. You may not remember, but when you got Scarlet Fever, Doda was at your bedside day and night.

"Of course I remember. You were off in America and Father was running down to Antibes every weekend."

"I meant the original onset of the illness, after your thirteenth birthday party. But yes, she was there for the recurrence as well." Madeleine paused. "Unfortunately, that time she faltered."

"Faltered?"

"Brigitte, you're too old to be coy. We both know if Doda had been there that night, everything would be different—*everything*."

Madeleine's upper lip quivered. Just as she was about to say something else, Brigitte asked, "Is that why she followed me to Elba—guilt?

Even in such a vulnerable state, Madeleine did not mince words. "Partially, yes." Again, Brigitte started to interrupt but this time Madeleine was not so easily curtailed. "But mostly because she wanted to protect you. She was devastated by our decision to send you to Elba and offered to go live with you. She beseeched us to let her be our surrogate. At first, Christophe was worried about her influence over you, but she promised that she would abide by our wishes."

"You mean *his* wishes. What wishes did *he* have after I had gone? What—did he insist Doda not corrupt me with her Judaism?" Brigitte meant it as an insult and only realized the truth of her words as they were coming out of her mouth.

"Yes, that was the main issue. Brigitte, your father is Catholic. And while we've never been religious, we wanted to ensure that if there was ever another Holocaust, you would be spared."

"My God." Brigitte lifted her hand to her mouth.

"Dear, I know this is overwhelming. I know it must seem like deceit after deceit, but what else could we do?"

Though Brigitte's hand remained covering her mouth, her words were clear. "So you never saw Doda again?"

"As you know, your grandmother didn't like to travel . . ." Madeleine hesitated before continuing. ". . . but we did see her once."

"When?"

"You were visiting Padua. We came to see Mother and meet Sophie."

"No!" Brigitte's exclamation was barely audible. She gripped the armrest. Every word from Madeleine's mouth was surreal and painful, and the chair's coarse tufted fabric felt good in her hand.

"Dear, we had to see our granddaughter. By that time, you had turned the Vigliettis and La Roccas against us and we had to arrange our meeting with Mother in secrecy. We arrived just after you left and stayed for only a few hours. Mother showed us where you lived and allowed us to see Sophie."

"You were on Elba and met Sophie?" Brigitte felt dizzy; her tongue was sluggish. Each word took effort.

"Yes and no. We didn't meet Sophie. Mother said that Sophie adored you and told you everything and that it would therefore be too risky to introduce us, even as strangers."

Brigitte recalled the day she left for Padua. After Brigitte's ferry had set sail, Doda had supposedly run errands, but she'd never returned home. The following night, they had found her wandering aimlessly in the lighthouse at Fort Stella. "So then you knew of Doda's condition."

"Not then, no. We had no idea she was ill until much later. Somehow she managed to hide it in her phone calls and letters. I'm not sure exactly when we fully realized that she was losing her mind, and we didn't know the extent of it until we heard from Sophie."

A new burst of anger resuscitated Brigitte. "You heard from Sophie or you contacted her?"

Madeleine uncrossed her legs and took a deep breath. It appeared that she was having as much difficulty as Brigitte in maintaining her composure. This provided some perverse comfort to Brigitte. "Brigitte, first let me stop for a moment and thank you for taking care of Mother. Had I known the magnitude of her illness, I would have had her moved back to Paris and looked after her myself."

"Really? You would have stayed home to care for her?" Brigitte fought to remain resolute. She was not yet ready to abandon her conviction, on which she had based everything.

"Yes Brigitte, I would have. And I would have done the same with you and Sophie as well, if you would have let me."

The two women stared at one another until the moment passed without resolution. Finally, Brigitte broke the silence. "We strayed from Max."

"Yes. Pablo tried his best to get your father to save Max, but it was too risky. Max was too well known."

The room began to spin. Brigitte's words fell from her mouth, like spittle. "*L'agneau sacrificiel.*"

"Yes, it was that terrible day that Pablo came over to advocate for Max's life. You were so traumatized. To make matters worse, Pablo drew that sketch and sent it to us afterward. You must remember the sketch, you hated it so." Brigitte nodded. "I'm sure it was meant to punish your father, but I think it was also meant to honor him. Pablo knew how much Christophe had sacrificed and how many lives he had saved."

Brigitte could take no more, but neither could she end the conversation without hearing Madeleine's final confession. She steadied herself for the ultimate assault, and asked, "And after Drancy?"

"After Drancy, everything went so wrong. You were so sick and we didn't know what to do."

"So you left?"

"It's not that easy Brigitte. We were trying to rebuild. The world was trying to rebuild and we needed hope."

"And sacrifice?"

"Yes, we made mistakes. We weren't perfect. Your father has suffered dearly for his imperfections. My one wish is that he doesn't take his guilt to the grave. Last night you said 'fair is fair.' If after hearing this story you believe your irrevocable condemnation of him is still fair, then you have the right to tell him. I will not stop you. I only ask that you wait until tomorrow morning. He's resting right now and mustn't be disturbed."

Brigitte went to respond but Madeleine interrupted her.

"And now, dear, I too must rest." The hour was up. Madeleine stood and turned to go to her bedroom, leaving no further recourse for Brigitte's reprisal.

66

Rome, February 1, 2000 - Early Evening

After the conversation with her mother, Brigitte took her time getting ready for Maria's birthday party. When she was finally dressed, she went to her suitcase that lay open on its stand and pulled the sketch from its torn lining. The night before, after her tour of Rome, Brigitte had purchased a beautiful gilded frame in an antique store near the hotel. She watched herself in the mirror as she methodically framed and wrapped her gift. She then went down to the lobby to wait out the remaining two hours before the party.

Because she wasn't yet ready to suffer a conversation with either Sophie or Maria, Brigitte sought out the seclusion of the hotel's library. The small room was empty and dimly lit, a perfect escape if not for the computer's screen saver that beckoned her attention. When she ventured out to the front desk, the same receptionist was stationed there yet again. Brigitte wondered when he slept.

"Can I have an access code to the computer?"

"Certainly *signora.*"

"Can I also order a martini from the bar?"

"I'm sorry, but we do not serve cocktails in the lobby area."

"Then I'll have an espresso. Is it possible to have it served in the library?"

"Certainly."

Brigitte returned to the library, sat down at the computer and entered her access code. The browser had been left open by the previous guest and awaited her command.

"A little something for your espresso." The receptionist materialized from nowhere and, along with the espresso, placed a miniature bottle of Bailey's beside the monitor. With a mischievous wink, he said, "Let's keep it our secret."

"Thank you."

"My pleasure. My name is Francesco, should you need anything else. And may I add that you look particularly stunning tonight."

Brigitte wore the black evening gown that she and Colette had purchased years earlier. Brigitte remembered wondering when she would ever have the occasion to wear such a dress. "*Grazie*, Francesco."

Sophie, who must have just come back from her day, intercepted Francesco mid-lobby. She inquired about the availability of an ironing board. While Brigitte could not see them, she could hear their conversation clearly through the library's open door.

"Certainly, but we have an overnight laundry service if you'd like."

"No thank you, it's for a birthday party tonight."

Francesco's voice took on a more playful tone. "Is it your birthday?'

Chloé responded, "No, though I couldn't be happier if it were."

Brigitte typed *"Max "Pablo Picasso""* and clicked through the *Gertrude, Alice, and the Lost Generation* link to the *Max Jacob* link and continued to read the article that she hadn't yet finished the night before.

> On <u>February 24, 1944</u> Max Jacob too was arrested by the
> <u>Gestapo</u> and put into <u>Orléans</u> prison holding camp in <u>Drancy</u>
> for transport to a <u>concentration camp</u> in <u>Germany</u>. However,
> said to be suffering from bronchial pneumonia, Max Jacob
> died in the <u>Drancy deportation camp</u> on March 5th. Among
> Jacob's novels are <u>Saint Matorel</u> (1911) and <u>Filibuth ou la
> Montre en or</u> (1922). Prose and poetry are combined in the
> play <u>Le Siège de Jérusalem: drame céleste</u> (1912-14) and in

his *Défense de Tartufe* (1919), which includes one of his most well-known poems, *Antibes and the Antibes Road*. His critical study, *Art poétique* (1922), had wide influence.

Brigitte gasped when she read of Max's death. When she had asked her mother about Max, Brigitte had no idea that he had died at Drancy just five months before they'd been interned there. Of his listed works, one in particular caught her eye. She clicked on *Antibes and the Antibes Road*. It was an odd poem about nothing, but it perfectly captured her memory of the town in two of its short lines:

> The Vauban fort looks like a ship
> The Gothic church spire lustrous as wax

Brigitte was suddenly overcome with an unexpected rush of adrenaline and experienced a heightened emotional state that approximated relief. She picked up Maria's gift, returned to the reception desk and handed Francesco the bottle of Baileys. "I don't think I'll need this, but thank you."

Francesco nodded. "Again, my pleasure."

"Well, then, I've another favor to ask."

"My pleasure."

She felt strangely giddy, so much so that her subsequent request appeared as if she were returning Francesco's earlier flirtation. "Can I make that two favors?"

"Of course."

"First, can I print something from the computer?"

"Yes, it's easy. Would you like me to show you?"

"Please."

While the poem was printing, Francesco asked, "And the other favor?"

Brigitte placed Maria's gift on the reception desk. It was beautifully wrapped in hand-stenciled paper and a large crimson bow with tendrils of ribbon sprouting out all sides. "Could you take this to my suite and personally deliver it to Madeleine Crémieux?"

"Of course. Any note?"

As he took the gift, Brigitte noticed his wedding band for the first time. "Yes, please fold and tape the poem you just printed to the front."

Before Brigitte turned to leave, she added, "You should tell her that she may want to open it in private. And I'm sorry, it's not Madeleine Crémieux, it's Madeleine Sureau."

Outside, Brigitte descended the Spanish Steps and, with still an hour to kill, she decided to stroll. In heels unsuited for Rome's cobblestone, her pace was slow, and she took in the minutiae of the evening: streetlight-casted shadows disappearing into dark alleys, random snippets of chatter and laughter, aromas wafting from overly perfumed passersby, and countless other sights and sounds of urban life. She stopped at the Trevi Fountain and sat on its edge, near one of the majestic seahorses. Its deafening splash was too much and she stood and walked around the fountain, to its calmer waters where coins carrying the wishes of children and tourists glittered from bottom of the fountain's shallow basin.

Before going to the dinner, Brigitte first returned to the hotel. She was late and hurried past the front desk without glancing in Francesco's direction. In her room, she sat at her dresser and picked up the telephone.

"Donovan, it's Brigitte." As Brigitte spoke, she stared into the mirror.

"No, no, nothing is wrong. It's just . . . can I ask you a favor?" The phone was an old-fashioned rotary dial; the weight of the receiver felt good in her hand. "My plans have changed and I was hoping you could check on the café and change the sign to indicate that it will remain closed until next Friday." Brigitte coiled the phone's cord around her finger. "No, I may be gone longer, but Paolo should be back midweek." Brigitte picked up the phone and walked to the window. Across the way, Grey and Maria stood talking on the terrace. "To Paris." Brigitte backed away, out of view. "That's a long story and unfortunately, I'm in a hurry. No, nothing else except . . . " Brigitte watched as Grey took Maria's arm in the crook of his and walked her back into the flat. " . . . I just wanted to hear your voice."

67

Rome, February 1, 2000 - Evening

Grey pulled his chair out from the table. "I'm gonna start the lamb."

Even in Brigitte's anxious state, she was awed by the apartment's decadence. It achieved the perfect stylistic balance of antique and modern for which she'd tried to strike in the renovation of Doda's flat. Here, though, every piece of furniture and art was museum quality. She couldn't imagine a better atmosphere for Maria's birthday party. Even so, it was difficult for Brigitte to keep her eye from wandering out to the flat's terrace, to the small, lit bedroom window just across the street.

"I am able to help." Brigitte stood and joined Grey in the kitchen.

The last to arrive at the party, Brigitte assuaged Maria's and Sophie's apparent concern by exuding enthusiastic vigor. If they weren't convinced, they knew better than to question her, and so, in wordless compliance, all three women gave themselves over to the celebration at hand.

Grey was a different matter. Her offer to help him serve the dinner had put them in the kitchen alone together. It was the perfect time to ascertain his intent, but much had transpired and it was, after all, an evening of celebration. Instead of demanding his contrition, Brigitte confessed her decision to accompany her parents back to Paris.

"Wait, are you moving?"

"No, but they are old and Chloé is young. There is much to share." Brigitte suddenly realized she was not prepared to have this conversation with him and began mixing the salad.

Grey was not so easily distracted. Pulling the tray of lamb skewers from the oven, he asked, "Have you forgiven them?"

Brigitte dodged his question. "Forgiveness is an American concept."

"Oh, and in Europe you never get mad at each other?"

"No, I am serious. Not like America, we are old. We see'd so much unforgivable that we now do not stop to forgive. We keep going."

As they carried the food into the dining room, Brigitte wondered whether, in her attempt to elude the truth, she had discovered it instead.

The party was a success: old memories were shared and new ones forged. Sophie invited Maria to Paris for her birthday in May, and Maria agreed to come. The thought of sharing Paris with Maria almost made Brigitte forget the ordeal she must endure between now and then. She dared not think of that now, because, in truth, nothing could quell that anxiety until she confronted her father. It was a conversation for which, no matter how many times she rehearsed it in her head, she would never be prepared—an exposure that would force her to face what she had spent her entire life denying. But that conversation would not be tonight. Tonight she would celebrate the birthday of her dearest friend. Brigitte turned her attention back to party and reveled in the laughter that conveyed the love and joy with which she had been blessed for so many years.

The night's mood dipped when Maria unwrapped the restored wedding photos that Paolo and Juliana had given her. Fortunately, Juliana had thought to wrap photos individually, and after Maria realized the gift's contents, she chose to open the photo of Antonio at a later time. The lull was brief, and Maria handled it with grace.

When it came time for Brigitte's gift, she handed Maria a manila envelope and apologized for not having wrapped it. She admitted that it was not meant to be a gift but rather a discussion that she'd planned to have with Maria after the party. She went on to say that she was so caught up in the good cheer that she decided to share her surprise with the entire party (she neglected to divulge that she had given Maria's intended gift to Madeleine). Realizing the intimacy of the moment, Grey excused himself to the terrace to smoke, and the conversation switched to Italian.

From the envelope, Maria pulled a single sheet of paper. "Brigitte, I don't understand. What is this?"

"It's two account numbers and the contact information to a Sig. Ricci at Banca Antonveneta, in Padua. It appears that Le Voci never went bankrupt, that the new ownership continued to be backed by your grandfather after the Ansóphia disappeared."

"But that's impossible! You were with us when we received the notice from the bank."

"It was apparently a ruse. The Peratas never owned Le Voci. They were just the company's new management designated by your grandfather. They were paid by him and continued to be paid by his estate after he died."

"I don't understand. What does this mean?"

"Well, for whatever reason, your grandfather didn't—or couldn't—change the company's beneficiary designation and so when he died, two accounts were formed under yours and Antonio's names. Sig. Ricci assured me that notification had been sent to the address on file (which he would not disclose to me), but I'm assuming since you never mentioned it that you never received any notification."

"Never."

"It wouldn't have mattered anyway because the accounts were empty. Sig. Ricci told Le Voci's bylaws mandated that all corporate profit be reinvested back into the company. He said this wasn't too uncommon, and knowing Angelo and Ugo, I imagine Le Voci was that way from the beginning."

"So I still don't understand—if all profits are to be reinvested, what do these accounts mean?"

"I said they *were* empty. That changed with the sale of Le Voci to Scaccia Navi. According to Sig. Ricci, upon Le Voci's transfer of ownership, the contractual requirements of the original loan required that fifty percent of the proceeds above and beyond the cost of sale were to be deposited into these accounts."

"Are you saying what I think you're saying?"

"I don't know exactly what I'm saying because Sig. Ricci wouldn't tell me anything else except that Le Voci's former management team has filed a legal suit challenging the statute of limitations on unclaimed beneficiary accounts of this type. Again, he wouldn't disclose the details. He told me that for any additional information, you would need to go there in person. If I were you, I would extend your trip a few days and go to Padua to talk with Sig. Ricci face to face."

Grey had returned from outside and with Maria's invitation, rejoined the group. The conversation reverted to English with Juliana speaking first. "A mysterious inheritance and a trip to Padua? Absa-fuckin-lutely!"

Paolo chimed in. "I'm in! I say we rent a car and—"

Maria interrupted, holding up one hand. "Wait, hold on. I can't stay. I can't afford to take any more time off from work."

Juliana moaned in protest.

"I'm not ruling it out, but it makes no sense to waste a nonrefundable ticket and, besides, I have to go back to work on Friday." She leaned over and asked Brigitte, "Can Paolo and Juliana represent me? They can go check it out, and I'll call or fax or do whatever I need to do from New York."

Brigitte had anticipated Maria's resistance. "Yes, I asked at the bank what to do if you are not able to travel to Padua. Sig. Ricci says it is possible that a child of you can see the accounts. But you will need to call to Sig. Ricci with your permission."

"Brigitte, I can't believe this. What if my inheritance is there? What made you think of this after all this time?"

Brigitte nodded toward Grey. "Something more to thank for Grey. The first day we meet he asks me of you and I remember you never receive your heritance. I remember this discussion and call my lawyer. He finds these two accounts and I go to Padua to talk to Sig. Ricci."

Maria turned to Grey. "Grey, there is no way I can ever repay you for all you've done for my family. When we're back in New York, you must come to the restaurant and let me host a party for you. Bring along your partner and whoever else you would like to invite."

Grey's eyes filled with tears and his voice quivered as he replied, "I would love that."

"It's the least I could do." Maria reached across the table and took Grey's hand. What she remembered or knew still wasn't clear. What *was* clear—at least to Brigitte—was that it no longer mattered.

While Maria and Sophie cleared the table, and Juliana and Paolo conspired their trip to Padua, Brigitte joined Grey on the terrace. After again thanking him for everything, she asked, "Will you be returning to Elba or staying here in Rome?"

Grey did not immediately answer, but instead turned from her and stared out across Rome. At last, he said, "I think it's time I go home."

Brigitte's gaze did not join his but was again drawn to the Hotel Hassler, to the now dark window of her parents' room. "I understand."

68

Rome, February 1, 2000 - Late Evening

After the party, Brigitte's celebratory mood gave way to apprehension about the night's conclusion. As they were exiting the apartment building, Brigitte turned to Sophie and said, "Let's not go back yet. We've had no time alone."

Instead of crossing the street to their hotel, they ventured out to the landing of the Spanish Steps. Brigitte began with a casual observation. "I read somewhere that for over two centuries these steps have been a social cross-section for Rome. This afternoon, I sat at my window and witnessed just how true that is. It's fascinating to see how people from all walks of life come here to read, or meet up with friends, or just sit and think." Brigitte lifted the hem of her dress off the ground. "I know we're not dressed appropriately but do you mind if we sit?"

"Of course not." Sophie took her mother's arm, and the two women walked down a few stairs to a secluded spot.

Once settled, Brigitte said, "I'm sorry I've never visited you. *Mon Dieu*, I never even visited you when you were here in college."

Sophie tried to interrupt but Brigitte continued. "I would've loved to have seen Rome through your eyes back then. I remember how excited you you'd become whenever you talked about your classes or your new friends. And when you became infatuated with the *Brigate Rosse*— remember how scared I was? I was certain that you'd get mixed up in some political uprising. At the same time, I thought how proud your Uncle Ugo would have been."

Sophie laughed, "God, that was a lifetime ago. I thought we were going to change the world. Little did I understand the sacrifice required by idealism."

Looking up at night sky, Brigitte shivered. "Ugo used to say, "if you're not a communist at eighteen, you can't be a dreamer at fifty."

"I wouldn't say that I'm much of a dreamer. Remember, I am a lawyer." They both laughed softly.

Brigitte stroked Sophie's hand. "Do you know how proud I am of you? You have made your own way despite all of the obstacles I put before you."

"Mother, please."

"Well, I did. I was too blinded by my own problems to really be there to help you through yours. But fortunately, you have managed quite well without me."

Sophie let go of her mother's hand to gesticulate a rebuttal. "Mother, you must be kidding! You gave me everything. I was the selfish one for not understanding the full scope of the trauma you suffered." Sophie refolded her hand into her mother's and chose her next words carefully. "I realize now what you sacrificed."

For a moment Brigitte didn't respond, but then she tightened her grip and asked, "Did you ever come here when you were in university?"

"I used to study here on the weekends. The first date I had with Etienne, we sat over there with a bottle of wine and . . . " Sophie's voice trailed off.

"Dear, I'm so sorry about you and Etienne."

"No Mother, you were right all along. In the realm of selfishness, I think the French bear the highest standard."

"*D'accord.*"

Sophie chuckled. "*Merde*, I never think of you as French."

"*Meerci bowcoop.*" Brigitte mocked an Italian's bad attempt at a French accent and the two women giggled like schoolgirls.

When their laughter subsided, Brigitte said, "Dear, I love you more than you'll ever know. "

Sophie laid her head in her mother's lap. Out of the corner of her eye, Brigitte saw Paolo and Grey emerge from the darkness. Deep in conversation, they didn't notice Brigitte and Sophie's huddle. They descended the steps and continued on their way into the night. Brigitte reached down and stroked her daughter's hair.

On the short walk back to the hotel, Sophie asked Brigitte, "Mother, did the man from the bank give any sense of the size of the inheritance?"

"I didn't want to say this in there but Sig. Ricci told me Scaccia Navi has four lawyers working on the case. I think that says something."

Sophie opened the lobby door for her mother. "It certainly does. You know what I'll do? When I get back to Paris, I'll make some calls and see what I can find out. Maria may need counsel to get through this."

Brigitte's laughter was filled with pride. "Dear, of course, that's what you will do. Now, go ahead to the room without me. I'm going to sit in the library for a bit."

"Are you okay?"

Brigitte leaned in and kissed her daughter on the cheek. "I have never been better."

As they waited for the elevator, Brigitte said, "Sophie, thank you for bringing them. I would have gone to the grave with regret had you not intervened."

Sophie was too choked up to reply.

After the elevator doors closed, Brigitte returned to the lobby. Francesco was reading a book and appeared not to see her approach, but as she neared, he lifted his head. The twinkle in his eyes matched Brigitte's.

"I trust you had a wonderful time."

Brigitte winked. "That, *signor*, is an understatement. I'm sorry to be a burden but can I trouble you one more time for a computer pass code?"

"You, dear woman, could never be a burden."

When Francesco reached under the desk to get the code, something on the counter caught his shirtsleeve, ripping it open. With impeccable grace, he managed by slight of eye to obscure his newly bared arm from Brigitte's view while writing the computer pass code with his left hand. The result was barely legible.

In taking the code, Brigitte said, "I'm sorry." She didn't want to embarrass him with any additional indication that she had seen the numbered tattoo on his inner forearm.

He did not meet her gaze but lowered his eyes in apology. "Don't worry, it is a tear easily mended."

As she pulled her hand away, Brigitte began to say something else but then decided against it and quickly turned before he raised his eyes.

Again at the computer, Brigitte brought up the *Le Monde* "Reconciliation" article and read it in its entirety. It focused on the devastation of the war and challenge of rebuilding any semblance of unity among France's fractured people. Madeleine was certain in her response:

> France will overcome this as we have overcome our past tribulations. We are a proud people who will always remain resolute in the face of adversity.

After finishing the article, Brigitte drifted among once safeguarded memories without constraint. She thought back to the 1949 train ride from Paris to Antibes, where she had stared out the window to the war-blemished towns and wondered about her new life on Elba. This memory conjured forth another from even further back in time, a memory of the same journey nine years prior. She was almost five years old and had sat in Christophe's lap, looking out the window as the idyllic French countryside sped by.

"Daddy, how big is the ocean?"

Beside them, Madeleine leaned in to be cheek-to-cheek with her daughter. Her tone was coy. "Yes, dear, tell us."

Christophe looked up from whatever he was reading and kissed each of them on the nose. "Not as big as my love for my two favorite girls in the world."

69

Rome, February 2, 2000 - Predawn

"Alors, comment c'est passé la fête?"

Brigitte couldn't sleep and when she walked into the suite's living room, she didn't see Madeleine on the sofa staring out into the night. So surprised was Brigitte by her mother's voice that she dropped the glass of water she was holding.

"I'm sorry, I didn't mean to frighten you."

Brigitte went to the bar to find a towel. "That's what happens when one is confronted by an unexpected voice from the dark at two in the morning."

"Well, that was some present you left. I couldn't sleep either." Madeleine's manner was dismissive, as if Brigitte's gift had been flowers or a box of chocolates. "Where on earth did you find one of Max's poems?"

"On the Internet. I've become rather proficient over the past month."

Madeleine dropped her aloof pretense. "And the sketch?"

On her knees dabbing the carpet dry, Brigitte said over her shoulder, "That doesn't matter. It's yours and I wanted you to have it."

"I'm not sure what to do with it. It's far too painful to display."

Brigitte rose and stood over her mother. "As I said, it is yours to do with as you wish."

"Well, thank you. It must have brought up many confusing memories when you found it."

Brigitte sat on the sofa next to Madeleine. "Yes, it did."

Madeleine reached out as if to take her daughter's hands but then thought better of it. "Brigitte, I wish I could take back those memories. Your father and I wish we could take back a lot of things. I also pray that you try to understand that we did what we thought was right in order to protect you."

"Mother, please don't! *Nom de Dieu*, don't you think we've said enough?"

"There is one more thing you should know."

Brigitte bolted up, withdrew from the sofa and turned to face the bar, thus shielding herself from Madeleine's view. She begged, "Mother, *please.*"

"He's dead, Brigitte."

Brigitte spun around. "Dead?"

"Yes, he died six months ago."

"Six months ago? Who?"

"Dr. Godard."

Brigitte barely recognized the name. "I'm sorry, but how does that matter?"

"I know how you must hate him so I thought you should know."

"Why would I hate him?"

"Brigitte, please, I don't want to talk about this any more than you do, but I thought you would want to know."

The realization began slowly. Brigitte collapsed back onto the couch.

"After we found out you were pregnant, your father wanted to kill him. I convinced him that revenge would only make things worse. With so much pain, I was desperate that we focus on healing. The world needed to heal."

"So Dr. Godard is . . . "

Madeleine lost her composure and her voice raced with the urgency of words too long unsaid. "You must believe that your father did his best to protect us. After Drancy, he wanted to ensure that we were not scarred in any way. That is why we hired German staff, bought from German stores, and you had a German doctor. He wanted us to learn not to cower in their presence—not to be ashamed. Most of them were as horrified as we were by what their Fatherland had done. They were contrite in their servitude. Dr. Godard was different. He took revenge."

Brigitte could barely speak. When she did, her words were that of a child. "And Sophie?"

"*Elle ne sait pas.*" Tears muffled Madeleine's response. It was the only time in her life that Brigitte would ever see her mother cry. Madeleine took a moment to recompose herself before continuing. "She met him once, about five years ago. We were waiting to be seated at a café and he was standing in line in front of us. He was so hunched and frail that I didn't recognize him, until his lunch companion, a former colleague your father's, introduced him to us. I couldn't speak. When Sophie greeted him, I thought I would die. Fortunately, as he was about to respond, the maître d' appeared and seated them at a nearby table. I was desperate to leave, but I didn't want Sophie to suspect anything. He stared at us throughout lunch, staying long after his friend left. After we finished eating, when Sophie went to the bathroom, he approached me. Before he spoke, I told him that if he ever so much as looked again in her direction, I would expose him. He left before Sophie returned."

Brigitte lowered her head and exhaled a long, labored breath.

"From the restaurant window, I watched him hail a taxi. I was numb. When Sophie asked who he was, I told her that he used to be the family doctor whom we had stopped seeing because of his incompetence. Brigitte, I never told your father about this incident. We thought that he had fled Paris after the first time Christophe confronted him. For years, we had Mother on the lookout in case he turned up in Elba. But then, after running into him, I did some research and found out that less than a year after your departure for Elba, his wife and only daughter were killed in an automobile accident, and he closed his practice and lived in Neuilly as a recluse. He died last year. I only know this because it made the papers. His death was cited as an example of France's widespread neglect of the elderly. Apparently he fell down his stairs and wasn't discovered for a month, until a neighbor noticed a stench coming from the house. The coroner said he didn't die from the fall but from starvation."

Brigitte stared at her hands that lay folded, upturned in her lap. It was as though she had never really looked at her palms and only noticed now that they were riddled with lines, crisscrossing every which way, like the face of the nun from the *gelateria*.

"Brigitte, there are no apologies that will suffice for your lost youth, but you must know that we have never stopped loving you. And though it is selfish for me to ask you to forgive your father, that is what I am asking. He has lived with so much regret. I just can't bear to see him suffer any longer."

"Oh Mother." Brigitte buried her head into her mother's nightgown. Its silk was fine and smooth.

"Dear child, I've waited my whole life for this moment."

Long after Madeleine had gone to bed, Brigitte remained in the darkness and reinterpreted the clues from her past. At dawn, she rose and stood before the terrace sliding glass doors and watched the soft morning light blanket Rome. Below, a family descended the Spanish Steps. The father held a candle and the mother cradled an infant in her arms. Brigitte smiled. Maria had taught her the tradition of Candlemas, and Brigitte had attended both Giuseppe's and Juliana's first Candlemas ceremonies. Further provoking the memory, dawn's emerging light revealed Maria and Grey on the terrace across the way. As Brigitte backed away from the window to avoid being seen, a door creaked open behind her. Brigitte turned to find her father alone in the dark.

"*Papa.*" She said it softly so as not to startle him.

When he turned to her, his expression was one of impossible hope.

THE END

ACKNOWLEDGEMENTS

To those who told me that writing a second novel would be easier than the first, you lied. To be fair, it didn't help that I chose a protagonist who was born in a time and place that forced me to tread a pseudo historical fiction path. After spending three days researching whether, in 1944, the European car of choice (Renault's 4CV) had metal keys, I now have the most utmost respect for anyone who attempts true historical fiction. As for historical non-fiction, I can't imagine.

In light of this arduous task, I once again cast my editorial web widely across family, friends, friends' families, new acquaintances and even strangers. Thank you all.

First to Kristy Lin Billuni, my primary editor, whose guidance went far beyond editorial. I also want to thank those who provided secondary editorial assistance: Vikas Arora, Sandra Bullitt, Nello Carlini, David Gershan, Diane Perro, Sita Saviolo, Eliot Shrefer, Laura Sherman, Brianna Smith, Leslie Stern, Alex Teague, and Andie Trilo.

For additional creative and proof work: Sheila Von Driska for zillions of things, not the least of which was her cover design; Camilla Newhagen for the cover art; Duane Cramer for the headshot photo; and Pia La Rocca, Marco Gazzetta, Brigitte Benharrous Dean and Mathieu Sureau for Italian and French translation.

Others who gave me inspiration, advice and honest assessment were: Betsy Burroughs, Chip Conley, Jorge A. Colunga, Judy Lewenthal Daniel, Portia Dawson, Zaven Demerjian, Mavis DeWees, Peter Evers, Rebecca Fraimow, Dr. Lianne Gensler, Carole Hines, Claire Lewis, Camilla Newhagen, Helen Lin, Michael Pietsch, Monica Pressley, Margaret Ryan, Roberto Scaccia, Christopher Schelling, Paul Sekhri, Claudia Welss, and Julie Young.

Finally I want to thank my partner Nick Rubashkin who was there with me every step of the way. Full moons forever.

A NOTE ON RESEARCH

Like most historical fiction, *Ere I Saw Elba* includes fictional treatment of factual circumstances. I've attempted to represent such settings and people in an authentic manner, although I admit that I did not validate my research with academic rigor. In my fictional portrayals of historical personages, I've taken the most liberty with my three bald men: Christian Dior, Pablo Picasso, and Max Jacob. Christian Dior did introduce and tour America with the "New Look" (the "New Look" did feature a black tuxedo dress), but Madeleine Crémieux was not based on any of Mr. Dior's "new Look" models, nor do I know if Mr. Dior favored any of his models over the others. As for Pablo and Max, while they were roommates and friends, I've no idea if Pablo advocated for Max's life when Max was interned at Drancy (where Max did indeed die). In regards to Max's sexual irreverence, I did not base these scenes on actual incidents, but rather I have extrapolated from non-verified citations (Max was said to have joined the artistic community in Montparnasse to "sin disgracefully, " and was rumored to have arrived drunk at the funeral of Picasso's lover, Eva Gödel, and attempted to seduce the driver of the hearse). There are plot points in *Ere I Saw Elba* that are directly based on historical accounting or supposition: some of the Drancy internment details, René Carmille's subversion within SNS, James Joyce's birthday party at Shakespeare and Company, the assumption that Max Jacob was the model for Picasso's Man with the Lamb, etc. For this research, I relied mostly on the Internet (thank you Wikipedia and Google!), but I also want to thank Rebecca Fraimow for getting me started, Diane Perro for her Drancy and WWII research, Sita Saviolo for her incredible tour of Padova (especially for bringing the Teatro Anatomico to life), Sandra Bullitt for her unique lens as a Holocaust survivor, and again, Marko Gazzetta, Sita Saviolo, Pia La Rocca, Brigitte Benharrous Dean, and Matthew Sureau for their Italian and French cultural review.

THE AUTHOR

Drew Banks (drewbanks.com) is an entrepreneur and author. In both his business writing and fiction, Drew deconstructs behavioral patterns in an attempt to explore casual motivations and deterrents. While Drew's first two business books, *Beyond Spin* and *Customer.Community* examine organizational implications of various social psychologies, he is drawn to fiction as a more intimate medium for delving beneath the surface of the individual. *Ere I Saw Elba* is his second novel, as well as the second of The Elba Trilogy: *Able Was I, Ere I Saw Elba,* and *I before ì* (work in progress).

LaVergne, TN USA
19 August 2009
155219LV00002B/5/P